In Those

Dazzling

Days of Elvis

ISBN: 978-1-68313-077-2

First Edition
Printed and bound in the USA

Cover art by Josephine Rascoe Keenan
Interior design by Kelsey Rice

In Those Dazzling Days of Elvis

-BY-

JOSEPHINE RASCOE KEENAN

P

Pen-L Publishing
Fayetteville, Arkansas
Pen-L.com

Books by Josephine Rascoe Keenan:

In Those First Bright Days of Elvis
In Those Dazzling Days of Elvis

*Dedicated to the memory of
my uncle and aunt,
Victor Earl Lawton and Opal Neeley Lawton,
for their love and guidance,
and, as always, to the memory of the King,
Elvis Aaron Presley*

Contents

PART ONE

Consequences

CHAPTER 1

TROUBLE

Sunday, January 6, 1957, Elvis Presley made his third appearance on *The Ed Sullivan Show*. For me it was quite a different night from his first appearance, when all the in-crowd and their boyfriends were here to cheer him on.

This time only Mama and I perched in front of the dope machine, which didn't put her to sleep tonight. She leaned forward on the edge of her easy chair, her eyes sparkling with excitement.

"I think you've learned to like Elvis—and the TV," I said.

She waved a hand to hush me. "Ed's about to introduce him."

He was in the middle of "Hound Dog" before I realized what was different.

"Look, Mama, they're only showing him from the waist up!"

"They're censoring his performance."

"He's still gyrating, though," I said. "You can tell by all the applause and screams from the audience."

"You can't keep a good man down," Mama said with a naughty smile.

I bounced on the red couch. "Listen, listen! He's going to sing 'Peace in the Valley.'"

"A gospel song?" Mama said. "That's a switch. Wonder if he can do it."

"That's where he learned, singing gospel music in church."

When Elvis finished, Ed Sullivan came out, his hand extended.

"This is a real decent, fine boy."

The crowd went wild.

I loved Elvis's little knowing smiles at the audience and the fact that he was still moving and jiving, whether his lower part was visible on camera or not. Elvis was indeed a fine man. I wondered if I would ever see him again.

February 14, 1957, was a bad day for me.

It was bad for my chemistry teacher too. Miss Glovina Armstrong, whose appearance—from her salt-and-pepper flat top like the boys wore, right down to the top of her white socks and tennie-pumps—screamed "old maid schoolteacher."

That morning, our school's star Dilbert, Eugene Hoffmeyer, arrived ten seconds after the bell rang for third period class to begin, and that set her off. I was not sure what set off the queasiness in my stomach. The breakfast I swallowed too fast because I was late leaving to pick up the carpoolers, or something more worrisome?

Eugene skidded through the door and crashed into the lab desk I shared with Maylene McCord.

"Ouch!"

Clutching his knee and hopping on one foot in circles, he slammed into the blackboard, just beneath the giant slide rule.

Miss Glovina rubbed her elbows against her waistline and glared. She performed that action several times every day during our class, and rumor was she did it in other classes as well. To what end, no one had yet divined.

"Eugene Hoffmeyer, kindly remove your backside from my periodic table of elements and take your seat before I give you a tardy slip for detention hall."

"Oh no, Miss Glovina. It's Valentine's Day. I can't stay after school. I was late because I couldn't get my sousaphone to fit in the case and because the band director, you know, Mr. Nesbitt—"

"Spare me your palaver, and give me the common name for acetylsalicylic acid."

"Come again?" sputtered Eugene.

"Quickly, who knows the answer?" Without drawing a breath between names, she called the role, rapid-fire, allowing not a millisecond between one name and the next: "Louise, Mary, Helena, Diane, Ladonna, David, James, Frank, Maylene . . ."

Maylene gave a start and opened her mouth, but Miss Glovina had moved on. "Ju—"

Before she could bleat my name, I shouted through her droning litany, "Aspirin!"

She stopped and stared at me. "One intelligent student in this entire class? Is that all we have?"

"I'm smart, Miss Glovina," Eugene said. "You don't give a person a chance to think."

Again she rubbed her waistline with her elbows.

"I don't when there is no apparent evidence a person has the capacity to perform that act."

Eugene slumped.

"See if you can manage to find that little bottle of acetylsalicylic acid in plain view on top of my desk and fetch it to me so I can numb the pain of having to deal with you for the next . . ." She wheeled to check the wall clock. "Forty minutes."

"Would you like me to get you a glass of—"

"No!"

Eugene handed her the bottle of aspirin and slunk to his seat. She popped two, dry swallowed, stood tall, and frantically jabbed at her waistline with her elbows, at which time a pair of salmon-colored, old-lady panties slipped from beneath her dress and draped around her white socks. With a sigh, she stepped out of them, dropped them in her pocketbook, and snapped it shut.

"Now, as I was saying . . ."

The class covered their faces and shook with silent laughter. I'd have joined in, but my stomach chose that moment to convulse. Clapping my hand over my mouth, I tore out for the girls' restroom. Down the hall, across the dark-brown tiles I dashed, saliva welling in my mouth. Shoving the door with both hands, I barely made it past the lavatories to an open stall before my breakfast flew out in a splash. I heaved and spat until the last of the food gave way to yellow bile and dribbled to nothing.

When I could get my breath, I realized I was on my knees hugging the who-knew-when-it-was-last-cleaned toilet. Fighting not to gag at the thought, I got up and, stooped over like an invalid, made my way to the sinks. A little cold water splashed on my face made me able to return to chemistry class.

Miss Glovina gave me a sharp look when I slipped back into my seat but said nothing, for Principal Younger, who had been on my heels out in the hall, summoned her to the door.

"Are you all right? You've got puke on your pretty blue blouse," Maylene whispered, handing me a hanky.

"I'm fine."

"What's wrong?"

"Probably a touch of food poisoning," I whispered back.

"Hope you feel better," she said and patted my arm.

I forced myself to smile back at her, just as I had been forcing myself to respond to her for weeks. Whenever possible, I focused my attention on other members of the in-crowd without appearing to snub Maylene. I no longer hung on her every word, or took her into my confidence, like I had before she and Farrel went to the Christmas dance together. My aim was to give her the impression we were still friends and never let her know how I much I hated her.

At first, after the night they betrayed me, I'd vowed I would not run with the in-crowd again, but on second thought, I'd decided that to pretend nothing was wrong would be the best course of action. If I totally cut myself off from them, I'd be in Nowheresville again. So, to all appearances, I was still the same Julie—still in the carpool, still going everywhere with them, still pretending Farrel hadn't broken my heart.

At last the bell rang for the end of class. In the hall, Eugene jostled my arm.

"Happy Valentine's Day, Julie," he said. "I know Rhonda has my ring, but I guess I can still give my other girlfriends a valentine, if I want to."

He thrust a crumpled envelope into my hand and speed walked away from me without another word. Inside was a card covered with hearts that said:

"Roses are red, they're pretty, it's true,

But no rose on earth is as pretty as you."

It was signed, "Almost all my love (Rhonda has some of it), Eugene."

Word that Miss Glovina had dropped her drawers spread so fast it nearly set the schoolhouse on fire. During first lunch, Bubba John Younger swiped a key from the rack where his father, Principal Younger, kept spare keys to all the teachers' rooms. Knowing that Miss Glovina took pride in not carrying a load of clutter tucked under her arm in a handbag like the other female teachers did, Bubba John sneaked into the chemistry lab while she was at lunch and pawed around in her old black purse with the frayed handles. By second lunch, the salmon-colored, old-lady panties fluttered on the flag pole right beneath the Stars and Stripes.

In Advanced Junior English class, Miss Bolenbaugh, on tiptoe, danced around the room holding a copy of *Macbeth* in one hand and flailing her other like a nymph who had missed one too many ballet classes.

"'Life's but a walking shadow, a poor player, that struts and frets his hour upon the stage, and then is heard no more,'" she warbled. "To translate these famous lines into a modern rendition, let us say that, with his prize on exhibit beneath our flag, Bubba John now *struts* his hour upon this high school stage, but when his father gets after him with the razor strap this evening, no doubt Bubba John will *fret* his hour, seeing stars and accumulating stripes of his own."

That afternoon, I had another bout of nausea. Mercifully, I felt it coming on soon enough to get permission to go to the girls' room rather than having to dash out of study hall with my hand over my mouth. Still, I barely made it to a toilet before throwing up again. My thoughts ran to the conversation I'd had with Maylene about it being a touch of food poisoning. But I'd only had toast with mayhaw jelly for breakfast and nothing since. That couldn't have given me food poisoning.

"Hi, sis. What cooks?"

I looked up, startled. Carmen stood inside the wooden swinging doors of the restroom. She walked along the row of sinks to stand beside me, and we fell into our typical pose, side by side, fascinated by our duplicate faces in the mirror.

"I pinch myself every morning when I wake up," she said. "I've got a sister!"

Taking both my arms, she turned me to face her.

"Hey, how come you're so pale? Cramps?"

My memory jolted as hard as my stomach had moments before. A fact I'd been trying to ignore out of existence reared and planted its feet in full consciousness. Under the running water, my fingers twitched as adrenalin shot through me.

"Here," she said, digging into her purse. "Take a couple of aspirin."

"Acetylsalicylic acid," I murmured, drying my fingers on my skirt and letting her shake two into my hand.

"You fracture me! You've been in old lady Armstrong's class too long." She grinned. "Love her step-ins hanging on the flag pole. In my class, she had a mad spell and shoved the sliding part of the giant slide rule so hard it flew out the open window. Hit the lawn boy on the head and knocked him clean out. I gotta split, or I'll be late. Listen, what do you figure folks think, now that they know about us?"

The news we were sisters had spread like bubonic plague through town. Mama thought folks had known all along and had scraped up the decency to keep their mouths shut about our dirty laundry. I hoped so, but I had my doubts. When did people ever keep quiet about anything?

"Maybe they'll eventually forget about it and get interested in some other scandal," I said to Carmen.

She nodded. "I hope so. I'd like to be normal and not under the small-town microscope. I'd better tinkle while I'm in here. Hope the aspirin works."

I moved toward the door, so weak I wondered if I could make it back to class.

"Oh, listen," she called out from a stall. "Eugene Hoffmeyer stuck a valentine in my hand that he meant for you this morning. You should have seen the look on his face when I told him I was Carmen. He snatched that valentine back so fast! To think, I had to tell him I wasn't you. Don't that beat all?"

CHAPTER 2
Good Luck Charm

I drove the group that day, so after school Darcy, Maylene, Laura, and Lynn trailed after me out onto the campus.

"The carpool's not the same without Frances," Laura said.

Every day one of us made that same remark. It was true, but sometimes I thought I would scream if I heard it one more time. Our witty Frances, who kept us splitting our sides with her jokes and wisecracks, was gone, leaving us shocked and despondent.

"Are you sick, Julie?" Darcy draped an arm around my shoulder as we walked toward the car. "Maylene told us you tossed your cookies this morning."

"I'm fine!" I said, shrugging free of her heavy arm meant to be consoling.

But I wasn't fine. I was a wreck and chomping at the bit to get home.

"Look who's headed for his car across the street," Laura said.

My face burned hot. Justin Moore hadn't called me since the Christmas dance. The only reason he took me was because Maylene had gone with Farrel. There was nothing between Justin and me, but still, I felt put down that he hadn't called, especially since he and Maylene weren't going out anymore. Word on the grapevine was he'd dumped her, but she claimed she already had a date every time he called.

Only one of us had a class with him and the opportunity to wheedle out his side of the story, and that was Lynn. But she reported that the most he ever said was "Hi."

We watched him head straight for his car. Just when I thought he'd get in without so much as a glance in our direction, he looked up and caught us staring at him

He flicked a wave and reached for the door. Then, as though he'd had second thoughts, he headed over toward us.

"Hi, Julie," he said with a nod to the others, who stood looking at him with goofy grins smeared on their faces.

He is awful cute, I thought.

Maylene edged past Darcy and squeezed next to me.

"Justin, hi!" She gazed up at him with that innocent and at the same time provocative look she used on boys she was pursuing. "How have you been?"

"Busy. Listen, Julie, I—"

Maylene sidled close to him. "I hear you got accepted into Princeton."

He kept looking at me. "Yes, I—"

"Congratulations!" Maylene said with loud enthusiasm.

Justin finally looked directly at her. "Thanks."

After a long moment of searching each other's faces, they both averted their eyes.

"I've got to run," he said with a frown of discomfort. "I'll call you, Julie."

Maylene stood watching him cross the street to his car, but I jumped into the driver's seat of Mama's green-and-white Chevy and started the engine. Maylene barely had time to get in before I put it in gear.

"And awa-a-ay we go," Darcy sang as I pulled out.

"You know what, Darcy?" Maylene said. "You're way too cheerful. You're getting on my nerves with that bouncing and grinning like a Cheshire Cat. You need to be more anti-frantic."

"I'm just a happy girl. You should try smiling once in a while."

"Smiling makes wrinkles," Maylene retorted. "Did you know Diane de Poitiers of France never smiled or frowned, she was so afraid of getting wrinkles."

Darcy gave a heavy sigh. "We all know who Diane de Poitiers was, Maylene. I don't care to model myself after a loose woman, even if she was the mistress of a king."

I cringed. Darcy would think I was a loose woman, if she knew.

Darcy continued her lecture. "Maybe, if you mind your manners and act more ladylike, Justin'll call you again."

"He already calls me!" Maylene snapped.

"He didn't act like it."

Darcy ducked her head, as if to evade a blow.

I knew they'd both protest their sparring was all in fun but, in reality, the car was fraught with tension. All the girls knew how gone I was over Farrel, especially Maylene, and they all disapproved of her going to the dance with him. Supposedly, I was her best friend.

"Imagine," Lynn had said privately to me, "her finagling him into taking her. She absolutely could not bear for people to say that Maylene the Great didn't have a date. Hey, made a rhyme. See my fellow before bedtime. If she'd only cooled her heels, she could have gone with Justin. He got back in time to take her."

"Maybe it was Farrel who did the finagling," I'd said.

Lynn's eyes had grown wide. "I hope you're not taking up for her!"

"It's water over the dam," I'd said, but it wasn't. It would never be. I could never forgive either one of them.

"I like this car," Lynn said, shifting the focus off Maylene and Darcy.

Dear Lynn. She always tried to defuse a situation, but I felt she was just being polite about Mama's inexpensive car.

"It's no great shakes," I said.

She pointed toward the rear. "It has fins, even if they are little ones."

"Nowhere near as big and cool as the fins on Darcy's Dreamsicle," I said.

Laura leaned over from the backseat. "We all love the Dreamsicle. It's so spacious and comfy."

Maylene jumped in. "Almost too big. My daddy says it's definitely too flashy."

Darcy struck right back at her. "But your folks' car—that little Plymouth—has curved rear fenders with no fins at all. We could barely fit into it before, and now, even without Frances, it's still a tight squeeze."

Maylene's snide voice came from the backseat. "That's not a nice thing to say, Darcy. Maybe it's a tight squeeze because you're so big. If you're all that uncomfortable riding in it, you can just drop out of the carpool."

"I may be big boned and tall, but I don't have a roll of fat around my waist like you do."

Maylene bristled. "There's not an ounce of fat on me!"

"All right, you two, knock it off," Lynn said.

Laura joined in. "This car fits us fine, and so does Maylene's, and they always have, even when Frances was still . . . Oh dear, I'm going to cry."

"We can get eight in here," I said, trying to steer us away from the usual gloom that our conversations eventually settled into these days.

"Remember last Easter," Maylene said, smirking, "when we all picked up Larson, Justin, Don, and Farrel at the Dairyette and went parking in the woods?"

My heart twisted. That was the first time Farrel and I ever kissed.

"We didn't *all* go," Laura and Lynn said in unison, clearly still ticked off about it.

"Oh, right. Sorry," Maylene said. "But just think, if we'd *all* gone, you wouldn't have had the fun of hearing about it."

An uncomfortable silence enveloped us.

Was that the night when Frances had gotten pregnant? She and Don had left the car and disappeared, and it'd taken quite a while to roust them out of the woods when it was time to leave.

As I turned the corner onto Main Street, Darcy said, "Who have you asked for a date to the Sadie Hawkins dance, Julie?"

"To the what?"

"Gee whillikers, Julie, get on the stick. Next week is TWIRP week. Saturday night caps it off with the Sadie Hawkins dance."

"I forgot all about it," I said.

"Can you believe this girl?" exclaimed Darcy.

"I can," Maylene said.

Maylene had threatened me last year that, if I didn't get a boyfriend, the in-crowd would have to drop me. That was partly why I ended up doing IT with Farrel. I'd tried so, so hard to get him to love me, or even like me enough to be a regular date and get Maylene off my back.

"Julie, pay attention," Darcy said. "You know Al Capp's hillbilly comic strip, *Li'l Abner*, don't you? Sadie Hawkins Day and TWIRP week are the only chances a girl gets to ask a boy of her dreams for a date."

"And pay for him," Laura added. "TWIRP stands for The Woman Is Required to Pay. I'm planning to ask fourteen boys out for next week. I've been saving for months to buy cokes for them at the Dairyette."

"There are only seven nights in a week," Maylene said in her know-it-all voice.

Laura groaned. "I know that, Maylene, but there are also seven afternoons. I want to ask Bubba John Younger for one of my fourteen. He's so cute." Laura's voice turned wistful. "I wish he'd ask *me* out."

"If it hasn't happened yet, more than likely it's not going to." Maylene sounded like she was issuing a decree.

Laura sighed. "I know. In the end, I probably won't ask anybody. I never do. I'm scared they'll either say 'no,' or their parents will *make* them go, and they'll wish they didn't have to, and they'll make sure I know it, and we'll both be miserable."

Darcy poked my arm. "I bet that's why Justin's going to call you, to give you a chance to ask him. Everyone know you're shy."

Not anymore, I thought, remembering the day I called Farrel at school and told him I was "ready" to do IT. Madness had taken possession of me.

Darcy looked over into the backseat. "Who are you going to ask, Maylene?"

I held my breath, hoping against hope she wouldn't say Farrel.

The sensible voice in my head said, "What do you care if she asks Farrel? It doesn't matter anymore."

I wished it didn't. *If she says "Farrel," I might wreck the car.*

"I haven't decided yet," Maylene said. "Look, there goes Eugene Hoffmeyer in that crate he's been driving since the year one. I wonder if Rhonda still has his ring."

"He gave me a valentine after chemistry class this morning," I said. "You should ask him."

I could see Maylene's face in the rearview mirror, looking satisfied, like she'd thought of the perfect solution to my dateless state.

I flipped my hair. "Ask him yourself, if you think he's so cute."

"It looks like he's headed for the Dairyette," Darcy said. "Are we going, Julie? Let's do. We haven't been to the Dairyette since Frances. Life goes on, you know."

"I don't feel right about it yet," Laura said. "The carpool should still be in mourning. It's barely been two months. If you're going, take me home first."

"I know!" Darcy bounced on the seat. "Let's go to the cemetery. We can visit her grave. We haven't done that yet. We can say a prayer and then go to the Dairyette."

Lynn gasped. "Are you out of your tree? I'm never going back to that cemetery."

Maylene chortled. "You are someday."

"Come on, you all, don't be like that," Darcy said. "You know what? I've been thinking."

"That's a new twist," Maylene said.

"Shut up, Maylene. This is important."

"Okay, tell us."

"Frances died of the flu, right?" Darcy said, her voice taking on a mysterious tone. "But I haven't heard about another case of it since. Last time we had a flu epidemic, it was in the newspapers every day how many people were sick. Don't you all think it's strange nobody else seems to have caught it?"

"Hmmm . . ." Maylene said, and another thoughtful silence fell over the car.

My thoughts went into a silent frenzy. I couldn't let them get on that track. As far as I knew only Farrel, Don, Mama, Carmen and her mother, Frances's folks, and I knew the truth about what had killed Frances. But as Mama always said, "Two can keep a secret, if one of them is dead."

"We'll go another day soon, okay?" I said. "Darcy's right, life does have to go on."

Driving home after dropping them off, I thought maybe I should get out of the carpool.

I'm being hypocritical by staying in it when I loathe Maylene. I loathe her but miss her at the same time. She was my confidant, my best friend. Now I have no one I can talk to.

When I turned onto our street, the fear that had gnawed at me all day welled up into my mouth, and I thought for a minute I was going to throw up all over myself and the car. I had to get home fast and check something that had been eating at me all day. I had to do it, and yet every inch forward the car went filled me with more dread.

I'll check the mail first, I thought, heading straight for the mailbox on the front porch. Bills, bills, and again bills. In the middle of the pile was an envelope addressed to me. Tossing the rest on the commode, as Mama insisted on calling the hutch in the entrance hall, I tore it open and yanked out the red-and-white card, hoping against hope Farrel had sent me a valentine. But the name signed beneath the verse was "Elvis." *Not a bad substitute!* A note was handwritten on the opposite side.

Dear Juliet,

Hope this reaches you in time for Valentine's Day. You'll never believe it, but remember when you said you were all shook up over a guy and I wrote back that "All Shook Up" would be a good title for a song? Well, after that, I went to bed one night, had quite a dream, and woke up all shook up myself. I called my friend, Otis Blackwell, and before you could shake a bull by the tail he'd composed a song using those words. This is the best part—I get credit as co-writer because I said "All Shook Up" would make a good refrain! How about them apples? I recorded it on January 12 out in Hollywood. I'll send you a cut as soon as it's released.

I hope you are doing great and having a ball. Drop me a line, if you have a minute. Your letters bring my toes back down to the ground and remind me of real places and real folks. And, by the way, I sent you this card with the hope that, no matter who has your heart, you, my good luck charm, will always save a part of yourself to be my valentine. After all, as the first girl who ever screamed at one of my concerts, you get the credit for this incredible ride I'm on. I have to confess, sometimes I want to stop and get off, but I'm afraid it's too late for that.

My best,
Elvis

To him, I was still that innocent young girl he gave a ride home one night. I couldn't imagine why he was still writing me, now that he had the world at his feet. We were never more than friends, and barely that. We'd had so little time together—and yet it seemed it was enough to make us friends forever. I didn't understand it, but then, I didn't need to. It just was.

I couldn't put off any longer the deed I had to do. In my room, my personal planner was open to February. I knew what I was looking for wouldn't be there. I nearly ripped out the page, flipping back to January. Nothing there either. Then I realized I was looking at my 1957 planner. Last year's was the one that would tell the tale.

I had hidden it so well from Mama I couldn't remember myself where it was. I rushed to the box on the top shelf of my closet where I stored my stuff. Not there. I yanked open the drawer in my bedside table. Not there. Not in any of the dresser drawers. Not under the bed. One last place—my hatbox.

It was there, and what it told made my insides twist, even though I had known it all along—known, but repressed it—tried so hard to pretend it couldn't possibly be true. A small "p" was penciled in next to December 7.

I hadn't had a period since Farrel and I did IT.

CHAPTER 3
FOR A CAP AND BELLS

Two weeks later, I rehearsed my speech to Mama all the way home from Magnolia, but I could only get as far as two of the three words. Over and over I tried to recite all three. On the road. In our driveway. And on the walk leading to the house. Never getting any further than, "I am . . . I am . . ."

With her feet propped up on the old footstool, Mama was deeply immersed in the latest Mary Stewart novel when I opened the back door and went into the den. For some odd reason, I could only focus on the straw sticking out through the split in the stool's leather up-holstery and how it highlighted the shabby state we lived in so Mama could spend almost everything she earned on me.

She looked up at me over the top of her glasses and smiled.

"Hi, honey. What's up?"

"Nothing, much."

That's not what I meant to say.

I put my school books on the table in the breakfast nook and got a drink of water from the cooler the iceman filled every day. I sipped slowly to postpone the awful moment. Swallowing the last drop, I forced myself to go and stand over her.

"Just let me finish this page," she said, lost in the world of Merlin. At last she dragged her gaze up to me. "Okay. Now you have my full attention."

"Mama . . ." I paused, unable to get my breath.

"That's me." She grinned.

"I am."

The perpendicular frown line that lived perpetually between her eyebrows deepened.

"Am what?"

"Pregnant."

Too late I remembered that in her mind the word "pregnant" was not a socially acceptable term for my condition.

She blanched. Using both hands, she reached for the stale glass of tea on the table by her chair. She took a sloshy sip, wiped her chin with the back of her hand, and smiled.

"Now, now, let's not jump to conclusions. It's nothing to miss a period or two at your age."

"I had the rabbit test."

"Oh my God." Stark fear filled her eyes. "You went to a doctor?"

I nodded. "Twice. At my first visit, he did the test, and today at the follow up appointment, he told me my rabbit had died."

"Whom did you see?"

Even under stress of the worst kind, Mama never flubbed her grammar.

"A doctor in Magnolia. Gave him a false name." I held out my left hand. "I even wore this cheap wedding band I won at the county fair playing Go Fish. It didn't fool him for one minute. Oh, Mama, it was awful. First, I had to give them some tinkle. The doctor said they would shoot my pee into a rabbit, and if he died, then I was."

"Use the proper word, please, Julie, and the rabbit wouldn't be a 'he.' Only females are used, and they all die from the test because the lab people cut them open and check to see if their ovaries are affected by the hormone present in the urine of a woman who's expecting."

I stared at her, flabbergasted. "How on earth do you know that?"

"I was in the family way once."

"Right. With me." My attempt at laughter floundered. "The worst part was the nurse made me take off all my clothes! I thought he would only be concerned with the bottom end."

"You must not have minded removing your clothes when you performed the act that landed you in this predicament," Mama said, clipping her words.

"I didn't take off anything but—"

"Please, spare me the gruesome details," Mama said.

I couldn't look at her.

"Two trips to Magnolia, and I never knew. I did notice, however, that we were using an awful lot of gas recently. Why didn't you tell me?"

"I warned you at Christmas it could be."

Her face crinkled. "What are we going to do?"

"Mama, don't start. We aren't going to do anything. We knew this was a possibility. You said you could handle it, that I could stay home and have my baby."

"I wasn't myself that night."

"What do you mean?"

She leaped up from her chair, shrieking, "I mean, you can't stay here in El Dorado, pregnant!" She jerked open her pocketbook and dug around in it. "Why in God's name did I give up smoking?"

"I don't care what those people think. They can't hurt me."

"*Those people* can most certainly hurt you!"

"How?"

"For starters, no young man from a good family will want to marry you."

"I never cared about those rich, society boys anyway."

Mama looked at me like I was an alien from outer space.

"No young man from any family will want to marry you."

"I don't care. All boys think about is some stupid football game."

"The games are our primary form of entertainment in the South. And I'm sure the young men think about making money. Unless you can snag a man who'll make you a good living, and fat chance you'll have of that with a child, you'll have to work." Mama blew her nose. "*Those people* can keep you from getting a job. Who's going to want someone with loose morals teaching their children?"

"I don't have loose morals! And what makes you think I would teach school?"

"Then what do you plan to do? There's not much other than typing, teaching, or nursing that a woman *can* do."

I broke our locked stare. She had won.

"Go ahead. Tell me. What?" she demanded.

"I don't know. Be a musician, maybe. I hadn't thought much about it."

"Well, you'd better start thinking. I can't support you forever." She slung her purse to the floor. "Maybe there's an old pack left over in another pocketbook." She hurried toward the breakfast room. "God, please, I'll be good forever, if you'll just let there be one left."

"I only ever did it one time, Mama, and it was with the boy I loved," I shouted after her.

She stopped short. "Once is enough to make people call you a slut. That's why I didn't want you going out with Mr. Budrow. He's too old for you. I was afraid it would come to this. Have you told him yet?"

"I don't plan to tell him."

Mama smiled her cynical smile. "How did you think you could keep the baby and not tell him? I'm sure he'll find out, whether or not you ever deign to mention it. So marrying him is not an option?"

"No."

I thought of Farrel's comment on marriage: "Hell'll freeze over before I get married."

"In a way, that's good. At least you won't be saddled with a loser for the rest of your life. I have to check my other purses."

I put my hand on my abdomen. My baby was in there—and Farrel's baby. It was a miracle. I sat on one of the modern couches and struggled to twist the fake wedding ring on my finger. It didn't want to come off.

I could hear Mama in her closet, slinging purses. What would my father say if I told him? But that was out of the question. In spite of our meeting back on Christmas Eve, he was still a stranger to me.

Mama came back to the den, stoop shouldered.

"Nothing but some loose tobacco in the bottom of one."

She sank into her chair.

I tried to speak calmly. "I would *hate* teaching."

"With an illegitimate child, they won't let you type and take short-hand for them either, those hotshots in their plush, two-story offices downtown. I doubt if a one of them has ever been to New York and seen a real building."

"The guidance counselor says a woman can do anything she wants to," I said.

"She gets paid four thousand dollars a year to say that."

"How do you know?"

"She substituted at bridge club and bragged about her salary all night."

"What do you make, Mama?"

"Not nearly enough. Even with the hundred and seventy-five dollar raise that brought it up to three thousand a year, I'm constantly having to rob Peter to pay Paul. But that's because I stash something away each month for your college tuition and . . . your wedding."

That last word brought her to tears, but after a few sobbing breaths, she cut them off and sat up straight.

My gaze followed hers as it drifted through the den windows to the backyard. Outside, the chilly weather we in the South called winter draped its dismal gloom over the leafless sycamores and neglected perennial beds, blanketed with fall's unraked leaves.

"Just today, a traffic light caught me by the shop where I got my green dress back in December," I said. "The day Farrel and Maylene made their date for the Christmas dance. They both betrayed me. The hurt of that feels like it will be with me forever."

"One thing certain and two things sure," Mama said, "the shame and disgrace of being pregnant out of wedlock will be with you forever, and not exclusively in this town. Everywhere. That's how women who break the rules are treated in this world."

I mocked her. "Out of wedlock."

She turned on me. "What did you say, young lady?"

"Nothing. It's just that you're so old-fashioned."

"You'll think old-fashioned when you're shunned by everyone in this town. I'll contact some homes for girls in trouble." She yanked a fresh tissue from the box on the floor by her chair. "Oh God, everything is lost. Everything I've worked for, saved for all these years."

"Mama, I can't bear it if you send me away."

"There's no alternative, Julie. All my work to teach you the manners needed to be socially acceptable, how to set a proper table, how to make your home lovely so it will be a haven for your successful, socially prominent husband that now you'll never have. Lost. All *your* work and study to make honor roll and National Honor Society is lost. Wasted. You may have even ruined your chance to get an education. Pregnant girls are not allowed to attend school, in case you didn't know. And if, by dent and maneuver, we can keep this a secret and manage to get you through high school and into the university, what sorority will take a girl whose reputation is sullied?"

"I don't care about being in a sorority."

"You will when you realize that no decent boy will date a GDI."

"What's a GDI?"

"A goddamned independent. Someone not in a sorority or fraternity."

"Mama, I don't even want to go to college."

"You'll need an education to support yourself. I've sacrificed so you could enjoy your young years and not have to wait tables or work as a cashier at Safeway after school. And now . . ."

I could only sit and watch as Mama covered her face with her hands and wept. I was her great disappointment. I wasn't a bad girl. I wasn't a slut. But I had failed my mother completely with one mistake, and that cut into my heart.

After a moment, she wiped her eyes.

"I'm sorry, honey. I don't mean to hurt you any more than you are already hurt. It's just that I've had to bear so much in my life."

I leaned toward her. "But you're going to have a grandchild. Isn't that the joyful side of this nightmare? Doesn't that mean anything to you, Mama?"

"Given the circumstances, it only spells shame and disgrace." She crossed her arms over her chest and meandered to the far end of the room. Holding up a finger, she whirled around to face me. "I'll arrange for you to go to a home for unwed mothers, and we'll put out the story that you're away for a while getting special treatment for an illness."

I scoffed. "Who in their right mind will believe that?"

"The whole town believes Frances Latimer died of the flu."

"Do they? Just the other day the girls in the carpool were questioning that little fabrication."

Mama puckered her brows in her typical worried look.

"Besides, it's obvious I'm healthy. What illness would you have me come down with?"

"I don't know yet. I'll come up with one."

"Stop it! Just stop it, right now! I won't go! You can't make me!"

Mama came over and gathered me in her arms.

"Now, now. I'll protect you. We'll work it out. You made a mistake, but it was one of those wonderful impulses of the moment? Wasn't it?"

It wasn't. I'd done it deliberately, hoping to make Farrel love me. And I'd been so scared.

"Even though it didn't make him love me, being close to him that way was eighteen-karat gold."

Mama smiled her cynical smile again. "'For a cap and bells our lives we pay.'"

CHAPTER 4
I Got Stung

I needed a friend, a girl friend I could talk to. The only person I could think of was Carmen, of all people. She couldn't have been more surprised than I was when she opened the door of her grandmother's little house on East Third Street where she and her mother lived. Every time I laid eyes on her and saw a replica of myself, I felt the same shock.

"Come on in. Take a load off. Coffee?"

"Is your mother here?"

"At work."

"Then yes, please. I would like a cup. That is, if you're not busy watching after your grandmother."

Her face paled. "My grandmother died."

"Oh no! When?"

"A couple of weeks ago."

"Why didn't you tell me?"

"I didn't think you'd be interested."

"Oh, I'm so sorry."

"So am I. I'll miss her."

In the kitchen, I sat at the small table and watched Carmen set up the percolator and plug it in.

"So, to what do I owe the honor of your presence?" she asked in a sarcastic tone as she sat in the chair next to mine.

"I need to tell you something." I toyed with a stray spoon left on the table.

"Nothing bad, I hope?"

"Pretty bad."

For a long minute, I couldn't go on.

She leaned in toward me. "Yesss?"

I took a stunted breath. "That time in the girls' room at school."

"Yes, go on."

"It wasn't cramps."

Instant comprehension flashed on her face. "You're not telling me you have Frances's non-existent flu?"

"Pretty much, yeah. It was morning sickness."

"In the afternoon?"

I struggled to hold back tears. "I threw up that morning too. The doctor said it can happen anytime."

"Oh my God, the doctor. Then you're sure?"

"I'm sure."

It got so quiet in the kitchen, I could hear the faint ticking of a clock from another room off somewhere in the house. She chewed her lower lip.

"Don't take this wrong, but it is Farrel's, isn't it?"

"Yep. Only one guy. Only one time."

She squeezed my hand. "Boy, that's a real bite. Pregnant the first time out. You must really love him. I don't see you as the type who'd do IT with just anybody."

"I thought it would make him love me, but it didn't. And you're right, I did love him, but I don't anymore."

She snapped her fingers. "Over him, just like that, huh?"

"After he betrayed me with Maylene? Yes, just like that."

Carmen shook her head and got up to pour the coffee. I looked around the cluttered room. There were no cabinets, just an old hutch crammed with mismatched dishes, haphazardly stacked. On the table, an ashtray of Woolworths red glass variety held a mound of cigarettes smoked down to the last centimeter. The leftover smoke from the dead butts clung to the walls and seeped into my clothes, making it hard to breathe.

She opened the hutch and, after a few moments of surveying the crammed-in dishes, took out two mugs whose flowered patterns made them similar enough to pass as part of a set.

"We got these on a trip to Memphis," she said, holding them up. "They're my favorite. There used to be two more but . . . Mother threw one at my stepfather one night, and he threw the other one back at her."

I shuddered at the thought of living with such explosive people.

Returning to the table with the two steaming coffees, she added, "Mind you, my folks don't hurt each other. They just enjoy smashing things up. Oops, forgot the cream."

I took the glass bottle she brought back to the table and poured a creamy splash into my mug while she reached for the Pall Malls next to the ashtray.

"Shit. Empty." She crushed the pack in her fist. "I don't know if I can handle this visit without a weed."

"Coffee's good," I said.

"Deep breath, deep breath." She inhaled stale kitchen air and broke into a cough. "I sound like Mother. Now's a good time to quit, I guess. One positive thing about your whole mess."

"What could that possibly be?" I asked, rolling my eyes.

"At least now you know what a tallywacker looks like."

"A what?"

"A boy's ding-a-ling. I've never seen one. I'm a virgin, if you can believe it."

"That's the irony of it all," I said, taking a sip of coffee. "Farrel and I did it in the backseat of his car, and it was dark. I didn't get to see it."

"Shucks." Carmen made a face. "Here I was all ready to get a bona-fide description of one. No pun intended."

I giggled. "I remember the only time in my life I did get to see one."

Her eyes danced. She leaned forward. "Tell."

"I was down in New Orleans visiting Aunt Hattie."

"Who's that?"

"Mama's aunt. Anyway, I was only about nine years old, and she took me to visit a cousin who had just had a baby—a little boy. While we were there, his mother changed his diapers, and I got to watch.

You have to remember, I'd never seen anyone naked but girls. I about dropped dead when I got a load of his thing. The thought ran through my head that all babies must be born that way, myself included, then after a few months that part 'down there' must change somehow so they look like I look now. You realize Mama had never told me a thing. Still hasn't. Oh, she has plenty to say about most everything else, but she's always mute about important things, like the birds and the bees."

Carmen hooted.

"On the way home, I said to Aunt Hattie, 'He'll change, won't he, Aunt Hattie? It'll fall off, and he'll look normal.' Her mouth twisted all out of shape, and I could tell she was fighting tooth and toenail to keep from laughing. She said, 'No, honey, nothing's going to fall off. That's how you tell whether the baby is a boy or a girl.'

"'Oh,' I said to her. 'I thought you had to wait until they were old enough to grow hair on their bald little heads, and if it grew long, the baby was a girl, and if it stayed short, it was a boy.'"

"Stop, stop," Carmen begged, holding her sides as tears rolled down her face.

"I never told Mama about that incident. She's a real prude."

"No lie!" She opened the crushed cigarette pack and felt inside again. "Not even a broken one. I can't continue this without a cigarette." She dug in the ashtray and chose the longest butt. "Now, if I can light this without setting my eyelashes on fire."

"Or burning the end of your nose."

She took the only drag left on the stumpy butt and crushed it out.

"So, tell me. What about the baby?"

I frowned. "What about it?"

"Do you feel anything for it? I mean love or something like that?"

I put my hand over my abdomen. "I do, yes. Funny you should think of that. Mama didn't."

Carmen's curled lip matched the cynicism of her words. "I bet she's ready to kill you."

"That's the general idea."

"All mothers sing the same song. Don't get pregnant. You'll disgrace the whole family if you do."

"She wants to send me away."

"Where to?"

"A home for unwed mothers. Carmen, I don't want to be sent off. I want to stay here and have my baby."

She reached for my hand again. "Honey girl, don't cry. That won't help a thing. What does Farrel say?"

"I haven't told him, and I don't intend to."

"You have got to be out of your mind!"

"I don't want him to know."

"Don't you imagine he's bound to pick up the scent sooner or later?"

"He'll be away at school."

She shook her head. "He's home every weekend."

"If Mama sends me off, there's no way he'll ever find out about the baby."

"Won't he wonder where you've disappeared to?"

"Mama says we'll put out the story that I've been sent off to get treatment for some disease."

"Terminal! Tell her it has to be terminal. Pregnant girls who get sent away have to be on the brink of death. But whatever disease you pick, it won't fool anybody. The whole town will titter up their sleeves and say 'Boy or girl?'—especially when you have a miraculous cure and get back home just in time for your senior year."

"Oh no."

"You know it's true."

"You're right," I said, loathing to look back on my own insensitive treatment of a girl in my predicament. "A girl in the class ahead of us got sent off last year with a 'terminal illness.' Everybody laughed and screamed about it. They had a coke party for her when she got home, to celebrate her *miraculous* recovery. Afterwards, when we were on the way to the car, my own mother said she could tell by the mature look of the girl's upper arms that she'd had a baby. I laughed at her, but now I see it's not so funny. Genevieve Hayes. Poor thing. Hasn't lived it down yet."

"Never will." Carmen lit another butt, sucked the one drag left, and crushed it out.

"Why don't you just tell Farrel? I bet you a dollar he'd marry you. He's not a bad sort."

"He might marry me, but he wouldn't be happy."

"What's him being happy got to do with it? Are *you* going to be happy? That's the question. The goal here is to keep your life from being ruined."

"He'd feel his life was ruined, then mine would be too. When I asked him why Don didn't marry Frances instead of paying for the abortion that killed her, his exact words were, 'It would have ruined everything.'" The knot in my throat swelled, pushing tears into my eyes. "Besides, I don't want him to be unhappy."

"And you don't love him anymore," she said in a cynical tone. "Don't kid yourself, sis. You love him. Although, before God, I don't know why."

I took a shuddering breath. "There is no fire . . ."

"What?"

"Something Mama always says. 'There is no fire like that of the first love.' I guess maybe she is right about that, but she's not right about sending me off to a home and making me sign my baby away."

"You can't be planning on keeping it, if you don't even want to marry its father."

"Yes, I will keep it. I could never let my baby go."

"Then I guess you don't mind being labeled a 'bad girl' for the rest of your life." Carmen looked at me with sober eyes. "Face reality. You know you can't stay here pregnant out of wedlock, and you can't keep it either. If you don't tell Farrel and get him to marry you, you'll probably never get married at all. What decent man will marry a fallen woman with a child?"

"You sound exactly like Mama."

"It's how the cookie crumbles, sister-of-mine. And getting married is what a woman's life is all about, so they say."

She dragged a book from the opposite end of the table and flipped it open.

"This cookbook says it all. It's not how smart the woman is to create and test the recipe or pass it down from Grandma, it's how desirable she is to have caught a man and gotten him to marry her. That's more important than the recipe any day of the week."

Carmen flicked a polished nail on the open page. "Look here. Does it say Betty Cade contributed this soup recipe? No. It says Mrs. Jasper Cade, Junior, with Betty in parentheses next to her married name. It's like that all through this book, at the bottom of every recipe, except for the few who never married or who divorced, like your mother." She jabbed a finger at one of Mama's recipes. "Here, it includes this recipe for Crawfish Étouffée by Mrs. Elizabeth Lawrence Morgan. The Lawrence Morgan part tells everyone she's divorced."

"Let's not talk about that," I said.

"You're up against a wall, honey girl. If you stay here, unmarried with a baby, your recipes will never make the League of Socially Acceptable Women's Cookbook. You better go on to the home for the unweds, have the baby, and put it up for adoption.

"On the other hand," she continued, "if a pregnant girl gets married, all is forgiven because everyone who's anyone knows the second baby takes nine months, but the first baby can come any time."

I laughed and cried simultaneously, and Carmen laughed with me. Afterwards, we sat in companionable silence for a long time. She was right. I knew she was. And Mama knew it too. She was deceiving herself if she believed any amount of elaborate planning could prevent my scandalous secret from heading the gossip agenda of every bridge club or tea party in town.

Carmen looked up at me from lowered lids, as if she wanted to say something but was afraid to.

I leaned in to her. "What?"

"Nothing. It's just that I'm glad you came to me. It makes us more like real sisters. I'll do whatever I can to help you."

"That's sweet, but what can you do? Nothing. There's nothing anyone can do."

She looked past me, pensively.

"Maybe. Maybe not."

CHAPTER 5
Wooden Heart

Mama was standing at the commode in tears when I got home.

"I simply can't take any more!"

"What now?" I asked, weary of all the problems that had assailed us.

She held out a letter written on see-through paper and fragrant with old-lady perfume.

"Aunt Hattie is coming."

I rubbed my head that had developed a dull ache during my visit with Carmen.

"That's bad."

Mama shook her head. "Worse than bad. She's coming to inspect you—us—to see if we're living according to her standards of propriety."

"Who cares about her standards?"

"I do. If she finds us up to snuff, she might leave us a little something in her will."

"Are we her only kin?"

"The only surviving, since her nephew, Michael, and his parents died. You remember, his father was my brother, Hamilton Lawrence the third. We wouldn't be in her will at all if Michael were still living, you can count on that. He was her pride and joy. Michael Durell Lawrence."

"What did they die of?"

"A boating accident on Lake Pontchartrain."

"If we're her only kin, then who else could she leave it to?"

"The DAR, or the Colonial Dames of the Seventeenth Century, or the United Daughters of the Confederacy. They'd be the most likely candidates."

"When is she coming?"

"June fifteenth, for at least two weeks, maybe more."

"I'll be six months along by then!"

Mama flailed the air with both hands. "Why do you think I'm beside myself?"

"What are we going to do?"

"Send you to a home for unwed mothers, that's what."

"But where will you tell her I am?"

"I haven't the faintest idea."

The room swayed. I leaned against the commode. Mama grabbed my arm.

"Are you going to faint?"

"No, I just got a little dizzy. It's passing now."

She led me toward the den. "You need to sit down."

"How much would 'a little something' be?" I asked when I was sitting on the couch across from the windows.

"It could be quite a bit. Her father, your great-grandfather, left her well off. He was a prominent man in the shipping industry down in New Orleans. Did I tell you, she was once a Mardi Gras Queen? She's so old now, she might not have two nickels left to rub together. If she does have any money left, you'd think she'd fix up that rundown family mansion in the Garden District she lives in, if for no other reason than to keep up appearances. Money can buy everything in this life."

"Money can't buy happiness," I said.

She turned an astonished face on me. "But it can certainly buy a reasonable facsimile. Where did you ever hear such falderal?"

"Aunt Hattie told me herself, when I was visiting her that summer."

"Oh dear. Maybe that means she doesn't have much."

"You're always the pessimist," I said. "It could mean she has money and it hasn't brought her any happiness."

Mama eased down into her chair and gazed out the window.

"Funny you heard from her today," I said. "I was just talking about her."

Mama raised one eyebrow. "To whom?"

"Carmen."

"And what were you telling Miss Carmen about your Great-Aunt Hattie."

Even now, at sixteen and pregnant, I didn't feel I could tell Mama about seeing the diaper changed.

"Only that I'd visited her in New Orleans."

"Where did you run into Miss Carmen?"

I could scream when Mama quizzed me like that.

"I didn't. I went to see her. She is my sister. I guess I can see her when I want to."

Mama lifted an imperious chin. "I'd rather you didn't."

I looked her straight in the eye. "I'm going to see my father again too."

"You love to provoke me, don't you?"

"I didn't do it to provoke you. Is Aunt Hattie sick?"

"She doesn't indicate she is."

"Then why is she talking about leaving stuff?"

"She isn't. I'm just ruminating because she's old enough to be thinking about it. She turns eighty on June twenty-third."

"I'd forgotten we have the same birthday."

"If she gets wind of your condition, she'll think we live in moral degeneration, and she'll renounce us on the spot."

"She must already think that, given your scandalous divorce," I said in self-defense, deliberately trying to rattle Mama's cage.

She bristled. "To the self-righteous, who consider themselves morally superior, divorce pales in comparison to pregnancy out of wedlock. And now, just as she must be thinking enough time has passed since the divorce that she can visit us without bringing shame down on her own head by association, you turn up pregnant."

"She's an old maid, fixin' to be a great, great aunt. Won't a new baby carry some weight with her?"

"Not an ounce. Be serious, Julie. If nothing else has proved it to you, this letter from Aunt Hattie must. You absolutely have to go to a home or reveal the situation to Mr. Budrow and get him to marry you."

We sat in silence for a long while. Finally, I asked, "Seriously, if I do go to a home, where will you tell her I am?"

Mama's face shattered. "I don't know. I just don't know. Hand me that box of tissues, will you?"

"I guess you could say I'm at that girls' school in Dallas you once threatened to send me to."

"School is not in session in June!"

A knock sounded at the front door.

"Who could that be?" Mama said, jerking upright and wiping her eyes.

From the living room we could see the tall figure peeping in through the glass in our front door. The lights were off, in spite of the dreary afternoon. I didn't feel like having company. Maybe he couldn't see us.

"Whose face is that, looking in?" Mama asked from behind me.

"Julie," he called, knocking again, almost frantically. "Julie, I know you're in there."

It was Farrel. I moved to the door and opened it.

"Why do you all keep your doors locked in the daytime?" he demanded through the screen. "This is El Dorado."

An entire essay flashed through my mind explaining that we'd locked our doors for years because of my father's violence and the whole sordid story, but I only said, "Force of habit, I guess."

We stood, looking at each other, the damp cold of February seeping into the house. He shivered, and I pushed open the screen door.

"Sorry to bust in like this," he said, "but I've called and called. Don't you ever answer the phone? Finally, I decided this was the only way to see you."

He stepped inside and hesitated, looking past me toward the dining room. Mama stood there in the doorway, frowning like she had acute appendicitis.

Given the state she was in, the idea of latching on to him as a solution for my problem might overcome her. Temptation was working on me too. If he married me, it would get me out of this mess. People would still count on their fingers and know I'd had to get married, but I would no longer be unmarried and pregnant.

"I've left messages too," he said, staring accusingly at Mama.

I took a deep breath. "I got them."

"Then why didn't you—?"

"Sit down, Mr. Budrow," Mama broke in. "You young folks can talk in the living room. I'll go back to the den and my easy chair."

An inch of me relaxed once she was gone. Farrel sat on the antique sofa in front of the windows. His long legs made him appear weirdly out of place on that delicate piece of furniture. I perched on the edge of a chair on the opposite side of the room.

"I see," he said with a wry smile.

"You see what?"

"How it's going to be. You over there and me here."

I ignored his remark and pointed to the gas heater recessed inside the carved, wooden mantle.

"It's funny."

He cocked his head. "What is?"

"How, as a child, I believed Santa came down a chimney above that stove. But there is no chimney. My mind saw it as a real fireplace, complete with ashes on the hearth."

He stared at the flames running blue and orange up the platelets of the stove.

"I guess you're still ticked off at me about that fool dance."

"You mean your betrayal?" I said.

"I've told you it didn't mean nothing to me. She asked me to go. What was I going to say?"

"'No,' for starters, followed by 'I'm taking Julie.'"

"Yeah, well . . . I . . ." He broke off, looking aggravated.

Maylene said he'd asked her. He said she'd asked him. I would never know who to believe. It didn't matter. Betrayal was betrayal, no matter how it came to pass.

"So, what possessed you to come here today?" I asked, remembering the hundreds of times I'd have given anything if he'd dropped by to see me.

"Don't be like that."

"Like what?"

"Sarcastic. I came because I heard you were sick at school the other day."

"Who told you about that?" I demanded, shrinking at the sudden shrillness in my voice.

"A little bird," he said, his face sober.

"No, tell me who told you."

"Why are you getting upset?" he countered.

"I'm not the least bit upset."

"You're yelling, and you look like you're about to cry. Tell me what was wrong."

"Nothing was wrong. What could be wrong?" I said, straining every nerve to sound casual. "I just . . . nothing."

I hated the look of dread on his face. His gaze felt like a probe drilling into my brain, to ferret out the truth that lay hiding there.

"You know what could be wrong." He leaned forward. "Julie, is everything okay? Tell me."

What if I told him and he wanted me to get an abortion? I didn't think he would, but what if he did? I wouldn't be able to bear the heartbreak of hearing him suggest that to me.

"There's nothing to tell."

"You threw up because of nothing?"

"It was just . . ."

"Just what?"

On the other hand, maybe Carmen was right. Maybe I *should* tell him. Maybe, after the part he played in Frances's death, he wanted to do the right thing by me. Maybe he did have feelings for me, after all. Maybe he even loved me. Why else would he be quizzing me like this? If I were to trust him and tell him, I wouldn't have to go to a home. I could be Mrs. Budrow and have him and his baby. I opened my mouth to spill all, but he spoke first.

"Was it that time of the month?"

The gleam of hope flickering in his eyes felt like a dull knife cutting into my guts. He didn't love me.

"Uh . . . yeah. Right. That's what it was."

Relief swamped his entire body, evidenced by his slump into the back of the sofa.

"Thank God," he said.

Never in my life had I witnessed such relief.

"Well," he began, brightening up. "I have some news, then."

"What news?"

"I've got a job!" His whole aspect changed from fear to jubilation.

"A job?"

"Roughnecking with a drilling company out of Texas that bought up some leases to drill for oil here in Arkansas. It'll be great money! You know, Julie, I don't let many folks see who I really am. You're special to me, so I'm going to tell you something I've only ever said to one other human soul, and that's Don."

He dropped his head into his hands for a long, thoughtful moment. I waited, barely able to draw a deep breath. When he raised his head, he looked at me with intensity burning in his eyes.

"The driving force of my life is to pull myself up out of the mire of poverty me and my folks and my brothers and sisters are trapped in. My new job will make me enough money that, after only a year of living here at home and working the rigs, I'll have enough to go to the university next year."

His voice built with enthusiasm. "None of my folks has ever had a college education. I'll be the first. I want to get my degree in engineering. I'll have to go to school and work too. But maybe, IF I make my grades, and IF I can save enough money, I'll be able to get my master's and work for General Electric someday and have a big house on the right side of the tracks . . ."

He broke off. His face burned red. He was hurt by what people said about his family.

I felt numb. No way could I tell him now and shatter his dream.

"You're going to be living here in town for the next year?"

"Yep. How's that for good news?" He stared at me with bright eyes.

That left me no alternative except to go to the home for unwed mothers. I pulled out all the stops in the smile department and put on my best act.

"That's wonderful news, Farrel. I hope all your dreams come true. I'm glad you shared them with me."

He narrowed his eyes. "You're sure you're okay? You're not fibbing to me, are you? I want to do right by you."

That sealed it, left not a shred of doubt I was doing the right thing. No woman on earth would want that kind of proposal. All I could manage was a nod.

"You could make one of my dreams come true right now," he said.

I couldn't even muster a smile. "How?"

He patted the burgundy silk cushion beside him. "Come over here, and I'll show you."

"I can't," I said in a flat voice.

He looked puzzled. "Why?"

"You know why."

It seemed a struggle for him to speak the words.

"It's not like you think."

"What do I think?"

"That I've got a wooden heart. That what's between us don't mean nothing to me."

"You have a funny way of showing it, especially considering your theme song."

"What theme song?"

"Don't tell me, show me."

"Aw, I didn't mean nothing by that. I would tell you."

But he didn't. He clapped his knees and, with a big smile, heaved up from the sofa.

"I'll call you."

I followed him to the door. Bending, he put his lips on mine in the old way, the way that said he loved me, even if he didn't speak the words. The same familiar fire shot through my body as he crushed me close.

We broke apart, and he started out the door. Deep inside, the longing I always felt when I was with him reared up again, making me ache to pull him back and tell him the truth. To hell with his dreams! But I hesitated an instant too long, and he moved out of reach.

CHAPTER 6
THE SADIE HAWKINS DANCE

"Now, freckles."

"What?"

"On your nose. Freckles."

Darcy, who had taken it upon herself to costume me for the climax of TWIRP week, the Sadie Hawkins dance, plunked me down in the chair in front of my dresser and proceeded to dot my nose and cheeks with eyebrow pencil.

An hour before I had to pick up Justin, she'd bounded into the house, in her usual boisterous style, and cajoled me into changing into the comic strip outfit she'd pilfered from the drama teacher's costume room.

I silently thanked heaven I wasn't showing yet. Not even the slightest bulge was visible on my tummy as she'd tugged the short, black skirt with the jagged hem line around my waist and tucked in the off-shouldered blouse with the big, orange dots. Nonetheless, having her fool around with my costume like this made me nervous.

"What difference does it make what I wear?" I asked her.

"All the girls are dressing like Daisy Mae, silly. You've got to get hip, girl. I bet Justin is wearing overalls. He is so cute."

I looked at myself in the mirror. "Yikes! You surely don't expect me to wear this getup out of the house?"

"If you want to be cool, you have to."

Being cool had been my singular goal in life just a few months ago. Not anymore. How unexpectedly life can change.

"Now come on. Let me finish up your face."

While she worked, she talked incessantly about nothing, which is why I nearly flipped when she abruptly deviated from her stream of gossipy chatter.

"I think it's wonderful that you and Carmen found each other. I've always so longed for a sister, someone I could count on to always be my friend. You're not embarrassed about her, are you, Julie?"

Whenever anyone mentioned my tarnished family, I wanted to crawl under the house and sink down through the yellow-streaked clay all the way to China, where I would don a coolie hat and hide beneath it forever among people who didn't care that my mother had discovered my father *in flagrante delicto*, as she was fond of labeling it, with another woman.

Carmen, the offspring resulting from that infidelity, had barged into my life bringing her deficit—Mama's word—of manners and correct grammar, all things I had been taught to eschew—again Mama's word—just as I was finally being accepted by the popular crowd. The thought flashed through my mind that I was a horrible hypocrite. When the popular kids weren't around, I was perfectly willing to turn to her with my problems. And how two-faced I was to condemn her bad grammar while excusing the same fault in Farrel.

"The whole situation is difficult sometimes," I said, my voice tight with tension, "but that's how the cow ate the cabbage."

She leaned down, cheek to cheek, and looked at our reflections in the mirror.

"I'm sorry if talking about it makes you uncomfortable."

It made me want to claw her eyes out. *That's* what it made me. But I put on a fake smile and watched as the stain on my family's reputation manifested itself on my face as a ruddy blush.

At the same time, I knew Darcy meant well and didn't have a mean bone in her body. She was the kindest member of the in-crowd.

"And what about your father?" she went on. "I hear on the grapevine you saw him at Christmas. What was it like?"

I could only stare at her. *Where in the world did she drum up the nerve to ask me such a question? Next she'll be asking me how my pregnancy is progressing. That's when I'd drop over dead.*

"You know, my folks are separated," she said, looking away. Her lower lip curled, and for an instant I thought she was going to cry.

"Darcy, I . . . I didn't know."

Her smiling mask flashed back onto her face, incongruous with the tears pooling in her eyes.

"Yes, Mother left a few months ago."

I turned flabbergasted eyes on her. "Your *mother*? I never heard of anyone's mother leaving."

"We keep real quiet about it, but I think Daddy's going to file for divorce."

I patted her hand. "I'm sorry, Darcy. It must be awful not to have your mother."

"It is. She rode off on a motorcycle, hanging onto a tattooed guy with a bandana tied round his head. I haven't heard from her since. I shouldn't have mentioned it. Let's not say another word about it. Ever."

That's how most Southerners were: more than willing to never talk about anything truly significant in their lives.

She took a deep breath. "Okay, we have to blacken one of your front teeth."

"No way, José!"

Her face reflected defeat for only a moment before her eyes lit with her typical bouncy enthusiasm. I watched her in the mirror, beaming with delight as she beheld the fruits of having labored over me from head to toe.

"Perfect! That is, *almost* perfect. Will you let me tie up your hair in pigtails, one on each side of your head?"

"No. Daisy Mae wears her hair down. I at least know that much."

She smiled. "Okay. Gotta run. I'm late picking up Larson." She waved fluttering fingers. "See you all at the Y."

Guilt crept over me for always cringing at her enthusiastic behavior, sometimes so over-the-top it embarrassed those around her. She was good at heart and probably the best friend I had.

"Darcy," I said, stopping her in mid-bound.

She turned back with large, expectant eyes.

"Thanks. This was sweet of you. And I'm glad you felt you could confide in me."

Another slushy smile, and she was gone.

It was so weird going to the door to pick up a boy, then escorting him to the car and opening the door for him, like nice boys always did for girls. I even took Justin a corsage, which he actually pinned on his overalls.

His parents, an elderly couple at least in their forties, met me at the door and looked on with big smiles as I struggled with the corsage pin. I giggled all through the procedure, and solemn Justin even managed a half-smile.

"And there's the boutonniere," his mother said, a tender look touching her face. "I remember—"

"Mother, we need to get going," Justin said.

"Oh, this'll only take a minute, and someday you'll look back and wish you'd listened to more of what it was like in the good ole days."

Justin groaned.

She gestured to Justin's father. "This one had the florist deliver the corsage, and along with it in the box was another little flower. My mother and I worried all afternoon that it had come unattached from the corsage, or maybe I was supposed to wear it. But where? Didn't have a clue, as you kids say. We were country folks." She nodded toward Mr. Moore. "I'm surprised this one took a shine to a farm girl."

"Most beautiful farm girl I ever laid eyes on," Mr. Moore said. "Still is."

"Aw, go on." Mrs. Moore gave him a gentle poke. "Mother and I finally decided the little flower was for my hair. When this one picked me up, I thought he looked a little surprised, but he never said a word. At the dance, a nice lady chaperone took one look at me and whisked me off to the restroom. Turned out the little flower was a boutonniere for the boy's lapel. Thought I'd die!"

"Put a lid on it, Mother! We've got to hit the road."

Justin steered me to the door.

"Thank you, Mrs. Moore," I called back as the screen door banged behind us. "I'm wearing this one in my hair tonight in honor of you."

I could tell the minute we stepped into the large room at the Y that tonight would go down in my memories as a symbol of all that was good about school days and friends in our wonderful little town. The room glowed with colored lanterns. Crepe paper streamers dangled from the lights. Balloons and posters of Dogpatch characters decorated the walls. Our classmates, bedecked in Daisy Mae and Li'l Abner costumes, circulated among themselves, electrifying the room with their chatter and laughter.

For fear I would throw up again, Mama had tried to talk me out of going to the dance. But after my storm of tears and entreaties, she relented—against her better judgment. She had already sent letters to the homes for unwed mothers in the Dallas-Ft. Worth area, hoping one would be affordable and have space for me. That made this night even more important. Though I vowed I wouldn't go to a home voluntarily, she might succeed in forcing me.

From across the room, I picked out Laura, a snaggletooth grin made with eyebrow pencil taking over her face as she clung to the arm of Bubba John Younger. Lynn beamed from her perch on the edge of the shallow stage beside her date, Billy Jack Griffith, a football player who moved here last August in time for the start of practice. Carmen stood next to the food table with Della, Rhonda, Faye, and Eugene Hoffmeyer. She saw Justin and me from across the room and came straight over.

Her greeting, "Hi, sis," made me cringe with fear of what the in-crowd would think. But I didn't want to hurt her feelings by snubbing her, so I plastered on a smile. Standing opposite each other in the same costume, we looked absolutely identical.

Justin blinked at the sight of us. "Which one of you is my date? I can't tell you apart."

"Are you with Eugene?" I asked Carmen.

"Not on your tintype, even though he did offer to pay for his own coke and drive his car if I'd ask him."

Our partners for the first two dances were our dates, but the third dance partner hinged on a race.

"As you know," the Y Director said, "in the Li'l Abner comic strip, the town spinsters chased the bachelors on Sadie Hawkins Day. Any fellow who got caught and dragged across the finish line before sundown had to marry the girl. Our race will be for a dance, not a wedding, so girls, get ready to chase the boy of your dreams. And to be fair," she continued, "we're going to give you boys a head start."

"We don't need a head start," rang out through the room.

On the count of three, the boys took off, the girls hotfooting it behind them. Bedlam took over as boys turned over chairs and leaped across tables to escape undaunted girls, determined to catch them.

Justin and I joined the hilarity, scurrying in and out among other Abners and Sadies.

On my third trip across the hall, I lost control and skidded, crashing into Farrel, who was just arriving. He caught me by both arms, or I'd have fallen flat.

"You're the one who is supposed to catch me," he said, smiling into my startled face.

All evening I'd scanned the large room to see if anyone had TWIRPed him. *He must be up to his usual habit of stopping by our dances without a date so he would have no obligation to any one girl.*

I yearned to prolong my grip on his arms, but I forced myself to let go.

"Like it or not, you caught me," he said. "I'm your partner for the next dance."

"I'm not dragging you back to the finish line," I said, turning away.

"No," he said behind me. "I'm dragging you."

He grabbed me around the waist and picked me up, like he was carrying me across the threshold, and proceeded straight to the finish line.

"She caught me. The next dance is mine," he told the director.

"This is a switch," the director said, "but since there's no rule against it, you get your dance."

The jukebox fired up, and Farrel pulled me close. Elvis's latest song, "Tell Me Why," filled the room. Farrel's lips touched my hair.

"Tell *me* why," he said.

"Shuussh."

A collage of couples on the floor revolved around us as we danced. Justin stood on the sidelines, his face torn between understanding and hurt.

This was what I had longed for—to be once again in Farrel's arms. *At this moment, all three of us are together, maybe for the one and only time*, I thought, remembering my poor baby, who would likely never know his father. Farrel might be proud of a son or a daughter someday, but now the baby and I would only be in his way of fulfilling his dreams.

"Thanks for the dance," he said when the music stopped.

Thoughts of our child stirred emotions inside me that trumped reason. Seeing the passionate look in his eyes, the grip on my resolve loosened, and I opened my mouth to speak the forbidden words. The truth would have been spilled—and Farrel's dreams of the future shattered—had it not been for Eugene Hoffmeyer's boisterous intrusion into the time capsule of isolation Farrel and I stood in, clinging to each other's hands, alone together in the tumult of the crowded dance floor.

"I'm claiming the next dance, Julie," Eugene said, "even if it is girls' choice. You didn't ask me for a TWIRP date all week, and I want my turn."

Farrel dropped my hands and walked away.

"Eugene, you're such a ding-a-ling!" I said as an ear-piercing fast song rocked the dance hall.

"Come on, let's dance," and he jerked me out onto the floor where he stomped my toe and yanked me under his arm.

Nausea tickled the back of my throat.

"Isn't this the greatest?" he yelled over the music.

On the sidelines, Justin looked like a wall flower. A moment later, Laura snagged him for a dance while Eugene threw me back and forth, under his arms, and across his body, around and under, in time with the ear-splitting music.

The floor swayed, spots flitted before my eyes, and the room went black.

CHAPTER 7

TIME AND TIDE

I came to with a jerk, my throat and nose burning from the pungent fumes of the vial of smelling salts the Y director held up to my nose. A crowd of curious and anxious faces floated above me. Someone pressed a cold cloth to my forehead. Farrel and Justin stood watching like two scared boys, pale fright pasted on their faces.

"I'm sorry," Eugene repeated over and over. "I didn't mean to make her fall out."

Justin took him by the shoulders and steered him away. Farrel kept his eyes fastened on mine until the director and someone's dad helped me to my feet and led me toward the office. Carmen trailed close behind with Justin and Farrel. The three crowded with us into the small area, and they hovered around me.

When I was seated in the director's comfortable chair, she asked, "How are you feeling? Still faint? Does anything hurt?"

"Just my finger."

She gingerly took my hand and frowned over the finger.

"We'll call an ambulance and get you to the hospital," she said, reaching for the phone.

"She doesn't need to go to the hospital," Carmen said, meeting my eyes.

"Not for just a hurt finger," I added, panicked at the thought of my condition being discovered.

The director persisted. "But it might be broken."

"It's probably just a sprain. I'm fine, really."

I struggled up from the chair to prove it. Thankfully, the dizziness was gone.

"You're still none too steady on your feet. You need to call your mother to come pick you up," the director said.

"She can't," I said and cleared my throat. "I have the car. TWIRP week."

The director frowned. "Oh dear."

Carmen moved to my side. "It's okay. Justin's her date. He can take her home and call his dad to pick him up there."

Justin nodded his agreement, and the director audibly breathed her relief.

"Problem solved. It takes a woman." Abruptly, she turned back to me, then back to eyeball Carmen. "I know you're not twins."

"Half-sisters," I said.

The director tilted her head. "I knew that. This is the first time I've ever been around you two together. Amazing. I've never seen such a resemblance in non-twins. Just amazing."

"Broken," the doctor pronounced in the treatment room on Monday morning.

I wasn't surprised. It had throbbed all night after the dance, and I'd had such pain brushing my teeth Sunday morning that I had to tape it.

"But the fracture is stable," he added with a smile. "You're going to live. We'll splint it to the finger beside it for four weeks. After that you'll have limited use for two more weeks. Then, tip-top shape again. No excessive use of the hand. You're in the band at school, aren't you?"

I nodded. "The clarinet."

"You'll have to give that up for a while. I'll write you an excuse, not that you'll need one when they see your splint. Take a couple of aspirin when you need it for pain."

"Let's go, honey," Mama said.

She moved to help me get off the table. I'd noticed her leg jumping the whole time we were in the examining room. I knew that signaled her nerves were frayed.

My own anxiety leapfrogged when the doctor said, "I know you're eager to get her to school, but I'm concerned about a sixteen-year-old fainting. We'd better run some tests. Make sure nothing else is wrong."

Mama's eyes glazed over with panic. "That won't be necessary, Doctor." Her lips strained into a fake smile. "Julie's never fainted before. I'm sure it was the heat and the excitement of the dance. Besides, you had just started your period, hadn't you?" Her wide eyes commanded my confirmation.

"Right," I said, sliding off the examining table.

"That's no cause for a healthy girl to faint. I'd feel better about it if I checked her out," the doctor said.

"If it happens again, absolutely," Mama said. With a hand under my elbow, she swiftly piloted me into the outer office. "Put this on my bill, Betty Sue," she said to the clerk. "I'm in a hurry to get her to school before she misses any more classes."

"I'm sorry, Mrs. Morgan, but we're not extending any more credit," the girl replied.

Mama snorted. "Dear Gussie, what is the world coming to? Well, you'll have to wait until I can get home, get my checkbook, and come all the way back."

The girl held her gaze. "Yes, ma'am. But bring it by today."

"Whew, that was a close call," Mama said in the car on the way home. "Thank God I was able to stop him from examining you. That does it. We're under the gun. You're going into a home for unwed mothers if I have to open one up out in Texas myself. It's the only way to keep your life from being ruined. And mine. I just can't bear any more shame."

We rode a few blocks in silence. When we turned onto our street, Mama said, "Some years it seems like spring will never come."

I studied her profile. The determined chin looked out of place with her defeated posture.

"We'll tell people you're sick," she said.

"People aren't stupid. They'll figure out the truth when I suddenly disappear."

"No. That fainting spell couldn't have come at a more opportune time."

"They won't be fooled by that."

"They damn well better be!"

Wheeling into the driveway, she gunned the car up the concrete strips and slammed on the brakes. She held the steering wheel with both hands and looked down into her lap.

"I'm sorry. I'm at the end of my rope. You're right. The whole town will figure it out," she snapped her fingers, "just like that, if you disappear."

"Shouldn't I go to school today?"

Mama opened the car door.

"No, we can't take a chance on any more fainting or vomiting in public. We have to do something, quick. But what? 'Time and tide wait for no man.'"

We hadn't been inside two minutes when the phone rang. It was Carmen.

"Are you okay?"

"Broken finger. Why aren't you at school?"

"I'm playing hooky. Listen, I have an idea that might save you."

I sank down on Mama's bed. "What?"

"I don't dare mention it on the phone. You never know when the operator is listening in. We need to come over."

"We who?"

"Mother and me."

"Have you both gone stone crazy? Mama would have a cow before she'd let *you* into this house, never mind your mother."

"My mother isn't buck wild to do this either."

"So, obviously, it won't work. Come up with something else."

"*You* come up with something, if you're going to be so all-fired choosy. So far you haven't come up with diddly-squat. Now I have the perfect solution, and you won't even hear me out. You have until the count of three to say we can come over, then I'm hanging up, and you're on your own. One . . . two . . ."

"Wait! I'll talk to Mama, okay. We are pretty desperate. Give me some time to get her used to the idea of your mother being in the house . . . No, forget it. There's no way!"

"You have one hour." And she hung up.

"Mama!"

"What is it? Who was that on the phone?" she called from the kitchen.

"Carmen. She's thought of a plan to save me."

Mama came running. "What? Short of a doctor administered abortion, which is not to be had, there is no plan that is going to save you."

"She doesn't dare tell me on the phone. They want to come over here."

Mama arched one eyebrow. "They?"

"Carmen and her mother."

"Claudia?" Mama said in a faint voice. She looked upward. "Is this how You answer prayers?"

"We'd better let them come, Mama."

"Julie, you know I'd move heaven and earth, if I could, to save you from shame, but that is more than I am capable of. In your wildest imagination, how do you think I could allow that woman *and her child* to come into my house?"

I stood up and took Mama's hand with my good one.

"I know, Mama, but shouldn't we at least hear Carmen out? So far we've come up with exactly no way to save face or my reputation. Maybe she has something in mind that would work. After all, Claudia is a nurse. What could it hurt to just hear what they have to say?"

"It will hurt my pride. She's already ruined my reputation."

"What she and my father did is a bad reflection on them, not you."

Mama gave a short laugh. "Maybe you're right. And I would truly do anything for you."

"Then I can call and tell them to come on over?"

"Considering it may well be your only hope to get out of this unscathed, what choice do I have?"

"I'll call her back right now."

"So soon?" Mama's eyes pleaded.

"Yes. After all, time and tide . . ."

"Wait for no man," she finished, her sad eyes looking into mine. "And neither do babies."

CHAPTER 8
She's Not You

Mama stood in the center of the kitchen floor in a state of frenzied inertia, arms hanging limp, frazzled hair sticking out in all directions, and no lipstick.

"Hurry! Vacuum the living room rug. Oh no, better not. Your hand."

"Why aren't we going to sit in the den?"

"Julie, you don't entertain your ex-husband's mistress in the same room as your closest friends."

"This is not a tea party, Mama, and she's not his mistress anymore."

"Oh God, how can I let that woman come into my house?" Mama strangled a sob. "You'll never know what this is costing me."

And it's all my fault.

Mama glanced at her watch. "They'll be here any minute. Quick, dust the commode."

I sighed. "Mama, please don't refer to that piece of furniture while they're here. They won't have a clue what you are talking about."

Mama grabbed the Old Dutch Cleanser from a lower cabinet.

"Going to swish out the *real* commode?" I said.

"Enough of your sass!" she replied and headed into the bathroom.

"Work on your makeup while you're in there," I called out over the sound of running water.

She was still cleaning the bathroom when the knock came at the front door.

-

"They're here!" I cried, throwing off the apron I'd tied on to do the dusting.

Mama emerged with combed hair and fresh lipstick, but her cheeks were pale.

"God, give me strength," she murmured, but I could tell from the glitter in her eyes, a part of her was excited about meeting Claudia and Carmen face to face.

I followed her to the living room. There on the porch stood Eugene Hoffmeyer, puffed and confident, as if he were about to dole out favors to a cheering crowd.

"I came by to see how you are," he said, looking past Mama at me.

Mama bristled. "What are you doing out of school, Eugene?"

"I'm taking golf sixth period this year, in place of P.E. Thought I'd run by for a few minutes on my way to the club. I got worried when you weren't at school today, Julie."

I held up my splinted fingers. "The doctor." Looking past him I saw the mauve Chevy pulling up in front of the house. "Where are you parked, Eugene?"

"In the driveway." He looked over his shoulder. "Well, I'll be diddly-dog damned. Here comes Carmen in that old crate."

"You have your nerve, calling someone else's car a crate," I said.

He grinned. "I got you home that time, didn't I? Even if I did have to do it in reverse. That must be her mother getting out of the car with her." He scratched his head. "I never would've thought they'd come here. I mean . . ." His eyes crossed. "I don't know what I mean."

A brisk wind swept past us through the open door. I stole a glance at Mama, who looked totally out of her tree, what with Eugene on the front porch in front of God and everybody, stammering about our disgraceful family history, and Carmen, *with Claudia*, coming up our walkway.

Eugene glanced over his shoulder again. "Double doo-doo. They're coming in."

"Aptly put," Mama said.

"I'd better blow off this visit," Eugene said. "Unless you *want* me to come in." He looked at Mama, then at me with hopeful eyes.

Mama flipped out. "Dear God, no!" She took a moment before adding, "You'll be late for golf class."

He scowled. "At least I came by to check on you, Julie. I bet you haven't seen the likes of Justin Moore or Farrel Budrow at your front door."

"That was nice of you, Eugene," I said, "but you better hit the road."

On the way to his car, he flipped off his cap and performed a sweeping bow to Carmen and Claudia, who had hesitated at the end of our walkway. We all watched his clunker jerk and cough its way up the street and out of sight.

It took Claudia and Carmen only a few moments to come up the steps and onto the porch, not nearly long enough for Mama to regain her composure. She and Claudia stared at each other through the screen door. Like me, Carmen stood slightly back, waiting for the fur to fly, I supposed. Who knew what size eruption might occur as a result of our two mothers meeting face to face for the first time. The wait went on so long, I finally stepped forward and pushed open the screen door.

"Yes, forgive me. Come in," Mama said. "Have a seat here in the living room. Can I get you some coffee? I've just put on a pot."

"We didn't come to pay a social call," Claudia said in her usual sarcastic tone. "Carmen has a harebrained idea she thinks will save Julie's ass."

Mama blanched at her language. Carmen settled on the couch in front of the windows, but Claudia spent several moments looking at the porcelain figures on the commode and accent tables before moving on to the mantle where she studied Mama's cut-glass crystal pieces decorating the top. From there she observed the rosewood table that was my great-great grandmother's, and finally the towering grandfather clock on the side wall.

"Is it going to rain?" Mama asked.

Hope dwindled in me. Mama was following the same, acceptable routine all well-bred Southerners adhered to of never discussing anything but the weather, an upcoming marriage, or the arrival of a baby, within the bonds of matrimony, of course. Ironically, we wouldn't have to stray terribly far from acceptable conversation today in talking about a baby—just not an acceptable baby.

"So, what is the idea that is going to be Julie's salvation?" Mama asked.

"Yeah, let's get right to the point," Claudia said. "Understand, I don't like being drug over here any more than you liked opening that door and letting me in, Elizabeth. Come on, Carmen. Spit it out."

Carmen rose and stood in front of the mantle, like she was taking center stage in the Thespian Club play.

"First, we have to tell you that my stepfather has sent for Mother and me to come to England, where he's been stationed for a year."

"How, pray, does that pertain to us?" Mama asked.

"It *pertains* to you because I don't want to go," Carmen said. "I want to stay in school here in El Dorado. Now that Granny's dead, Mother can join my stepdad, but then I'll have no one in town to live with."

"What about your . . . father?" Mama asked.

Silence fell at the mention of Scott Morgan. I looked at Mama first, holding her hand over her mouth like she wished she could perform a vanishing act, then at Claudia, toying with the frazzling fringe on her blouse, then finally at Carmen, gazing blankly out the window. She was the first to speak.

"I could . . . stay with him. But I'm trying to help you and Julie out."

"I haven't heard a word about *how* yet," Mama said in a clipped tone.

"I'm getting to it." An instant later Carmen focused on me and did a double take. "Holy macaroni! I just now noticed your splint. Does it hurt?"

"A little," I admitted, grateful somebody was trying to comfort me.

"Julie, the doctor told you to keep that hand still," Mama said.

"That complicates things, maybe, a little," Carmen said, her brow puckered. "Oh well, never mind. We'll work it out."

"Get to the point, if there is one," Mama said.

"Okay," Carmen began. "If Julie doesn't go to a home for the unwed, she'll be ruined. Now here's the deal. What if . . . ?" She wriggled all the way from her feet up to her head. "I'm so excited. What if me and Julie change places?"

"Julie and I," Mama said, "and that is completely insane."

"It's not!" Carmen said. "No one would know she was gone. You wouldn't have to make up some lie about her being terminally ill."

"No one would be fooled," Mama said.

"They would," Carmen argued. "We can pass for each other. Stand here next to me, Julie. Put your sick hand behind your back. Now, look at us. If it wasn't for our clothes, could you tell us apart?"

"Of course I could," Mama said.

"Take off the blinders," Claudia said. "They could pass for identical twins. They look so much alike it's pure-dee, hard-down, flat-out shocking. Folks'll buy it. If anyone has any doubt, they'll write it off as them just being confused."

"How would it work?" Mama said, jerking upright in her chair and boring in on Carmen. "You and Julie—how did you put it? Changing places? Explain it to me."

"It's simple. I would move in here, instead of going to England."

Mama sank back. "You? Living in my house?"

"It's either that or *you* in disgrace with your society bunch," Claudia said. "Not to mention Julie's life ruined, if anybody gets wind of where you've shipped her off to."

The look Mama and I exchanged spanned more than just our living room, gloomy in February's winter light. We shared a glimpse into the future and what it might be like should my situation be discovered. Mama would not be on this earth forever. I'd be alone someday with no education, a menial job, and no husband. I knew Mama saw those same consequences for my life looming ahead of us if we didn't do something drastic, something impossible to glom onto, but something we both knew could not be avoided.

"The trouble is," Mama rose to her feet, "you two girls resemble each other in looks but . . ." She gave a nod toward Carmen. "You could never pass for my daughter. You are nothing like her."

"I know my grammar is Nowheresville," Carmen said, "so don't try to put me down by saying so."

Score one for my half-sister.

"She knows better," Claudia said. "She chooses to talk like I do to keep from hurting my feelings."

"I don't want to go to a home," I said, failing in my effort to hold back tears.

"Dry it up," Claudia said. "You don't have any other choice, the way I see it."

"Why can't I go to England with Claudia?" I spurted out to Mama. "Nobody would know me over there, and I could go to school and have my baby without fear of scorn or judgment."

Mama flipped her wig. "Not while I have breath in my body!"

"Ditto," Claudia said. "So, scrap that idea. You'll have to go to the home, and Carmen will come here and pretend she is you. It'll be fine."

I could tell Mama was mulling it over, in spite of her next words. "I don't know. Their choice of attire is as different as daylight and dark."

"I may dress like a Sukey Tawdry, but at least I'm a virgin," Carmen said. "Anyway, it doesn't matter 'cause I'll be wearing Julie's clothes."

It was my turn to blink.

"I don't know if I want her wearing Julie's clothes," Mama said.

"You know what?" Claudia got up and pointed a garish red fingernail at Mama. "I've had enough of you running my daughter into the ground. We've made you an offer. If you've got two brain cells to rub together to get a spark, you'll take it. If not, you'll suffer the consequences. Come on, Carmen, we've wasted enough time here."

"So you are or you aren't going to take me up on this?" Carmen managed to ask me as Candia dragged her by the hand out the door and onto the porch.

I shook my head. "I don't know. I just don't know."

"I know," Mama said. "The answer is NO, in all capital letters."

Worried that Mama would send me away, it was after midnight before I finally sank into a dreamless sleep. At five past three by the clock on my bedside table, something woke me. Instantly alert, I listened hard to hear the sound again. When it came, I realized it was too soft to have awakened me, but it had. I crept out of bed and followed it to Mama's room. No light seeped from beneath her closed door. From the darkness of the room came the sound of her weeping in the winter night.

CHAPTER 9

SURRENDER

Mama broke down and bought more cigarettes. After several nights of chain-smoking while calling homes for unwed mothers, she finally located one within a day's driving distance in a small town near Dallas, Texas. It wasn't her first choice, but it was the cheapest, and more important, it would take me at the end of March, when I would be going into the fifth month. Most homes only took girls six months along.

Risky as it was, Mama'd had to let me go back to school. There was no alternative. It was the state law of Arkansas that all kids must go to school—unless they're pregnant. Then they're not allowed to go.

When not on the phone at night, Mama spent her time pouring over a medical book she'd sneaked out of the law office where she worked, looking for an illness she could say I had come down with that would allow her to credibly stay in El Dorado while I was incarcerated. She'd lose her job if she stayed out in Texas with me, and she had to have her job to pay the fees for keeping me in the home. Even if she could have taken several months' vacation, she couldn't afford to stay in a hotel for so long.

"It could be polio," I suggested, looking up from my homework one evening. The scent of early daffodils drifted through the open windows of the den, making it hard to concentrate. "You could say I'm in an iron lung and can't have any visitors."

"Don't even think of such a thing!" she said, pulling at her hair with both hands. "It wouldn't work anyway. Nothing will! I'm at the end of my rope trying to think of a credible disease."

She got up from her chair in the den and sauntered into the break-fast room, where I sat at the table studying my French lesson.

"Maybe you could ask Claudia for the name of a suitable illness," I suggested.

"Don't make light of our situation. In the first place, no explanation on earth will convince Mavis MacAfee that I would leave my little chick alone and sick way out in Texas, no matter what the disease. I know Mavis. She'll see through that in nothing flat, and it's only a small step from there to concluding you're in a home for unwed mothers."

"Then I may as well stay here and have the baby."

"Oh, for God's sake, Julie. We've been over and under this a hundred times. You cannot, *must not* let anyone know the truth."

"Someone might already know," I said, pulling up my blouse and tugging down the waistband of my skirt. "Look."

Mama stared at my slightly increased waistline. "You're showing!"

"Only a little. My clothes still fit. Pretty much."

"What are you now? How many months?"

"Four. Maylene McCord asked me today if I'm putting on weight."

"God help us!"

"She's just being Maylene," I said. "She'd say that if I went from a hundred and fourteen to a hundred and fifteen."

"What are you up to?"

I dropped my gaze back to my French book. "A hundred and twenty."

"Julie!"

I laughed. "It's only five pounds."

Mama wrung her hands. "This isn't funny. We have to do something, *now.*"

She went into the kitchen and, lighting a cigarette, leaned on the edge of the sink and stared out at the finely tended yards of our neighbors, while my own eyes glazed over with scenes from that day at school. Maylene and I'd had a conversation longer than two minutes for the first time since she and Farrel went to the Christmas dance.

We'd been assigned to work as a team selling ads for the high school yearbook, and Mrs. Snyder, the journalism teacher, had given us permission to go to town during sixth period and try to persuade some of the local businesses to buy an ad.

El Dorado had bustled with shoppers on this first day of spring.

"Folks must be buying their Easter dresses already," Maylene had commented as she circled the square looking for a parking space. "Which is surprising, since it's still a month away." She turned a conspiratorial face to me. "I know what let's do."

"What?"

"Don't be so enthusiastic, Julie."

"How can I be enthusiastic when you haven't said yet what you want to do?"

I watched her silently count to ten. "Now," she said, exhaling, "I've made a vow not to be impatient with you anymore, no matter how rude you are to me."

I looked heavenward. "Just tell me your idea."

"Let's look for our own Easter dresses."

"Let's not."

"Jeez, Julie, you are so disagreeable these days. Oh, there's a space. Right in front of that new store, Earl Allen's. I've never been in there. Have you? I hear they have nifty threads for the teen set."

We had peered in the window of the new clothing store, and instantly I saw she was right. Bright skirts and tops in the latest fashions clung to sleek mannequins. Inside, the racks against the walls vibrated with color. A small section of high-styled shoes was on display. A guy who looked to be in his thirties moved swiftly from the back of the store to greet us.

"Welcome to Earl Allen's, young ladies. I'm Earl, the owner, and I have some perfect little numbers for both of you." He looked at me. "What are you? Size six?"

"I hope so."

His eyes switched to Maylene. "You can't be an inch over an eight."

Maylene bristled. "She and I are the same, size six."

"We're not here to buy clothes," I said, putting my splinted hand on Maylene's arm. "Would you buy an ad in the high school yearbook?"

"But first, we *have* to try on some of the clothes," Maylene cut in, edging away from me. "I can tell already they're just precious."

Earl's smile had lit up the store. "Sure, I'll buy an ad, but first, to the dressing rooms. Sorry, I only have one vacant right now, but it's a big one. Do you mind sharing?"

"Not a bit," Maylene said, pulling me along behind him to the back of the store.

She closed the curtains to the dressing room, and I watched in disbelief as she worked at unbuttoning her dress. She scowled at me.

"Don't be a party pooper."

We could hear Earl snatching garments from the racks.

"I can't afford to buy anything," I said to Maylene.

"We sell on credit," Earl called from outside the curtain. "Have a look at these."

Maylene stuck her arms through the closure in the curtains and gathered a pile of the cutest clothes I'd ever seen. Earl laughed at our coos of delight. In spite of my resolve, I couldn't help grabbing up a navy sundress in a soft cotton fabric with a pattern of little yellow stars. With it came a flowing, see-through coat of thin cotton in the same color and pattern.

"That's fantastic!" Maylene said, turning covetous eyes on the outfit. "If you don't buy it, I will. Try it on. I'll help. It'll take you all day to get it on by yourself with that broken finger."

The last vestige of my willpower evaporated, and in a jiffy I was stepping into the gorgeous dress.

"Take your slip off," she ordered. "That dress doesn't need one, and it'll only clump up underneath if you keep it on."

Mesmerized with excitement and forgetting everything except the fabulous outfit, I had wriggled out of the slip and had the dress above my head when her voice stopped me.

"You're gaining weight, girl."

The dress slipped from my good hand. She stood, staring at my waistline. Nothing was there, like an obvious bulge, to betray my condition, but my waist was definitely bigger. Most people would think I had simply put on a pound or two. I had sucked in and tried to twist away from her sharp eyes, but a mirror on both walls glared with my reflection.

In a split second, I knew I had to play it down.

"Too much cornbread and black-eyed peas."

"Step in it. I'll zip you, if it's not too tight, that is," she said, picking up the dress from where it lay in a soft heap on the floor.

Even with an extra inch around my waist, the dress fit, and I looked fabulous in it. Turning sideways and back, I preened in the dressing room mirror.

"Put on the coat," Maylene said, holding it so I could easily slip my splinted hand through the gossamer sleeve.

"Step out here and let me see," Earl said.

In the big three-way mirror, the outfit had lifted me out of teenage cuteness and into young adult glamour, despite my heavy saddle oxfords.

"Get those things off," Earl ordered, thrusting a pair of navy silk heels into my good hand. "Sit down. I'll get you into them."

Back in front of the mirror in the latest-style, pointed-toe heels, my first thought was of Farrel. What would he think if he saw me looking like this?

Maylene must have read my mind, for she called from the dressing room, "Farrel'll go ape when he sees you in that!"

I wanted to yank her "crown of glory" ponytail out by the roots.

"It's a miracle," she said, coming out of the dressing room in a pink number made of the same soft cotton. "We can throw away those scratchy screen wire petticoats."

I had to admit, she looked great.

"You should buy that."

"I fully intend to. And I'm buying yours, if you don't."

Not in ten lifetimes would I let that happen. Hesitantly, I turned to Earl.

"If my mother pitches a fit . . ."

"You can bring it back. Go ahead, try on some others. I'll go fill out the paperwork for the yearbook ad." We heard him murmuring to himself as he walked away, "I can tell already, the move from Little Rock here to Arkansas's oil town is going to put me in fat city."

I had bought the dress. Maylene bought the pink one for Easter. I couldn't imagine where I'd ever wear mine. It was way too mature-looking for our teenage scene. I didn't even know if I'd be able to get into it again, after the baby.

"Better skip dinner tonight," Maylene called when she and the rest of the carpool dropped me off after school.

That night at the table doing my homework I still hadn't told Mama about the dress. She had been at work when I got home, so I'd quickly hung it in the closet underneath my raincoat. I didn't have many wants anymore, except to wake up some morning and be like I used to be before Farrel—innocent again and this pregnancy just a terrible nightmare. Now, with the dress, I had just one more small desire—a crazy one, in light of the wish to be innocent, but nonetheless—I wanted Farrel to see me in it.

At the sink, Mama dripped water over her cigarette butt to put it out and turned.

"Julie, what are we going to do?"

"I'll think some more about it and tell you tomorrow. Right now there's something else I have to tell you."

"Lay it on me. After what you've plunked down on our doorstep already, I can take anything," she said with false bravado as I headed for my closet.

I returned to the breakfast room and held up the new dress. Her eyes grew misty.

"Oh, my poor darling." She looked it over from where she stood at the sink, then moved toward me, her arms extended. "It's the most beautiful thing I've ever seen."

"Thanks, Mama, for not murdering me. I can take it back. The salesman said so. I couldn't resist having it, even for just one day."

"You won't take it back. I won't let you. I'll pay it out."

"He said you could."

"And we'll keep it here, for when you come home. We'll make sure you get your figure back, and someday, you'll wear this. Go try it on for me."

I dabbed at her cheek with my napkin, still folded on the table from dinner, but her tears did not stop, even when I reappeared in the beautiful dress.

The next night I opened the door to what I knew was Carmen's knock and invited her in. I thought Mama would say "What's this all about?" but she didn't. She politely offered Carmen a seat—in the den.

This time I was the one who made the announcement, having finally decided to force the issue.

"This is my life, Mama, and I think Claudia and Carmen are right. Unless I stay here and keep the baby, Carmen and I have to change places. It's a way out, and it's our tough luck that there is no other way."

"But what if people see through it?" Mama asked in an anxious voice.

"We'll just have to make sure they don't," Carmen said. "Ain't it gonna be fun to try?"

Mama shook her head. "Yes, ain't it?"

CHAPTER 10
TRYING TO GET TO YOU

I packed only a few loose-fitting garments. Everything else had to be left in my closet for Carmen to wear.

We'd fine-tuned the "switch" down to the last instant. Ironically, Claudia was taking a plane to New York, then on to London, the same day Mama and I were leaving: Saturday, March 30, just as I was going into my seventeenth week. The plan was for Carmen to stay with our father until Sunday evening, when Mama got back home from depositing me. Mama wouldn't allow her to stay alone in the house.

Carmen, Claudia, Mama, and I met one last time to go over all possible details to keep our deception a secret.

"Just don't flub the dub and say something to Scott or your grandparents that Julie wouldn't say," Claudia admonished Carmen.

"He was so happy, he went ape when I told him I was coming over and would spend the night," Carmen said. "Thinking I was Julie, don't you see, you know. I don't like the idea of fooling him. Why can't I just be me until I move in here?"

"Use your horse sense," Claudia said, tweaking Carmen's nose. "I'll be gone. Then how would you explain that you hadn't gone with me? Besides, you're going to have to fool a whole lot of people. This will be good practice."

Carmen deflated. "At least *trying* to fool them. I'd feel better about this whole deal if I had a few days practice with Julie here to keep me on the right track. Why don't I go ahead and move in here now? That way I'll have a chance to watch her doing stuff, like putting on makeup, and listening to how she talks. You know, study her up close. And I'll be here to pack some of her clothes to take with me for the two days I'm at Dad's."

"That's right," I said. "She has to wear my clothes at our father's house. We didn't think of that."

"He hasn't seen either one of you often enough to recognize your clothes," Mama said.

Carmen glared at her. "You just don't want me here any sooner than I have to be."

Mama slapped her thigh. "Bingo!"

I stepped in. "Mama, she's doing us a huge favor. Don't treat her like that."

Mama shook her head. "I don't know. This whole business stinks to high heaven. I feel in my bones that something is not right."

"Because something isn't right," Claudia said. "It's a total lie, but I have no doubt you'll warm up to it quicker than you can sling a bull by the tail when you consider the alternative. That'll make it smell a helluva lot better—to high heaven."

Those two will always despise each other, I thought. And I understood why as Maylene flitted through my mind.

"What if someone comes to visit while both girls are here?" Mama mused, more to herself than to the rest of us.

"We'll just say she's spending the night with me," I said. "After all, she is my sister." I punctuated that with a squeal of delight. "I'm going to have a real sister for the first time in my life!"

Carmen and I grabbed hands and jumped up and down, screaming and laughing like girls without a care in the world.

"Don't do that! You'll jar the baby and bring on a miscarriage," Mama said.

I winked at her. "That would solve all our problems."

Mama gave me a dark look.

"Not by a long shot," Claudia said. "Word that you'd been treated at the hospital for losing a baby would go through town quick as that wink you just gave your mother."

"The secret of Frances's abortion seems to have been kept pretty tight," I said to Claudia. "The carpool girls are suspicious about why no one else has caught the flu, but they haven't suggested any other possible reason for her death."

"It gives a body hope this secret'll keep as easy," Claudia said.

"The carpool!" Carmen shrieked. "I forgot about your carpool. I've *got* to stay here a few days earlier so Julie can fill me in on stuff like that. I don't even know where all those girls live. How am I going to pick them up? This is like a spy movie. I need some training, like I'd get from the CIA, before I parade around in another person's skin. And that reminds me of something else. You're going to have to leave your driver's license with me, Julie."

"Why?"

"So I can drive, silly. What if, when I'm driving the carpool some day, I get stopped by a cop and have to show him *my* license because I don't have one with your name on it. That would be all she wrote. The jig would be up. Everybody in town would know I'm playing you, and it's only a baby step from there to the rest of the story, as Paul Harvey would say."

"What if I have to drive while I'm out in Texas?" I asked.

"You can take my license."

I shook my head. "But I won't be pretending to be you."

"Okay, I'll keep them both."

The license business did the trick. Carmen was allowed to move in three days before Mama and I were to leave. She shared my room, of course, and for the most part we delighted in the novelty of having each other around. Talking and giggling until late in the night and sharing secrets was like being real sisters.

She fit easily into my clothes and shoes and said they were classy. This came as a surprise to me from one whose own choice in clothes made her look cheap and loose. She especially liked the new dress I'd just bought at Earl Allen's.

That night before we fell asleep she said, "I want to wear the new blue one with the see-through coat to the junior class party."

"You can't wear that one. Even though Maylene was with me when I bought it, it's special to me. I've never worn it, and Mama and I are saving it for when I . . ." A knot swelled in my throat.

"Don't start," Carmen said. "I won't wear it, if you don't want me to, but won't it arouse Maylene's suspicions if you don't wear it to the party? Hey, girl, it's nothing to squall about." She patted my hand.

"I don't want to go away. Why can't I just stay here and have my baby?"

"You can, if you've got the guts," Carmen said, rolling over and reaching for the pack of cigarettes on her night table.

"You can't smoke in bed. Mama will kill you."

She jumped onto the floor, flipped her lighter, lit up, and took a long drag.

"Gee whillikers, that tastes good. Oh pooh! I'm going to have to quit. You don't smoke. This is my last one."

The next night, late, as we lay talking in the darkened room, I brought up something that had been worrying me.

"Carmen."

"Huh?" she said in a sleepy voice.

"What will you do if Farrel calls?"

"What?"

"If Farrel calls you . . . uh . . . me and wants to go out?"

"I don't know. Go out with him, I guess."

I sat straight up in bed. "Carmen, you can't! After what he did to me, I don't ever want to see him again."

"As I recall, he didn't do anything to you that you didn't invite. And besides, it won't be you seeing him. It'll be me."

"But he'll *think* it's me. No, Carmen, you can't. Promise me you won't."

"I don't understand why."

"He's mine, that's why!"

"I thought you never wanted to see him again."

"I don't, but if you go out with him, he'll think you are me, and that he can just walk all over me and I'll let him come running back."

"He's asked twice if you're preggy-poo-pie. That don't sound like treating you bad to me."

"Doesn't," I said.

She looked perplexed. "What?"

"You're here early to polish up your grammar. Do it, or you'll never pass for me."

"Okay, okay. It's not that I don't know better. It's just that talking like you and the rest of your in-crowd sounds so put-on, so hoity-toity."

She went to my desk chair and sat, smoking and looking out into the night.

"It might be better if I did go out with him."

I pulled my hair with both hands. "Jeez Louise! How could it be better?"

"It would definitely prove to him you hadn't gotten pregnant."

"Thinking it's me when he sees you around town will do the same thing."

"Look, Julie," she said, "there's a ton of things I'm gonna have to deal with, most of which will come as a huge surprise, no matter how much we try to plan ahead. You're going to have to trust me a little. I'll do the best I can, but sometimes I won't know until the situation crops up exactly what I need to do to keep your deep, dark secret from getting out. I'm doing you a favor, you know."

"Actually, Carmen, I'm doing *you* a favor too. Otherwise, you wouldn't get to stay here in town and go to school. Which brings up another issue. I'll be back right after the baby is born. Where will you go then, and how will we explain it when both of us are here in town and your mother is gone?"

The widening of her eyes was visible in the glow of her cigarette.

"Oops! Guess we failed to cover that base. It'll be September, won't it? We can say I've come back for the start of senior year."

I took hold of a handful of her long hair. "Here's another base we failed to cover. Your hair. We'll have to cut it ourselves. Word would get all over town if you went to Opal, my beauty parlor lady, and asked her to cut your hair like mine."

"Nobody's cutting my hair," Carmen said, folding her arms across her chest.

"Mama, get the scissors and come here," I called.

Dressed in my blue and white suit-dress for travel, I took a long last look around my room, which already bore signs of Carmen's invasion—like pinups of Paul Newman on the wall and forty-five records by rock 'n' roll singers other than Elvis. In the mail the day before, a note had come from him about his new purchase.

March 26, 1957
Dear Juliet,

I have the most out-of-sight news! I bought a house in Memphis! It's a mansion called Graceland after a girl named Grace who lived back during the Civil War. It used to be a farm where they raised Hereford cattle, but I won't be keeping cows. The house was built in 1939 and sits on 13.8 acres. It has 10,266 square feet inside, and my mama and daddy and my grandma are going to live with me. I always did want to get Mama a big, fine house. Hopefully, I can move in by June. I'm going to have a pool installed too, and maybe someday you will be in Memphis and can come swimming.

I'm off to Canada to perform in April, and in May I start shooting my third movie, Jailhouse Rock. *I can't believe all this is happening to me.*

Hope everything is going great for you, my good luck charm, and that you bring yourself as much luck as you have brought me.

As ever,
Elvis

I scratched out a hasty note, and Mama dropped it in the drive-by box at the post office. It didn't say much.

Dear Elvis,

That's great news about your house. I will do everything in my power to come visit you and swim in the pool someday.

Sorry I have to make it short and sweet this time. There isn't much news anyway—that I can tell—except I got a new dress. Maybe someday I'll get to wear it to one of your concerts. Meanwhile, I will always be thinking about you and sending all the luck I can imagine your way.

Juliet

Before dawn on Saturday, Mama and I sneaked our bags out of the house—both small, for I would get hand-me-down maternity clothes at the home, and Mama and Carmen would only be gone until Sunday night. Carmen put her stuff in a paper sack.

With me on the floor of the backseat and covered with a blanket, we dropped Carmen off at our father's house on the way out of town. I regretted not getting to visit him and my grandparents before leaving, but it couldn't be helped what with the last-minute scramble to bring Carmen up to speed on the technicalities of becoming me. We were nervous about whether they would buy into our deception, especially our father, but time had run out. There was nothing to do but go forward with the plan.

The road to Dallas was long and flat. To keep our spirits up, I read aloud the Burma Shave signs spaced along the highway.

"Dinah doesn't . . . Treat him right . . . But if he'd shave . . . Dynamite! . . . Burma Shave."

"Your voice is trembling," Mama said. "Get a hold of yourself."

"I'll try. Substitutes can let you down . . . Quicker than a strapless gown . . . Burma Shave. Oh, Mama, I'm so scared."

"Don't be. We can prolong it a bit if I take you to the motel with me to register, and after that I have a surprise. We're going to The Golden Pheasant for dinner. It's a special treat I've saved up for. Maybe you'll think back on it and not feel so lonely when I have to leave you."

I tried to crack a joke, but it fell flat. "Like a last meal?"

"Don't even think such a thing," she said.

Nowhere in El Dorado was there a restaurant as lush and highfalutin' as this one. The front doors, under bright-yellow awnings, had a sign over them advertising a new cooling system and were inlaid with stained glass pheasants. Two stuffed pheasants sat on top of big pillars in the foyer.

On tables covered with starched white cloths, silverware for every possible course had been laid. Although Mama had taught me what all the spoons and forks were for, I hadn't planned on getting to use them until I grew up. But maybe being pregnant made me already grown up. I did okay, except for giving my order to the waiter.

"A hamburger, please," I said.

He smiled. "Maybe the young miss would enjoy trying another version of our Texas beef."

I agreed, and the result was my first filet mignon, cooked to a perfect pink tint inside. Mama had wine with the meal, and we shared an order of cherries jubilee for dessert. She doled out her hard-earned cash, and we left the beautiful restaurant through the elegant doors into the evening and the hour of my exile.

PART TWO

I, Carmen

CHAPTER 11
DEVIL IN DISGUISE

With my finger bound in a phony splint, I got out of Elizabeth's car at Dad's the Saturday morning she and Julie left for Texas.

"You look a hundred percent better with your hair like Julie's," Elizabeth said through the open window.

"Great, 'cause with it hacked off I feel like a criminal who's been prepped for jail."

"Good luck," came Julie's voice from where she was hiding under a coat on the backseat floor.

"Same to you," I said and watched until they drove out of sight.

Right away, when Dad opened the door, he seemed taken in by our ruse. I never saw such spaced-out happiness as the look on his face when he thought it was Julie standing there holding a paper sack. Made me feel like dirt. I had always been worried that he loved Julie more than me.

"Hi, Chicken Little," he said.

"Julie! Come in this house!"

Grandma came rushing to the door, her bulk wobbling with each step, her arms open wide.

"What possessed Elizabeth to let you come? And for the whole weekend?" Dad asked as I moved into the warmth of Grandma's hug.

"A fit of wild abandon, I guess," I said to him over her shoulder.

His eyes widened. Too late the thought came to me that Julie wouldn't use that expression.

"Sit down, sit down," Grandma said. "Scott, put her sack in your room. What happened to your finger, honey?"

"Slipped and fell at the Sadie Hawkins dance."

Julie or no Julie, I wouldn't say I fainted. I had no patience with dames who fainted.

"That's a pretty pathetic cast," she said, taking my finger and examining it through her bifocals. "What's the medical world coming to?"

Grandpa—a long-legged, skinny geezer—wandered in and squatted into the droopy-bottomed easy chair.

"My springs are about to fall out," he said with a chuckle. "And so are the chair's."

Reaching over, he picked up a small pouch from the side table. Holding a piece of paper about three inches square between the fingers of one hand and using the forefinger of his other hand, he patted the pouch just enough to sprinkle tobacco onto the paper. Not a flake went astray. He rolled it up, licked along the side to seal it, and struck a match to light up.

"Smoke?" he said, looking straight at me.

Grandma swatted him on the head with a crocheted pillow.

"Don't put ideas into her head, you old buzzard. I'm fixing biscuits for breakfast," she went on. "You like biscuits, Julie?"

"Love 'em."

"Wanna go fishing this afternoon?" Dad asked.

"I've never been."

"I took you when you were about eight? Don't you remember? Your papaw went with us."

My brain went blank. "Papaw?"

He pointed his thumb at Grandpa. "Papaw!"

In a flash, I realized Julie must call him that. And was Grandma called Mamaw? I did a two-second racking of the brain and came up with nothing. Of all the trivia Julie had tried to instill in me, she'd forgotten one of the most important details.

"Right," I said, slapping on a fake smile. "I'm not awake yet."

"You could have slept in and come later. Why'd you have Elizabeth drop you off so early if you hadn't gotten your nap out?"

"She had to do it on her way out of town."

Oops. I wasn't supposed to say that. I could feel my eyes widen in shock at my slip of the tongue.

"So that's why she let you come for the weekend," Dad said. "She needed to leave you somewhere."

"No, that's not it at all. She'd have let me stay home by myself." *A total lie.*

"Where's she off to, Little Rock?" Papaw asked. "She still go up there every time the wind blows?"

I blanked again. Nobody had ever mentioned Elizabeth going to Little Rock, except on an occasional shopping spree.

"Uh . . . not much anymore," I stammered. "No money to spare these days."

"Why didn't she take you with her?" Dad pressed.

I thought quick. "I didn't want to go. I'd rather spend some time with you."

That seemed to satisfy them because Grandma got up and started for the kitchen.

"I smell my biscuits. They must be might near ready. Y'all, come on. By the time you get to the table, I'll have the eggs fried. The sausage and bacon's done."

"Can I help you?" I asked, not daring to risk calling her anything.

She turned a glad face to me. "Your old Mamaw welcomes all the help she can get, sweetheart."

I did have a guardian angel after all. Pure joy made me dance into the kitchen behind "Mamaw."

When we were all seated around the table, she asked Papaw to say grace.

His eyes glinted. "Bless the meat, and damn the skin. Open your mouth, and poke it in!"

I burst out laughing.

"Odell!" Mamaw yelped. "Julie'll think you're a heathen."

"It was pretty funny," I said. "Eliz . . . uh . . . Mama wouldn't like it, but she's not here, is she?"

After breakfast, Dad, Papaw, and I tied the rowboat on the roof of Dad's old jalopy, loaded up with tackle boxes and beer, and headed north of town to Calion Lake. Harsh sunlight danced in ripples on the green water. Lily pads and scum fringed the edges of the narrow inlet where Dad pulled up and stopped for us to unload.

Once in the boat, Dad grabbed a bottle of beer and downed half of it in one long glug. Papaw sneaked glances at him while fiddling with his fishing pole. Reaching for the can of worms, Dad let out a huge belch that echoed across the lake.

"Bring it up again, and we'll vote on it!" Papaw said.

I cracked up. Dad scowled and tossed back what turned out to be his first of many beers that afternoon.

"Calion Lake was man-made, long about thirty-eight," Papaw said. "In school, did they teach you that old Hernando de Soto wintered in this region, Julie?"

"The only de Soto I know anything about is the car," I said and bit my tongue. I'd almost told them my stepdad drives one.

When Dad shook out some worms next to me on the plank seat, I flipped, once more betraying that I'd never been fishing in my life.

"Get those things away from me!"

Dad laughed. "You can't catch a fish without a worm on your hook."

"I can't bait it with a broken finger."

He sighed but threaded a worm onto the hook and jumped up, holding the pole out to me.

"You're rocking the boat!" I said. "We don't want to go tail over tea-kettle into the drink."

Papaw pushed up the brim of his hat and studied me.

"Well, now you sound like regular folks," Dad said. "Elizabeth had you talking like a Harvard graduate before you were five years old."

His comment set off a warning bell in my head. I'd better polish up my routine if I planned to be convincing.

As the day wore on, I grew more and more uneasy about the situation. I was living a lie. I longed to drop the pretense and just be myself this weekend with the family. I could turn into Julie again on Monday at school. But how could I put the brakes on now? Besides, I'd given Julie and both our moms my word I would never reveal to a soul I was Carmen, and I intended to keep my promise. Julie's future depended on it.

But after three miserable hours in that ancient boat, with Dad tossing down one beer after another and Papaw growing silent and remote, I slipped again.

"I'm sweating like a pig."

"Elizabeth always said Southern ladies glow, not sweat," Dad said, his words slurred. "Take a dip and cool off."

That instant the cork on my line took a deep dive. Dad waved his arms.

"You've got a bite!"

One side of the boat tipped clear down to the water.

"Watch it, Scott!" yelled Papaw.

It didn't take much effort to plop the forlorn little fish into the boat. It flopped across my bare feet, and I squealed again. When it finally lay still on the boat floor, I took a deep breath.

"I actually caught one. I can't believe it. I caught a fish!"

"Big enough to keep, but barely," Papaw said. "Put him on your string."

"No way am I touching that thing."

"Think you can manage to eat him?" Papaw said and chuckled.

Even in his cups, Dad caught fish. Between them, he and Papaw got sixteen fair-sized bream. Mamaw fried them up for supper, making sure to put the one I caught on my plate. When I tasted the cornmeal crispness and the sweet white flesh, together with hot water cornbread dripping with butter, all the afternoon misery slipped into forgetfulness. We were halfway through the meal when Dad passed out, his face plunging flat down into his turnip greens.

Mamaw flushed and put her hands over her face. It took all three of us to get Dad into bed, still dressed, with snores rattling from his throat.

On top of being exhausted from too much sun, the effort to keep up the charade was wearing me out. At least I'd get to take off the mask of pretense in bed in the dark, but I'd thought wrong. With only two beds in the house, Papaw had to bunk with Dad, and I had to share the other bed with Mamaw. On and on she clapped her gums about life in the good ole days until I thought I'd go crazy.

When, at last, her snores rose in volume to compete with Dad's, I slipped the splint off my finger and tiptoed into the living room. A butterfly night-light kept me from crashing into the furniture. Praying the springs wouldn't choose this moment to go clattering onto the floor, I eased into Papaw's chair and fiddled with his tobacco paraphernalia until I managed to roll a small cigarette.

I reached for the packet of matches lying next to the tobacco pouch. Not a single one left. Impossible, after all this effort.

He must have more matches.

In my frenzied search, I sent the Bible crashing off the end table and onto the linoleum floor. I tensed. Someone was sure to come running with a gun. Not a sound, except the snoring.

At last, I spotted extra matches on the floor next to the splayed-open Bible. I snatched them, but before my shaking hands could strike one, a flame flared at the end of my squishy cigarette.

"Practice a little, and you'll be able to roll them as tight as mine."

"Papaw! You scared the hooty out of me."

"What do you think you did to me, prowling around and helping yourself to my tobacco?"

"Sorry. I couldn't sleep for the snoring duet."

"I know what you mean. Your dad's inhaling the bedspread."

"I didn't think you'd mind if I bummed a cig, since you offered me one earlier."

"I don't. Help yourself. Anytime."

To ease my anxiety that he might be seeing clear through me, I turned away from his penetrating eyes and took a long drag.

He signaled me to follow him.

The front door squeaked as we opened and shut it.

"Dadgummit!" he said when we were safely outside and on the way to the bench in the yard. "I've told Scott to oil them hinges a hunnerd times. Sometimes he ain't worth the powder to blow him to hell. Drunk half the time." He turned his face to me. "Now, missy, you want to explain what the deuce is going on here?"

Think fast, I silently ordered myself and sat on the bench, adopting the modest posture Julie used, my feet crossed at the ankles. I looked at him with fake innocence.

"I don't know what you mean."

He scrutinized my face. "Don't kid a kidder, sugar. You've changed. You ain't nothing like the Julie I know, except in looks."

My heart skipped beats. I felt like I was going to crack. It would be so easy to confess I was Carmen and then pretend it was a game Julie and I were playing, since people said we looked so much alike, and to involve him in the deception by making him promise not to tell anyone. But I didn't dare. What if he spilled the beans? He was sly. One of the last things Julie had said to me was, "No one must find out I'm pregnant." So be it.

"I'll clue you, Papaw. I'm Julie. Who else would I be?"

"You act more like the other one."

"Carmen?" I feigned surprise and talked fast. "It's been so much fun to find her and have a real sister. People are always getting us mixed up. We were thinking it might be fun to see just how far we could go pretending to be each other, but, of course, we're too different to get away with that." I forced a laugh and sucked hard on the cigarette.

"Julie don't smoke," he said.

The lie spouted out of me. "Carmen got me smoking."

His eyes grew hollow and filled with disbelief.

"I'm too old for these shenanigans. Where's the splint for your finger?"

Adrenalin shot through me as another lie popped out. "The doctor said I could take it off at night."

He stared out toward the "eternal" flame burning at the Lion Oil Refinery, just a few blocks from the house.

"That stink coming from over yonder is hovering all around us," he said. "You know what folks say when they smell it, don't you?"

I could feel the clueless look on my face.

"Everybody knows that," I said with bravado.

"Okay, let's hear it."

This whole charade had been my idea. I couldn't blow it the first day. "Is this a test?"

"It might be." He looked sideways at me.

"Quit trying to rattle my cage, Papaw."

"There's another whiff of it," he said.

I pinched my nostrils. "Phew! It goes all over town. I've smelled it clear to our house." An image of the house mother and I lived in on East Third popped into my mind. I quickly replaced it with a mental image of Julie's home. Stuff like that could cause me to blow the whole project.

"Do you know it?" he persisted.

I put on an innocent expression. "Know what?"

"The saying."

He had me, and we both knew it.

"So you never heard of the Lion lifting its tail?"

"Oh, that. Mama won't let me say it. She says it's crude."

Once again, confusion took over his face.

CHAPTER 12
Treat Me Nice

Late in the afternoon on Sunday, Elizabeth came to get me on her way back home from Texas. When Dad walked with me out to the car, I watched her face for a sign that she still loved him. My own mother got "that look," complete with misty eyes, when someone so much as mentioned his name. After three scotch and waters, and if my stepfather was safely out of earshot, like across the ocean, she would admit she'd never had a lover like Dad, but she always denied it when she sobered up. Elizabeth's reaction to him would best be described as a sheet of white marble. She barely glanced at him when he rapped on the car window with a knuckle and said, "Roll 'er down."

While he talked and she replied with low, grunting uh-huhs, I threw my sack into the backseat and crawled in. The raincoat Julie had hidden under was gone, a forecast of how empty the house would be without her.

"It was good of you to let her spend the night," Dad was saying as he leaned on the lowered window. "We hope you'll let her come again soon."

Elizabeth shrugged and turned her face toward the windshield. "We'll see."

"I sure had a good time, honey," Dad said, looking at me in the backseat. "And so did Mamaw and Papaw."

"Me too."

"How are her grades?" he asked Elizabeth.

"Not as good as Ju—" She broke off. "As they should be."

From where I sat, I could see her face redden. She was thinking of me as Carmen.

I jumped in. "Thanks for taking me fishing. It was fun, even in that old boat."

He turned on his engaging smile.

"You'll catch more next time, now that you've got the knack."

I waved. "Bye, Dad. See ya."

Elizabeth goosed it, and we shot off so fast he barely had time to step back. I watched him through the rear window until we turned at the end of the block and he slid out of sight.

"How did it go?" Elizabeth asked, a note of anxiety permeating her voice.

I shrugged. "They sort of bought it, but not totally."

"What happened?"

"Nothing to sweat. Papaw caught me smoking, that's all."

"We're done in!" she said.

"No, we're not. Simmer down, and I'll give you a blow-by-blow. Watch out!"

The tires screeched. I braced myself against the back of the passenger seat as we slammed to a stop.

"Jeez! You almost flattened that lady."

Elizabeth fanned her face with her hand. "She was jaywalking."

"The punishment was too great for the crime."

"I didn't hit her."

"A miss is as good as a mile, huh?" I said, trying to get my breath.

"Just tell me what happened at Scott's this weekend. Then I'll tell you about Julie."

She spoke the name "Scott" in that special way women speak the names of men they love. I'd heard mother say his name just like that. He was a looker, my old man. Probably great in the sack too. No wonder neither mom had exterminated him from her heart. The rest of the way to the house I filled her in on the events of the weekend, leaving out nothing, not even the Lion lifting his tail.

"Maybe you'll become more convincing with practice," she said, pulling into the driveway.

"There won't be a next time for the fishing scene," I said.

"Can't say I blame you. By the way, Julie would never address me as Elizabeth."

"Okey dokey."

Inside, the first crisis occurred when the telephone rang and I answered.

"Morgan residence."

A long, empty pause followed.

"Who is this?" came the voice on the phone.

"Julie," I said.

"That's a falsehood, if I ever heard one."

I began to doubt I would ever succeed in playing Julie if I couldn't even convince people with a one-worder. We had decided nothing had to be changed about my voice to persuade people. It would be next to impossible anyway. Although we didn't sound precisely identical, our natural pitch tones fell into the same range, with only the slightest variation in vocal patterns.

"Who is it?" whispered Elizabeth, wide-eyed and hands trembling as she held them out for the receiver. She listened only a second. "Mavis, what seems to be the problem?"

I didn't dare so much as twitch. Elizabeth's eyes went from pale gray to a dark storm color as the voice clattered on the other end of the line. Although I couldn't make out what she was saying, I could hear the railing tone in Mavis MacAfee's voice, no doubt about the one word lie I'd uttered: "Julie."

"We went out of town," Elizabeth said. "To Little Rock."

A tirade must have erupted on the other end, for Elizabeth's cheeks ripened into red patches.

"I just forgot to tell you," she said with a weary voice. "You do that. Come on over. I'm unpacking, but Julie can make us a pot of coffee.

No, come on. It's fine, really." Another long silence on Elizabeth's end. Then, "Okay. Okay. Un-huh. Fine. See you next weekend."

She slapped the receiver onto the hook and sank down on her bed.

"She doesn't believe it was you. Uh . . . Julie. God, I'm getting so mixed up. She doesn't believe Julie answered the phone."

"It would take someone with perfect pitch and a trained ear to detect the differences in Julie's and my voice," I said, sitting next to her.

"Just such a person was on the other end of the line," Elizabeth said. "Mavis MacAfee?"

"Is a musical genius. She could have sung at the Met, but she got married instead. And yes, those miniscule differences could betray you."

She leaped up and ran to her closet. Rummaging around, she threw hat boxes aside, tossed shoes out into the bedroom, and rattled coat hangers until she emerged, triumphant, with a tape recorder.

"I have a recording of Julie reciting a poem for English class finals last year. You must listen to it until you can mimic her exactly."

"I sound almost like her now," I said, hoping to weasel out of such a boring chore.

"Almost won't do it, obviously," Elizabeth said, thrusting the machine into my arms. "Take it to Julie's room and turn it on. Listen day and night, and master it."

"This is going a little too far," I said, my arms trembling with the weight of the machine. "Why don't we just go get Julie and bring her back and let her have the baby here? Facing down El Dorado's snotty society folks couldn't be any harder than all the tap dancing we're doing."

I meant it to be funny, but Elizabeth didn't take it that way. Her hand flashed out, and she slapped my face, hard. I was stunned. No one had ever slapped me before, not even my sometimes-volatile mother, who wouldn't hesitate to swat me on the rear end. "Never hit a child in the face," she always used to say as she prepared to give me a sound spanking on my bare bottom.

Elizabeth gasped. Her eyes opened wide, and she threw her arms as far as she could reach around me and the tape recorder.

"I'm so sorry. I don't know what came over me."

I drew back and stared at her.

"Don't ever hit me in the face again. If you do, I'll walk right out of this house and tell the world what you're up to."

"I said I was sorry. You must never, ever say anything like that again. El Dorado people are good people who don't deserve your condemnation."

"You are the one who condemns them. When you sent Julie off, you were condemning them. You're the one who won't give them a chance to forgive her for making a mistake."

"They wouldn't. She'd have been ruined for life," Elizabeth said.

"Then how 'good' are they?"

"They can't forgive her for something like that, don't you see? It's the way they've been taught—the way we've all been taught."

"Still, you'd better treat me nice if you want me to help pull off your black deception."

"You're not lily-white, yourself," she countered. "It's too bad you are so different from Julie in every way except looks."

I held up a hand and said, "I dig," and turning away, I carried the tape recorder to Julie's room. Elizabeth followed on my heels.

"Tell me what happened out there in Texas," I said, pulling from my pocket one of the two emergency cigarettes I had pilfered from Papaw.

"I took her out to eat at The Golden Pheasant," she said with a stifled sob.

"Like a last meal?" I quipped.

She blinked. "That's exactly what she said."

"So maybe we're not so different after all."

She shook her head and pulled a packet of matches from her own pocket.

"Would you happen to have another one of those?"

I took out the other cigarette I'd intended to save for three A.M. desperation.

She took it between her thumb and forefinger, making a face, as if it might be riddled with germs, coming as it did from my father's house.

"It's limp. What is it? Odell's roll-your-own?"

"Beggars can't be choosers, now can they? If you don't want it, give it back."

She stuck the firmer end between her lips and struck a match. I leaned toward her.

"Light us up, Mama."

CHAPTER 13

Suspicious Minds

That same night, I flipped out.

"Is it my turn to drive the carpool tomorrow? Julie told me where everybody lives, but she didn't say when it would be my turn to pick up. Think, did she drive last Friday? Or did someone pick her up?"

"So much has happened since then," Elizabeth said. "Seems like a lifetime ago."

We spent twenty minutes pacing around the den, racking our brains to remember.

Finally, I said, "Let's go for cigarettes. We'll never figure this out without them."

"You can't run around with tobacco breath. And I promised Julie I'd quit. It's coming back to me. She drove the carpool on Friday. She had to drop me off at work first, and I was worried about getting the car gassed up for the trip the next day."

I exhaled relief, wishing it was smoke.

It was Darcy Doyle driving the Dreamsicle who honked in the driveway that Monday, my first day of school as Julie. Wearing a "Julie dress" of the variety the other in-crowd girls wore, I went out onto the front porch with Julie's school books in my arms and the fake splint on my finger.

Maylene was the first to greet me. "Your hair's a mess."

Knowing I couldn't answer her without rancor in my voice, I merely smiled.

Laura Meade leaned forward, and I squeezed into the backseat, scared to death and excited out of my skull at the same time.

"It looks like you cut it yourself," Maylene said.

"I did do a little whacking."

Laura turned to look at me. "Get thee to a beauty parlor."

So far, no one seemed to sniff me out. I was on my way to becoming one of the in-crowd. Julie hated Maylene, but she hadn't done anything to me. I needed her. I intended to use all the energy I could no longer put into sucking on cigarettes to suck up to her. I wanted dear old May-lene in the palm of my hand. This was my chance to be popular, and I was going to make the absolute most of it.

"I'm so glad you've swapped your saddle oxfords for loafers," May-lene said, leaning over and pointing at my shoes.

Another two seconds of skipped heart beats. I'd automatically stepped into my own brown shoes this morning instead of putting on Julie's. Too many slip-ups would be fatal.

"Thanks, Maylene. I always value your opinions."

She blinked, surprise on her face.

"But you don't have pennies in their slots," Lynn said. "Maybe I've got a couple." She dug around in her purse. "Nope, but I do have a dime. Put it in one of them for now. You can't run around without money in your loafers. You'll look like your lookalike." She shook her head. "I keep forgetting you two are half-sisters. Hope I didn't hurt your feelings. It's just that you don't want to make fashion mistakes like she does."

I swallowed. "No, no I don't. But I imagine she thinks the way we dress is a bigger fashion mistake. At least she wears loafers."

I reached down, ostensibly to put the dime in one of my loafer's coin slots, but mostly to hide my anxious face. It was hard to talk about me, Carmen, while I was pretending to be Julie.

Laura sat up straight and preened. "Wonder why, with your finger still gimped, Mr. Nesbitt doesn't just let you sit in study hall during first and second period band class?"

"I guess he thinks I can at least learn the music, even if I can't play my instrument."

"You're a philanderer, you know that?" Maylene said. "I bet you could play that clarinet if you wanted to."

"The word is 'malingerer,' Maylene," Lynn said in her laidback way from the other side of me. "Miss Bolenbaugh is going to have your head on a spike if she hears you butcher the king's English like that."

Maylene blushed to her hairline. This was an opportunity to butter her up. Sitting next to her made it easy to nudge her in the ribs and give her a look that said I wouldn't have known the difference in the two words either. Her nod back to me said she was pleased. *Score one.* To hell with how Julie felt about her. In the long run, what I planned to do to cement my friendship with Maylene would benefit Julie too, when she came home.

"Julie, you're not yourself today," Lynn commented, a thoughtful look on her face.

My heart did its flutter act, like when Papaw caught me pilfering a cigarette.

"How so?"

She gazed out the window. "Oh, I don't know. You just seem different, somehow. Forget it. I'm not awake yet."

The school administration had been informed that I, Carmen, was leaving to go abroad with my folks for the rest of the year.

In the band hall, while they squeaked out the opening of some classical ditty, I, as Julie, surreptitiously studied the worn class schedule Julie had carried in her purse. We both took chemistry, so no problem there. No problem with Bolenbaugh's English class, unless I used the wrong past participle or something. In American History I could hold my own. As I scanned to the bottom of the paper, alarm bells went off in my head. How had we overlooked her French class? As Carmen, I had been enrolled in the Spanish class. To me, French might as well be Hungarian.

At the break, I rushed up to Mr. Nesbitt.

"I need to be excused," I told him, casting my eyes downward, as though trying to convey that I was referring to the condition girls didn't mention to male teachers.

He nodded, and I flew down the steps of the band hall, down the main steps, clear to the office on the first floor.

The clerk, wearing her typical "I hate everybody" face, paid no attention to me. For five whole minutes I stood at the counter, tapping my foot, while she continued arranging schedule cards in a big, green file box.

"'Scuse me," I said.

She lifted aggravated eyes to me. "Hold your horses, Madam Queen. I'll be there in a minute."

"I'm going to be late to class," I said.

"You're already late. What's the emergency?"

"I . . . uh . . . I need to drop French and sign up for Spanish."

Suspicion darkened her face. "Smack in the middle of the semester? And why, pray, would you be allowed to do such a thing?"

"I'm not doing good in French but—"

She cut me off. "You're not doing *well*."

"Yeah, yeah, but I'd be great in Spanish. I already know some. Adios, amigo. That's Spanish. You have to let me change."

"No can do. And that's English."

"But I *have* to!"

She got out my file and perused it.

"It says here you've got a B average in French." She looked at me with questioning eyes.

"I . . ." *Oh God, what excuse to give?* There was no way I could go into that class and convince the teacher I was Julie Morgan when I didn't know a word of French. "My mother wants me to take Spanish. We might go to Mexico."

"Note?"

"Wh-what?"

"Do you have a note from a parent stating the reasons why we should move you from French class to Spanish this late in the year?"

I lowered my eyes. "I can get one."

"Come back when you do. That's all."

Beaten, I turned and slunk out of the office. That one class could ruin everything. I had to call Elizabeth—Mama.

The nearest pay phone booth sat across the street in front of the Wildcat Café. No one was allowed to leave school until the first lunch period at eleven thirty. I'd have to scoot over there and pray no one saw me.

A directory hung on a wire beneath the phone. At least I remembered the name of the law firm Elizabeth worked for. I found the five-digit number only to realize I'd left my purse in Julie's locker. No alternative but to work the dime out of the coin slot of my loafer. The receptionist put me right through.

"Mama," I began, but she cut me off.

"Julie! What's wrong? Are you calling long distance?"

"It's Carmen," I said under my breath, in case, by some magical means, my voice was being broadcast out into the world.

I could hear her relief. "What's the problem?"

I told her, and she promised to call the school immediately.

"But it may not work," she warned. "When Principal Younger says he wants a note, he won't accept anything else. Oh, Lord! I can't take much more."

At that moment, who should come sauntering out of the Wildcat Café but Bubba John Younger. I told Elizabeth I'd call her back and leaped out of the phone booth right into his path. His eyes popped.

"Julie Morgan! What are you up to, sneaking out here to use the pay phone?"

"You sneaked out here yourself, it would appear," I said with a smirk.

He cocked his head. "My mom says anyone in a small town like El Dorado who uses a pay phone is having an affair. Folks who aren't up to no good just knock on somebody's door and ask to make a call."

Astonished, I blinked.

"I know, I know," he said, draping one of his big-muscled arms around my shoulders. "You're not some grown-up sneaking around using pay phones to call your squeeze." He lost his joviality and peered into my face. "But what the hey *are* you doing using the pay phone?"

"Bubba John, do you like me?" I asked, turning on the coy approach, complete with batting eye lashes.

He laughed. "A lot more today than I did last week. You've changed, girl. Warmed up." He squeezed my shoulder. "You must have had quite a good weekend."

If you only knew.

"Listen, Bubba John, would you do me a favor?"

"Sure, honey. The backseat of my car or yours?"

I pulled away from him. "That's not what I mean."

"I was afraid of that," he said with a yuk.

"I need a note to get transferred out of French class. Would you write it for me?"

"You mean get out of French for good? Won't your mom write it?"

"She will, but she can't until tonight. I need it now. Today."

He raised one eyebrow. "Why the big rush?"

I scrambled for a believable explanation. "I'm going to flunk if I have to take the mid-semester test today. I want to take Spanish. I'd be good at that."

He thought a minute. "If I write this note for you, will you go out with me next Saturday night?"

"It's a date."

I grabbed the notebook tucked under his arm and yanked out a clean sheet of paper.

"My old man reads every friggin' one of these notes, you know. What if he sniffs out that it's my writing?"

"I'll risk it, but hurry up. I have to get back up to band class."

"I guess it'll be worth a whuppin' since I'm getting a date with you out of it."

He took my splinted finger and held it up for examination.

"When you gonna get that bandage off, honey?"

"Four more weeks," I said, wiggling the finger from his grip.

"At least you won't be able to fight me off with only one good hand," he said, giving me the hen-scratched note. "Pick you up at seven, and wear something low cut, will ya? My big fingers are clumsy with the little bitty buttons you girls wear."

CHAPTER 14
Oh! What a Tangled Web we Weave

After lunch, Bubba John stopped me to exchange a brief word in the hall.

"Did that old biddy in the office swallow the note?"

"Hook, line, and sinker," I said, grinning all over my face at how cool it was I'd gone fishing just the day before yesterday and learned what that expression referred to.

The old biddy in the office only had to switch Julie's American History class in order for me to go to Mrs. Brandon's fifth period Spanish class, which I had attended every day as Carmen.

When I swung into the room, Mrs. Brandon spoke with only a glance at me.

"Buenos días, Carmen."

Like a shot, I tensed. That same instant she did a double take, her papers splaying onto the floor.

"I thought you went abroad with your mother," she said, amazement on her face.

I took a momentary pause, in order to keep straight in my own mind who I was.

"Carmen did go abroad." I yanked open Julie's purse—which I had decided to keep with me at all times in case I needed more dimes—and handed the transfer slip to her. "I'm Julie, and I'm transferring from French to Spanish because I'm having trouble parlez-vooing."

Mrs. Brandon rubbed her forehead. "I'm confused."

I made a throwaway gesture. "Everybody is always getting us mixed up. You're by no means the only one."

She studied my face with semi-frantic eyes. "And you're . . . ?"

"I'm Julie Morgan."

"Well, Julie . . ." She thought a moment before stooping to gather up her papers. I dropped down to help her. Meeting my eyes, she said, "You shouldn't give up your French. Besides, you'll be behind starting Spanish this late, even if it is only first year."

"I won't be behind," I said, carefully choosing my words so as not to blow it. "Carmen tutored me in Spanish before she left. She said I was a real quick study."

Mrs. Brandon studied my transfer slip. "I guess, if the office approved it, I have to go along." With a quick glance at me, she pointed to the back of the room. "You can keep your old seat."

We exchanged startled looks.

"I mean, Julie, you can take Carmen's old seat."

It didn't occur to me until later that I hadn't asked which seat was Carmen's, nor had Mrs. Brandon's expression changed when I, as Julie, went straight to it and sank down, exhausted. I was getting all tangled up in my lies.

It got tougher when the school day ended and I headed out to join the carpoolers at the Dreamsicle. Della, Rhonda, and Faye, looking like three harpies in their bat-winged sweaters, turned dark eyes on me as I passed the flagpole, their perpetual hangout.

When I waved, Della beckoned to me.

"Come here, Carmen. We thought you'd gone to England."

Uh-oh. Those three Dilberts had been my only friends up until today. We'd done everything together. No wonder they thought I was me. Doing some fast thinking, I hung a detour toward them.

"I'm Julie," I said in the friendliest manner I could muster. "You're right. Carmen has gone to England."

Doubt filled their faces.

Della laughed and shook her head, as if to get rid of cobwebs in her brain.

"Julie? Come on, cut it out."

"No, really. I am Julie."

"She is," Rhonda said. "I remember that dress she has on."

"Then what's different about today that you'd bother to talk to us?" Faye said in a snide tone.

Belatedly remembering the tension that had existed between Julie and them since she got into the in-crowd, I powdered down my friendly approach.

"What can I do for you?"

Their reason for the breakup between Julie and them was they'd thought she was trying to steal Eugene Hoffmeyer from Rhonda. I knew better, and so did they, now, but resentment of Julie's ascendance on the social scene had turned them bitter and hostile toward her, long after Rhonda had Eugene's ring on a chain around her neck.

"Tell us about Carmen," Della said.

I frowned. "Tell you what about Carmen?"

"Why did she move away?" Rhonda asked. "She said she didn't want to."

"Her mother went to join her dad in England, and she had to go too. I thought everybody knew that."

"Kind of sudden, huh?" Della asked. "Couldn't she have stayed here?"

I shifted Julie's books under my arm. "Alone? I hardly think so."

"You're her sister. Why couldn't she have stayed with you?" Faye said.

"Can you imagine my mother going along with that scene?" I said, scanning the mobs of kids streaming out of the building. "Listen, I see Maylene and them heading for the car. I gotta run."

"I knew that first night at Elvis's show at the stadium that you and Carmen must be sisters," Faye added. "I never saw any two people look so much alike. Remember, I was the one who pointed her out to you."

"Yes, Faye, I remember."

"I miss Carmen already." Faye's face drooped. "And I miss you too."

"We had some good times in the old days, Julie," Della said. "Now that Rhonda and Eugene are an item, we would let you go to the Dairyette with us once in a while."

Not in this new world I now live in skittered through my head, but I only smiled and said, "Sure. I gotta dash."

Hope sprang into their faces.

"You've changed, Julie," Della called after me. "We'll call you sometime. I like you much better like you are now. Almost as much as I liked Carmen."

With a joyful heart I skittered, like the thoughts in my head, off to join the carpool group. How wonderful to be accepted at last. At the same time a part of me felt sorry for those three. They weren't bad sorts. What a shame they couldn't break out of the Dilbert category.

Maylene accosted me the minute I caught up with them.

"Why weren't you in French class today?"

I was ready for her question, but not for what followed my answer.

"I hate French. I transferred into Spanish."

"Oh," she said, her voice taking on the snotty tone she was so famous for.

"I thought you were getting on better in French II than any of us," Laura said.

"I was only getting Bs. Uh . . . Mama didn't like that."

Maylene shot me a look. "My folks would think a B in French was great."

"Well, Mama didn't."

"Then you won't be studying with us at night anymore," Maylene said.

"Well, I guess not. But couldn't we study English some nights, or chemistry?"

"We're not having trouble in those classes," she said. "Listen, Lynn, do you want us to come to your house again tonight, or is your mother sick of us?"

"She's sick of us," Lynn said, climbing into the backseat of the Dreamsicle. "And so is my sister, the old hag. I hate her sometimes. Julie, you ought to be glad you never had to live with your sister."

"I'd have loved it!" I spouted, thinking back on those nights with Julie when we were prepping me to take her place. "Sharing a room and talking all night. Me and my sister. How great!"

"I guess you do need to study English some nights," Maylene said.

A chill ran through me. I must have made a grammar mistake. But what? I must have looked as confused as I felt, for the next thing she said was, "Me and my? Really, Julie. You've obviously spent too much time with that new sister of yours. It's a good thing she left town before everything about her rubbed off on you."

"Don't forget your own flubs," I said. "Philanderer instead of malingerer?"

Maylene tossed her ponytail.

"I'm sorry you aren't going to be studying with us anymore, Julie," Laura said.

"Me too," I said, feeling a bit empty, even though I had never studied with them.

I'd struck out already. Lost one of my connections—the weekly study group with them. For the first time it occurred to me that, when Julie came home, she wouldn't be able to take French anymore, and she loved it. She didn't know a word of Spanish. Oh well, we'd have to cross that bridge when we got to it.

Darcy chimed up. "I'll study English with you, Julie. I need all the help I can get with Shakespeare. And didn't you get an A on Bolenbaugh's last test?"

"Uh . . . okay."

How could I ever pull off helping her, when I, Carmen, had a C average in grammar and I hated Shakespeare? My disguise as Julie was not long for this world if I didn't shape up.

"Where are you going, Darcy?" Maylene asked.

"To the Dairyette. Where else? Hang loose. It's time we got back in the groove."

CHAPTER 15
Treat 'Em Rough and Tell 'Em Nothing

When we pulled into the Dairyette, the first person we saw was none other than Farrel the Great. Julie sarcastically referred to Maylene as "the Great," but I thought the tag fit Farrel better, the louse. In my opinion, he hadn't done Julie as wrong as she thought he had, but I knew he wouldn't win the school yearbook title for Most Considerate Boy. He glanced over at the Dreamsicle but didn't move from the table where he sat gobbling up a hot dog.

Parked next to his car was Bubba John's sleek red-and-white convertible. Leaning over the table with animated gestures, Bubba John appeared to be trying to get a reaction from Farrel, who, in turn, was reacting solely to his food. When he saw us, Bubba John strutted right over and rested both hands on the lowered window of the passenger side.

"There she is," he said, his brows lifted and a broad smile covering his face. "Did I tell you what time Saturday night, Julie?"

Maylene turned surprised eyes on me. "*You* have a date with *him*?" she mouthed.

I gave a brief nod.

Laura's face fell. I'd forgotten she had the hots for him.

"You told me seven, Bubba John."

"I talked to old Farrel over there. He says you've got plenty of blouses a fellow can get his hand down into without struggling with buttons."

"The son-of-a—" I caught myself in the nick, "gun!"

Lynn reached forward from the backseat and slapped his hands. "Farrel never said that. You've got a dirty mind, Bubba John."

He laughed. "A guy's gotta try. Anyway, Julie, I'm bugging out. Later, gator."

"You can kiss off any plans we ever made!" I yelled out the window.

He stopped in his tracks. Farrel glanced up toward us. In the car, all eyes turned on me.

"Aw, Julie," Bubba John said, moving back to the car, his face crinkled like he was about to cry. "I didn't mean nothing by it. You know I wouldn't try to put the make on you." He leaned into the car and said low, "You better not blow me off, not after what I done for you."

I was on the horns of a dilemma. I didn't want to make him mad. I needed dates with cute boys to maintain Julie's position in the in-crowd, but no nice girl participated in any hanky-panky. And going out with him might give the impression I was loose.

"I don't know, Bubba John. I'll have to think about it."

"All right." He scuffed off toward his car. "I'll call you tomorrow," he said over his shoulder. "Be ready to give me a big yes."

"What on earth did he do for you?" Laura demanded the minute he was gone.

Another lie bubbled up to my lips. This might be getting easier.

"He loaned me a dime for the pay phone."

Lynn turned her cat-that-swallowed-the-canary smile on me. "I thought you used the one from your loafer. I saw you take it out beside the phone booth."

"I . . . uh . . . dialed the wrong number and didn't have another dime. You saw . . . you saw me . . . at the phone booth?"

"I did. I went to the little girls' room the same time you asked Mr. Nesbitt for permission to go. Remember, in band this morning during the break?"

The look she gave me said "Gotcha!"

"When you weren't in there, I took a look out the restroom window and saw you heading to the pay phone."

I managed a shrug. "I had to call Mama. I needed a note to get out of French."

"Is that what you and Bubba John were writing so frantically?" Lynn asked.

In an instant I decided the truth, or part of the truth, would be better than another lie.

"Yep. Mama said it was okay to transfer out of French, but she naturally couldn't write the note until tonight, and I didn't want to flunk that test we were having today."

"You knew we weren't having a French test today," Maylene said, her voice oozing suspicion. "We always study together for French tests. And why didn't you call her from the office?"

Another lie popped up. "The clerk was on the phone, and I didn't have time to wait for her to get off."

I needed to flee this scene, and fast.

"Laura, let me out for a minute."

I pushed the seat forward and accidently clomped Maylene's toes as I climbed out of the Dreamsicle.

"Ouch!"

"Sorry."

"Where do you think you are going?" she asked in a huff.

"To see Farrel for a minute. Do you have a problem with that?"

"What do I care what you do?" she snapped.

"I just thought you might, since Justin isn't beating down your door."

Her eyes shot daggers at me. This was not the way to stay on her good side.

Without a clue what I was going to say, I headed for the table where Farrel, in the process of getting up, stood straddling the bench.

"I was fixin' to go, but if you're gonna sit and talk to me for a while, I'll get you an ice cream and have one myself."

"Just a coke," I said.

He returned with my drink and a banana split for himself.

"How can you stay so skinny?" I said.

"From working in those oil fields. I burn off everything I eat." He took a huge bite. "Hey, I got put on the same crew as your old man the other day. He's something else."

"Was he . . . okay?" I asked.

It was common knowledge that Dad often couldn't stay off the sauce long enough to put in a day's work.

Farrel's eyes softened. "He wasn't drunk, if that's what you're asking, but he talked about the beer he had in the Frigidaire waiting for him when he got home. He told me you spent last weekend with him."

I blinked. "Why would he tell you that? Does he know who you are?"

Farrel wiped dripping chocolate off his chin.

"I couldn't hardly keep him from knowing my name, and I told him I go out with you."

What did Dad think about Farrel?

"Him and my grandpa took me fishing," I said.

Farrel looked surprised. "That's the spirit."

"What is?"

"Dropping all that fancy talk when you're not around your mama."

In a flash, I realized my mistake. "I mean, he and my grandpa."

We both laughed, but my laugh was fake. Slip-ups like that could blow my cover, big time.

"Well, now that you're an expert fisherman, how would you like to go out on the lake with me to set a trot line Saturday night?"

"No, thanks. I hate fishing."

"Scared a snake might follow the flashlight beam and get in the boat?"

"There'd already be a snake in the boat. *You!*"

He gave me a sly smile.

"Besides, Bubba John told me what you said," I went on.

"About what?"

"Me, having plenty of blouses a fellow can get his hand down into without a struggle with buttons."

"What?" He put down his plastic spoon. "I didn't say nothing like that to him! You gotta believe me, honey."

I did believe him, in spite of what I said next to bait him.

"I can't believe you'd take our relationship with such a grain of salt."

He reached across the table and laid his hand on mine. "I don't, Julie. You know I don't. I take it very serious."

For a long moment, we looked at each other without saying a word while my mind raced. Did he love Julie? Did he plan on trying to get me to do IT with him, thinking I was Julie? Once a boy got to first base, he expected to get there on every date. My mother had beat that into my brain, and I believed it 'cause she was on the ball when it came to the male sex.

His face gave me no answers. Farrel was a cool one.

"I'll pick you up at seven thirty. It'll take me that long to get home and get showered and doused up with Old Spice. That smell is what makes you hot for me, isn't it?"

What my sister saw in this guy was more than I would ever know. I moved my hand from underneath his.

"I already have a date."

"With Bubba John? You broke it. I heard you yelling that all over the parking lot. I don't want you going out with him."

"You have no claim on me." I remembered something Julie had told me the night before she left, and I threw it at him. "You've never so much as sent me a valentine."

"I don't do stuff like that. Has Bubba John Younger sent you one? All he wants is to get in your pants."

Right then and there, I decided to do what Julie should have done a long time ago with Farrel and maybe with all boys. Obey Frances Latimer's dictate of "Treat 'em rough and tell 'em nothing."

"I thought that was all *you* wanted." Again I borrowed from Julie's secrets she'd confided to me those nights of my training to become her. "You had dropped me flat until I called you that time and said I would do IT. Frances, herself, told me you said taking me out felt like 'robbing the cradle.'"

His wary face said he was thinking fast.

"I'll show you on Saturday night what going out with you makes me feel like."

"Don't you ever learn?"

He glanced over at the Dreamsicle. "Keep your voice down. I can't fight my basic instincts."

"You'd better."

"Listen, Julie, I promise I won't try nothing. You know I wouldn't, not after . . . Frances." His voice broke saying her name. "I still can't get over it. 'Specially with Don talking me to death about it every time we go out for a beer together. And that's practically every damn night. He's still all tore up."

He certainly sounded sincere. Maybe he did care something about my sister. My opinion of him softened a little.

"I'll think about it." I got up from the table with a tilt of my head toward the car. "I don't want to hold them up."

"Wait. Are you still mad about me and Maylene going to the dance?"

Julie should never have let on it had hurt her so much.

"Of course not. Justin is a much better dancer than you."

He flinched. For a minute I thought I'd gone too far, but Frances's motto proved true. Treating him rough made him want me more.

"I wish I hadn't done that, taken her to the dance."

I laughed. "Like I said, no sweat. I have to go. They're waiting."

"Will you go out with me on Saturday?"

"I might. Eat your ice cream. It's melting."

He gave me a shrewd look. "You're not yourself, Julie."

No kidding.

CHAPTER 16
PICK YOUR POISON

I waited until Thursday to tell Elizabeth about the dates. She flipped her lid.

"You can't go out with Farrel Budrow!"

"You can't tell me what I can and can't do."

"While you're living under my roof, I can and I will!"

Standoff. I pressed my lips together, tight, to keep from talking. Neither Elizabeth nor I said a word for a full minute. *Next one who speaks loses.*

I lost.

"Elizabeth, I have to go. If I don't, he might get suspicious, figure it out that I'm not Julie," I said, trying to threaten her enough to give in. I wanted to go out with him—see what all the fuss was about. I had only spent about three hours total in Farrel's company one night when he got in my car at the Dairyette and we rode around a while. Nothing happened, except a lot of talk about how Julie was chasing him. I wanted to find out exactly what this cat had going that would make my sister go so ape over him.

My own mother had made it plain to Julie that her missing relationship with our dad had driven her to unsuitable substitutes for a parent's love and support, like Farrel, a guy way too old for her. I wondered why I hadn't gone in search of those substitutes. Maybe because of my stepdad, who, when he was around, showered me with affection and treated me like his own.

"Carmen, you need to call me Mama."

"And you need to call me Julie."

"I know, but it's hard." She stifled a sob and reached for the box of tissues beside her easy chair. "My darling is so unhappy in that place. It's all I can do to keep from going back out there and bringing her home."

I eased down on one of the red couches. "You got a letter from her?"

"Yes. I'll share it with you, but first, promise me you won't go on a date with that boy. What will I do if you get pregnant too?"

"I am *not* going to get pregnant by Farrel Budrow, or anyone. I'm not even going to let him feel me up."

Elizabeth shuddered. "Can't you say 'engage in a petting session'?"

"Mama E, I'm not you. I have to talk like I talk, not like some frustrated grammar police. Hey, how about me calling you that—Mama E?"

She expelled a quick breath that reeked of frustration. "It might do. We have to practice saying 'Mama something,' or we'll surely get caught when she arrives."

"You're rattling my head. When who arrives?"

"Old Aunt Hat."

I couldn't take much more of this household. No wonder Julie turned to Farrel.

"Who's Old Aint Hat?"

"My Great-Aunt Hattie Lawrence. I was a Lawrence before I married Julie's, uh, your father. Aunt Hattie lived here then, just up the street a few houses. Her sneeze was so loud you could hear her a block away." Elizabeth chuckled and gazed out the window into the backyard. "Look, the zinnia seeds I planted are up."

"Well, it is April." I shifted with impatience. "So what about Old Aint Hat?"

"She lives in New Orleans now, and she's coming for a visit. She says because it's been so long. But I know better."

"What do you mean?"

"She's coming to make sure we're living up to her rigid standards. To put it bluntly, she's coming here to inspect."

"Oh, Lord. Inspect what?"

"Julie, to see how she has turned out—to make sure that, under my tainted guidance as a divorcee, she has become a 'fine young lady.'"

"Whoa! That's heavy stuff."

"And since you girls have changed places, *you're* the Julie she's going to have to inspect."

"Lord, give me strength."

"Look at it as a kind of test."

"What happens if I don't pass?"

"There can be no question of your not passing. You *have* to pass. If you as Julie live up to her rigid standards, she might leave me a little something in her will, instead of giving it all to charity, as she is wont to do."

"On second thought, with money at stake, I believe I can call you 'Mama' after all."

"That'll be a help."

"I wouldn't want to make you lose out on inheriting some bread. But how about I call you Mama E until she gets here? If I get in the habit of that, then that is what I'll say if I have a slip and forget to call you just plain Mama. We can always say Julie has taken to calling you that."

Elizabeth finally smiled. "Right on."

"You're getting hip, Mama E! Now, will you let me go out with Farrel?"

She opened a note-sized envelope. "I'll read you Julie's letter first. Then we'll discuss it."

April 2, 1957
Dear Mama,

Just a note to let you know I'm doing okay. It's hard to believe it was only day before yesterday that you brought me here. I'd have written yesterday, but they kept me pretty busy.

She paused, frowning. "Doing what, I wonder?"

There are lots of girls here, so I don't think I'll be lonesome. It's reassuring to know that I am not the only girl in the world to make a mistake.

Elizabeth looked up at me, tears welling in her eyes. "Poor baby. Where was I? Oh, yes."

They let us go out if we want to, but only as far as we can walk, of course, so you can tell Carmen she was right. I have no use for my driver's license.

"What makes you think she's so unhappy?" I asked.
"Hold your horses. I'm not through yet."

We have to make up our own beds every day, but I expected that. We also have to clean the bathrooms, but that seems only fair. The food is good, but mostly vegetables and cornbread. The girls say that on Sundays we have something special, like chicken and dumplings or beef brisket. It's not The Golden Pheasant, by any means. Ha.

I hope everything is going well at home and Carmen is not having too much trouble turning into me. I hope you are well too, Mama. Write soon. I live for the day I can come home.

Much love to you and Carmen,
Julie

P.S. They are already after me to sign the papers to give the baby up for adoption. I am taking my own sweet time reading them over, though. I remember the advice you got from the lawyers you work for: Read thoroughly anything you sign.

Elizabeth wept into her already soggy tissue. I went over and tentatively patted her on the shoulder. She reached up and squeezed my hand.
"I'm sorry." She yanked several fresh tissues from the box beside her chair. "I'd give anything for a cigarette."
I would have given the same thing for one, but I forced myself to ignore both our cravings. I backed to the couch and sat again.

"She's not complaining," I ventured.

"She wouldn't," Elizabeth said, "but you have to read between the lines. Meat only one day a week. And then brisket or rooster."

I raised questioning eyebrows. "Rooster?"

Elizabeth answered me like I was a total idiot, which I was when it came to cooking.

"You don't know that many a tough old rooster is used to make chicken and dumplings?"

"Oh, guess I didn't."

We sat in silence another full minute.

"And she's forced to clean the bathrooms. They should have help hired to do that." Elizabeth shook her head. "What is she not saying? It's clear that conditions there are, at the very least, not what she's used to."

Fear of setting Elizabeth off made me duck my head when I asked, "It's not supposed to be a resort, is it?"

"Some places like that are. I didn't have the money to send her to one of those."

"When does Aint Hattie get here?"

"In early June."

"School'll be out by then. Will I have to be here alone with her all day while you're at work?"

Elizabeth sat up straight and said with authority, "No, you're going to summer school."

"Whaaat? No, I'm not!"

"It'll get you out of the house for half a day."

I jumped up and paced across the room.

"Summer school lasts for six whole weeks. Is she coming for a visit or moving in?"

Elizabeth laughed.

"They're not offering anything in summer school but American History. I'm taking that now."

"And making Ds. Your mother gave me your last report card before she left. You'll repeat it. I don't allow a child of mine to make Ds, especially in American History, the most important subject offered in school."

"I'm not a child of yours."

Elizabeth's eyes seemed to dilate. "Oh my God. I must be losing my mind."

"I'm losing mine too," I said. "I've got two boys beating on me for a date this coming Saturday."

"Who's the other one?"

"Bubba John Younger."

"You aren't going out with him either."

"Why not?"

"Any boy who has handled the panties of a school teacher is not fit company for a nice young lady."

"You heard about the undies on the flagpole, then?"

"Yes, I heard."

"But he saved my ass."

"Don't say it!" Elizabeth cried out too late. She composed herself. "You mustn't use expressions like that. How did he save you?"

"By forging the note supposedly from you that got me transferred out of French class and thereby saved both our you-know-whatses, because if I'd gone into that class not knowing a word of French, our little ruse, as you refer to it, would have been blown sky high, and Julie's and your reputations smeared forever, not to mention mine and my mother's and maybe even your ex-husband's. There! Put that in your pipe and smoke it. And I am going out with one of them on Saturday. Bubba John or Farrel. Pick your poison."

CHAPTER 17
Hard-Headed Woman

She picked Bubba John.

"Having hung Glovina Armstrong's panties on the flagpole pales in comparison to getting my daughter pregnant."

I didn't voice my thought that her daughter had played a role in the pregnancy bit.

I picked them both. I'd go out with Bubba John first, before he got liquored up, make him bring me home early, then I'd call Farrel and tell him he could pick me up in twenty minutes. That would fit nicely into my scheme of treating Farrel rough and telling him nothing. Also, I wouldn't piss either of them off by turning one down. Nor would I have to be with either of them so long I'd increase the chances of blowing the ruse.

On Saturday night, I took two hours to get dressed. I was starting to like being in Julie's room without her. It became mine then—all the pretty clothes, the perfume bottles on her dressing table, the earrings she hadn't taken with her, and the silky underwear. Most of all I liked the pink walls and fuzzy white throw rug at the foot of her bed. It was my bed now, at least for a few months.

After soaking in a hot tub, I stood naked in front of the mirror and beneath the ceiling fan, allowing its slow-whirling blades to dry me off. Mama E had the attic fan going, so it was cool, despite the 98 degree temperature outside, and it only early April.

My body was firm like Julie's, but my boobs were fuller and my hips slightly wider. We were the same height. I probably weighed a few more pounds—until she got pregnant, that is.

My conscience needled me. She wouldn't like it that I was going out with Farrel. Sometimes at night I lay in bed and imagined what I would say to him when we were alone together in his classy car. I would continue the deception and pray he bought it. I'd make him burn for me, let him lure me to the backseat thinking I was Julie. Then, since I was me and not her, slap his face off.

I sorted through her underwear drawer and chose a pair of lacey white panties and a matching bra. They weren't satin, but they weren't cheap either.

At the closet, I flipped through the sundresses, the skirts, the pretty blouses. The outfit I longed to wear was the midnight-blue dress with the tiny gold stars and the see-through coat. I took it out of the closet and held it up at the mirror to see how I'd look in it. It turned my eyes dark blue, like it had turned hers. I laid the coat on a chair, slipped the dress on over my head, and pulled it straight.

I looked sensational. Good enough to be a junior class beauty. Quickly, I pulled the thin coat on and checked in the mirror again. I really was Julie in this dress, except for a barely noticeable pulling across the boobs. I would wear it tonight.

"Take that dress off this very minute, or you aren't going out with anybody!"

Shocked, I turned toward the door. Elizabeth stood glaring at me.

"Did you hear me? Take it off!"

"I'm sorry, Mama E," I said, stretching out my arms to fend her off as she stormed toward me.

"Surely you weren't thinking of wearing it?"

"No! No! I just wanted to try it on. It's so pretty. I never had anything so pretty."

"You don't have it now. But I'd like to know why you've never had a dress that nice. Your stepfather makes a good salary."

"He's a tightwad."

"You mean frugal?"

"Hell, I don't know!" I let her help slide my arms out of the coat. "He buys me clothes, but this is a dream."

"Well, dream on if you think you're ever going to wear it," Elizabeth said, pulling the hem of the dress up and peeling it off over my head.

At the closet, she pulled out a lemon-colored cotton dress with puffed sleeves and tiny buttons running from the top of the white lace collar down to the waist and threw it on the bed.

"There, that ought to keep you out of trouble."

"You've got to be kidding," I said.

"Not in the least."

"You've got to be kidding," Bubba John said, staring at the buttons when he came inside to get me.

"Not in the least," I said with a grin.

Flying down the street with one of the coolest boys in school in his red-and-white convertible brought the mauve Chevy to mind. How the lowly had risen. The wind blasted my face and decimated the curls I'd worked so hard to create with Julie's curling iron.

"I should've told you to bring a scarf," Bubba John said. "Forgot all about it by the time my old man got through wearing me out the second time for that flagpole stunt. It was worth it, though. My mama saw old lady Armstrong in Samples at the lingerie counter, buying a new set of britches, white. Miss Glovina said she'd never again wear salmon undies. I said to Mama, 'White makes sense. She's bound to be a virgin. No man would have the old bag.' My old man heard me, and that's how come I got a second whipping. You a virgin, Julie, honey?"

And so it went, for an hour, until I broke the news to him that my mama had told me I had to go out with Farrel for part of the night, to be fair to both of them.

Bubba John pouted, but he took me home. At the door, he took my hand and held it up.

"Where's your splint?"

I got way too many adrenalin rushes these days. I'd forgotten my fake finger splint.

"Oh, I got it off early. Thought you'd never notice."

He gave me a look but said only, "Later, gator."

He was probably glad to be free to chase another skirt that night, maybe one with fewer buttons.

Farrel showed up dressed in blue slacks and a cotton shirt with pale-blue stripes. His hair was still damp with comb tracks, and he smelled divine.

"I wore your favorite, Old Spice." He smiled. "This feels like old times."

I turned on the tough act. "It's new times, big boy, and don't get any ideas."

He clearly had some, for his face fell. In the car, he backed his ears and tried again.

"Shall we go to our place?"

I had no clue what "our place" was.

"Absolutely not. Mama's let me out until ten thirty. If I'm not in by then, I can't go out with you again—ever."

He shot an anxious look at his wrist watch. "That won't give us much time."

"We don't need much. I'm just going on this date to prove I'm not mad anymore about you and Maylene. In fact, I'd almost forgotten about it until you brought it up at the Dairyette."

While he drove, silent and brooding, I studied his profile. This was the father of my little niece or nephew to be. A part of me bore guilt for not telling him about Julie and the baby, but it wasn't my place to do so.

He made right for the oilfields. When he pulled onto the dirt road and parked near a plum tree, I instinctively moved farther away from him, my back pressed against the door. He flipped on the radio, and wouldn't you know, Elvis's voice singing "I Was the One" floated out into the mellow night.

"Don't be scared, honey. I'm not going to try anything."

He put his arm on the seat back and shifted to face me. I only smiled.

"Not that I don't want to. I do. I want you so bad, Julie. You've always done that to me."

"Done what?"

"Made me want you, you know, like in the backseat."

Being careful about my phrasing, I said, "Now that you've been told I didn't get pregnant that time we . . . did IT, you're more than willing to put me at risk again."

"I said I wouldn't try anything."

"I know what you said. I also know you will if you get half a chance."

"You're a hard-headed woman, Julie. Come on. Let's get out and wish on a star."

With his arm around my waist, we walked across the clearing to the plum tree.

"Remember the first night I brought you here?" he said.

My heart sped up. Of course I didn't remember a thing about it, nor had Julie mentioned it.

"I spread out that blanket I always carry in the trunk."

"That must make things convenient for you."

He sputtered. "I mean, my old man always carries. Please, honey, go with me on this. I'm trying to make things right with us again. Just think back with me. Remember how we kissed and how you were scared to take home the plums we picked 'cause your mama would put two and two together? You told me I'd better take them home to my mother."

I answered with the truth. "No, I'm afraid I don't remember. You look like it makes a big difference to you that I don't."

"It does. I'm not a man of words, Julie. I'm a man of action, but you won't let me act. And you're right. We shouldn't mess around at all but . . ." He exhaled. "I don't know what I'm supposed to do anymore."

"Just fantasize, I guess."

I had never felt like such a conniver in all my life. It was a good feeling—a feeling of power—and I liked it.

"Okay," he said, taking my hand and looking up at the stars. "Let's wish. I wish you would let me—" he began.

"Better hush up. If you tell your wish, it won't come true."

He looked at me with wide eyes. "That's my line."

I tensed. "Your line?" Maybe he had led me into some secret ritual he and Julie acted out with the star-wishing bit.

"I've always been the one that told you not to say your wish out loud."

"Whoever's line," I said. "You're the one who better not say your wish out loud, if you want it to ever come true."

He was breathing hard.

"I do want it to, Julie. I do."

He put his hands on my waist, stared into my eyes, and bending down, pressed his lips to mine. With calculated detachment, I let him go into a deep kiss I knew would lay bare the magic he had that drove Julie nuts. I found out, all right. His kiss was good. No, it was better than good. It jazzed me up. No wonder she flipped over him. This was the finest kissing I'd ever had.

His hand slid up from my waist. The way he touched my boob, only on top of my clothes, mind you, turned me into putty. I was almost unable to resist when he reached to pull up my dress—almost, but not quite.

I slapped his cheek and demanded he take me home. To my surprise, he agreed.

At the door, he surprised me again.

"You know something, honey, your knockers have grown. Did you know that? In just this short time since we were together last, they've gotten bigger."

"It hasn't been a short time. We haven't been out since last December."

"Naw." He cut his eyes away. "It can't have been that long."

"You must have mine mixed mine up with Maylene's."

He laughed. "Maylene's too uptight to let a boy fool around with her."

"Then you did try."

"Naw, now. Don't go cooking up stuff. Hers are so little that when we were slow dancing I felt a tiny bump on her back and I thought one of them had slipped around behind, but it was only a mosquito bite."

I watched, solemn, while he guffawed.

"Come on, honey, lighten up. You know old Maylene would never let me mash her. But I'm telling you, yours have gotten bigger. If that don't beat all."

CHAPTER 18
Old "Aint" Hat

She traveled by train. Mama E and I met her at the station on a bright Saturday morning in June.

She "disembarked," as she called it, wearing a black-and-white polka-dot dress and a wide-brimmed white hat. She wore one white glove and carried the other and gripped the handle of a large bag that looked to have been made from an old Persian rug. I lightly ran my fingers over the fabric.

"It's an authentic carpet bag, left over from Reconstruction days," she said. "My great-grandmother passed it down. Her daddy shot a carpetbagger who was attempting to steal the last mule the family had left after the war. The Yankees took our mules, our horses, and our cows, but he got that Yankee's carpetbag."

"She means the Civil War," Mama E said low to me as we stood watching Aint Hat collect her trunk and two suitcases from the brakeman in charge of baggage.

Right off the bat, I nearly blew it with what was meant to be a friendly gesture.

"Let me carry something, Aint Hattie."

The old bat turned arrogant eyes on me, chin aloft, expression scornful.

Mama E jumped in. "*Aunt* Hattie will be pleased with any help you can give, I'm sure, and let's hope it will all fit in the car."

I about died, but I got the message. I had to switch from Aint to Aunt, PDQ.

"I'm having the trunk delivered," Aunt Hattie said. "And don't worry, I'm not moving in. I'm on a Southern pilgrimage. After I finish up with you two, I'm heading to Paragould to visit Cousin Nettie and her family, then on to Hot Springs to take the baths. Let me hold onto your arm, Julie. I'd hate to take a tumble before I even get to the house."

"Isn't Paragould up near Memphis?" I asked, hardly daring to say anything at all, but thinking I would draw more attention to myself if I didn't join in.

"It is," she said. "And no, I won't be visiting the new star of rock 'n' roll. Are you a fan of Mr. Presley, Julie?"

"I'm not only a fan, I'm a friend. We've been writing for over a year." I had my mouth open to tell her he sent me his records too, when I caught Mama E's wide eyes and slight shake of her head.

"You're corresponding with a person who exhibits himself on the stage? I'm sorry to hear that, Julie."

The increased pressure of Aunt Hattie's grip on my arm with her ungloved hand riveted my attention on her ring, half encased in her fleshy finger, its enormous diamond glinting in the sunlight. To a girl like me, whose mother wore only a gold band and a pair of dangling earrings my stepfather bought her on their honeymoon, it looked to be at least fifteen carats.

"Four," she said, reading my mind. "Four carats, and don't gawk. You've seen it before. Every time you've been with me, in fact, given that I haven't been able to get it off my finger since nineteen ought nine."

A frenzied need to perform a vanishing act seized me.

When the polka-dotted hem was tucked safely out of the way, I shut the door of the front passenger seat and crawled in back, grateful to have my face behind her so it couldn't betray me again. On the drive home, she and Elizabeth chatted about the world situation, which Aunt Hat declared was deplorable with the cost of gasoline at thirty-one cents a gallon.

"How much do you make a year, Elizabeth, working at that old law office?"

"It's not an old office, Auntie, and I make thirty-five hundred dollars a year. Look how pretty the courthouse is with all the flowers planted around it."

"Thirty-five hundred dollars a year! How do you keep the child in clothes?"

Elizabeth sighed. "I manage."

"Those cheapskates ought to at least pay you a living wage. After all, without you and others like you to type their so-called erudite briefs, they'd never darken the doors of a courtroom."

Elizabeth gave a little bounce behind the wheel. "If women could unite and form a union like the coal miners, we'd have some clout behind our struggle for higher wages," she said, her breath coming in quick jerks. "Not to mention health care and a pension."

Aunt Hattie turned her face toward Mama E, allowing me a view of her profile.

"You haven't turned Communist, have you, Elizabeth?"

Mama E shot a quick look at Aunt Hattie. "How could you even think such a thing?"

"People in unions are Communists."

"Just because people unite to have strength in numbers doesn't make them Communists," I said.

She turned raised eyebrows at me. "Is that what they're teaching you in school these days?"

"We'd best change the subject," Mama E said.

Aunt Hattie whipped her head around to face the front.

"What about alimony? Couldn't you squeeze a few dollars out of Scott Morgan now that he's sobered up enough to hold down a job?"

"How do you know about that?" Mama E asked.

Aunt Hattie's hat bobbed. "I have my sources."

I could see the blood drain from Elizabeth's face. That comment must have struck her to the core, as it had me. Could Aunt Hattie's "sources" have informed her about me and Julie switching places?

Mama E slammed on the brakes at a red light.

"I wouldn't take a dime from him!"

"Pride goeth before a fall," Aunt Hattie pronounced, turning again to look back over the seat at me. "Do you see your father at all these days?"

"What do your sources tell you?"

Mama E shouted, "Carmen!"

Aunt Hattie straightened. "What did you say, Elizabeth?"

Mama E cleared her throat. "I started to say, Carmen Newton, Julie's half-sister, is living here in town now, and she and Julie have gotten together of late. Isn't that so, *Julie?*"

"Uh . . . yes." I held my breath that her sources hadn't told her my mother had left town.

"I shouldn't think you'd allow the child to associate with riffraff," Aunt Hattie said.

"Carmen isn't riffraff!" My voice was way too loud.

"I was referring to your father, Scott," Aunt Hattie said. "I've never so much as laid my eyes on Miss Carmen. But I don't imagine she could be anything other than riffraff herself, considering her background and lineage."

My voice trembled with rage. "Half of her background and lineage is the same as mine!"

"But your other half is not the same, and half is enough to save you," the old biddy said.

It wasn't easy dealing with people in Julie's social class. Hypocrites, all. If Mama E hadn't turned into the driveway right then, there is no telling what else I might have said.

We hauled the suitcases to the guest room, and while I went to check the mail, Mama E fixed three glasses of iced tea. There was a letter from Elvis, and a letter from Mother. Glancing over my shoulder, I tore into it, knowing it was imperative, as Mama E would say, to keep it hidden from Aunt Hattie. All Mother said was she had arrived safely in London and that my stepfather sent his love. I didn't know what to do with the letter from Elvis.

Aunt Hattie was still in her room when I joined Mama E in the den. "Any mail?" she asked.

"A letter from Mother," I mouthed.

"Take it to the incinerator in the backyard and burn it. Now!"

"Don't get so rattled. It's safe in my pocket. I have to copy down her address before I get rid of it."

"You're not doing well," Elizabeth said in a low voice. "Calling her 'Aint' Hattie."

"It's your fault. You never told me to pronounce it 'aunt.' As for who isn't doing well, you called me 'Carmen.'"

Mama E wiped her brow. "Thank God you'll be in summer school most of the time. Any other mail?"

"A letter from Elvis."

"You didn't open it, did you?"

"No, I didn't open it," I said, my words dripping with disgust at her lack of trust.

"I promised I'd forward any letters from him. She wouldn't like it if they were opened." After a few minutes, she asked, "Where did you put it?"

"I left it on the doohickey."

"The *doohickey* you're referring to wouldn't happen to be the antique commode in the living room, would it?" an imperious voice said from the breakfast room. Aunt Hattie was making her way into the den, holding the letter aloft.

Me and Mama E both lost our cool.

"You know how kids are," Mama E said. "Julie can't bear to call it by its proper name."

"No, I absolutely cannot," I said.

"I presume this is from Mr. Presley," Aunt Hattie said, waving the envelope, "since it bears a Memphis postmark."

"May I have it, please?" I asked, putting on my polite voice.

"Since you put it so nicely, here." She thrust the envelope into my outstretched hand and settled herself on the red couch next to me. After a few moments, she asked, "Aren't you going to open it?"

I had her now. Aint Hat, the old bat, was curious about Elvis. That meant she liked him but would die before she'd admit it.

"Do you want me to?" I turned on my innocent face. "I thought it might not be good manners to open it in front of you. That's why I left it out there on the doo . . . commode."

She sighed. "At least you're making an effort." She patted my hand. "Go ahead, Julie, dear. Open your letter. I wouldn't mind hearing what Mr. Presley has to say myself."

Mama E's mouth flew open, and she burst out laughing.

"After all, Elizabeth, times are changing. Hurry up, Julie. I always did want to read a letter from a king."

CHAPTER 19
MINT JULEPS IN THE AFTERNOON

I didn't want to open Julie's letter from Elvis any more than Mama E wanted me to, but Aunt Hattie's eyes brightened as she eyed it. There was no excuse I could give for not reading it to her. Mama E and I exchanged looks that spelled doom. Taking my cue from a slight shrug of her shoulders, I slipped a fingernail under an edge of the flap and slid it across the envelope, taking care not to tear it, and not to let Aunt Hattie see that my nail polish was chipped.

A little thrill wiggled through my innards as I withdrew the folded note. *Elvis Presley had touched it, held it in his hands, written it to me!* I paused. Actually, he had written it to the real Julie, but for now I was she, as Mama E had taught me to say. It got my goat when she answered the phone and the person on the other end asked for her. She always said, "This is she." Drove me nuts. I told her, "It don't sound right." For which I was given a hearty scolding and made to write, "It doesn't sound right" two hundred times.

"Hurry up," Aunt Hattie said, nudging my arm so hard it caused me to leave a tiny rip in the last inch of the flap.

"Cool it!" I exclaimed. "I'm keeping it for posterity, and it'll be worth a lot more someday if it's intact." Maybe it could be glued back and Julie would never know it had been opened.

"Speaking of which, are you still 'intact,' young lady?"

"Intact? You mean . . . ?"

I could feel the flabbergasted look on my face. Never in all my born days had I heard anybody talk like that. And these folks I was hobnobbing with were supposed to be high classed. Maybe I wasn't squatting in such tall cotton after all.

"Well?" Aunt Hattie's bifocals made her scrutinizing eyeballs the size of walnuts.

In for a penny, in for a pound, I thought.

"If you mean have I had sexual intercourse, the answer is no."

I thought to goodness she'd fall out on the floor.

When she caught her breath again, she said, "We don't use language like that in proper society."

"What do you want me to call it? IT?"

"Call it what Elizabeth has taught you to call it."

Mama E said, "Petting gone too far."

"In the backseat of a car?" I asked.

Aunt Hattie drew herself up. "Or anywhere else?"

"The answer is still 'no,'" I said and flipped open the note Elvis had sent.

June 12, 1957
Dear Juliet,

Aunt Hattie interrupted. "What's this Juliet business?"

I sat there in a clueless state.

"He calls her that," Mama E said, automatically reaching for her cigarettes that were no longer there. I couldn't help snickering at the defeated look on her face.

Aunt Hattie poked my arm. "Read on."

I am still out in California shooting Jailhouse Rock, *but we're taking a break, so I have a minute to write to you. In only two more weeks I'll be moving into Graceland. Mama and Daddy and Grandma are already living there.*

On June 28, I'm doing a benefit appearance in Memphis at Russwood Park for St. Jude's Hospital. There'll be other celebrities appearing with me: Lou Costello, Jane Russell, Ferlin Husky, and even that gorgeous actress, Susan Hayward. (She's not as gorgeous as you, however.) I wish you could come up for it. Ever been to Russwood Park? Maybe you know, that's where the great Babe Ruth played ball.

Can you believe I am a real celebrity now? I remember not too long ago having a pig sandwich with you at the Old Hickory in El Dorado. These are dazzling days for me, but you have no idea how often I wish I was back there in that little town that so represents America, just having fun with the gang. You're so lucky to live there. Everything I wished for that night has come true. That's how I know I was right when I got the notion you were my good luck charm. I'm even a movie star now! Jailhouse won't be released until the fall, but you gotta put it on your calendar and see it. This summer you can see me in Loving You. It's scheduled to be released in early July.

Listen, honey, I gotta run. They're getting ready to shoot a real important scene of mine. You take care, you hear? And write! Send it to Graceland. 3764 Highway 51 South, Memphis, Tennessee, and Mama'll hold it for me till I get there.

As always, remembering,
Elvis

Everybody was quiet when I finished. I knew Mama E felt the same way I did—like Julie had died or something, and we were here reading a letter meant for her that we had no business seeing. Even Old Aunt Hat, in her ignorance of the situation, kept silent for about a minute and a half.

"Well, well, well," she said at last, smoothing the lap of the polka-dotted dress. "He sounds like a fine young man. That letter has made me revise my opinion of him. He must be a good person to have for a friend."

She patted my arm. "And I'm glad to hear that you're a nice, honest girl with high moral standards. Your grammar could use a little touching up, but I'm sure we can attend to it."

With that she began the struggle to get to her feet from the couch, which wasn't low, but for an elderly person with maybe arthritis or something the cushiness made it not the easiest seat to get up from. I reached out to steady her.

"I don't need any help," she said. "I'm going to take a nap. Wake me up if I sleep longer than an hour, Elizabeth."

At that very minute, the telephone rang. Mama E jumped, and so did I.

"I'll get it," I said, bounding past Aunt Hat to the extension in the breakfast room.

"Hello."

I wasn't expecting the voice that answered me. My knees went flimsy, and before I could get a grip, the one word that could taint all my efforts popped out of my mouth.

"Julie?"

Mama E's face registered shock, and Aunt Hattie, I'm sure, nearly dropped her drawers.

The next instant, my brain performed emergency resuscitation on my tongue and shot lifesaving words out of my mouth.

"This is Julie. I mean, this is she."

A look of pride accompanied by relief came over Mama E's face. Her efforts to polish me up had not been in vain. Aunt Hattie looked confused but said nothing.

"Carmen, what's going on?" Julie demanded over the phone.

"Can I call you back later? My Great-Aunt Hattie just got here from New Orleans."

"Oh my God," Julie said. "But I need to talk to Mama."

"Not possible at the moment," I said, throwing a smile to Aunt Hat. "It would be rude of me to talk on the phone now. Maybe while she's taking her nap I can call you back."

Julie's voice sagged. "Oh. Okay. Carmen, is everything all right?"

"I hope. Till later, then." And I hung up.

Mama E looked like she was about to have a stroke, and Aunt Hat looked pleased enough to call the lawyer and leave more than a little to Elizabeth. She hobbled the rest of the way through the den, left a kiss on my cheek when she passed me in the breakfast room, and went for her nap.

When we heard the click of her door shutting, I staggered to a couch and fell on it, totally wiped out. I had just survived what Aunt Hattie would call a situation similar to the siege of Atlanta. I hoped with flying colors. I looked questioningly at Mama E, who, slumping in her easy chair and fanning herself with her hand, looked none too able herself to plow the south forty, like Scarlett O'Hara.

I squirmed. "Did I do good?"

"You mean, did you do *well*? Yes, except for a few close calls. Was that Julie on the phone?"

"Yes," I whispered.

"As soon as we hear Aunt Hattie snoring, we'll call Julie back. Did she sound all right to you?"

She hadn't, but I didn't want to tell Mama E. It might upset her so much it would be the last straw, and the last straw could not fall now.

"She sounded fine. We shouldn't risk a call back with Aunt Hattie here. She mustn't pick up even a fragment of the conversation. After all, it isn't every day the opportunity comes to inherit a little something, is it, Mama E?"

"What did you call your mother?" came a voice from the dining room.

My heart paused, then fluttered. How much of what I'd said had Aunt Hattie heard?

"She called me 'Mama E,'" Elizabeth said, picking up the ball and running with it. "I forgot to offer you a toddy, Auntie," she said, obviously to distract her. "Would you like one? It'll help you fall asleep."

"That's what I came back for," she said. "The Champagne they served on the train had a moreish flavor."

Elizabeth's smile was too bright. "I'm afraid I can't offer you Champagne, but how about a mint julep?"

"If you have the silver goblets to serve it in," Aunt Hattie said.

Elizabeth got up and headed to the kitchen to dig out the Kentucky bourbon.

"I have the ones my mother left me, engraved with an *L* for Lawrence."

"Thank goodness they aren't engraved with an *M* for Morgan," Aunt Hattie said.

My temper flared. "Would an M change the flavor of the booze?"

Both Aunt Hattie and Elizabeth raised one eyebrow at me.

Being like Julie was harder than I had ever imagined, but I had to keep working at it so in the eyes of everyone I'd do more than be like her, I'd *be* her.

PART THREE

1. Julie

CHAPTER 20
THE TRUTH COMES OUT

I hung up, disappointed enough to cry. Phone calls were restricted, and Miss Oldenburg, the matron, had a list of people each girl was permitted to be in contact with. Only two phones for our use in the home made for a constant line of girls in the hall, where the phones sat out in the open, affording no privacy. Curious ears could always overhear every word of a girl's conversation.

I'd expected Mama to answer, so it was a shock when Carmen picked up, and more of a shock to learn that Aunt Hattie was there. I instantly remembered she was coming for a visit, but so much had happened since I came here, it was a wonder I remembered anything about my past life, as I refer to it now.

I'd so wanted to hear Mama's voice that, when Carmen abruptly hung up, I came close to sliding to the floor and sobbing. But already I was at the point of needing help to get up again, and there was no help anywhere in this hell hole. If Mama knew, it would kill her.

That first evening when Mama had brought me here, the matron was on her best behavior. She had escorted us into the designer-decorated visitor's salon, where girls are allowed to go if and when they ever have a guest.

"I'm Olivia Oldenburg, house matron. We are so glad, Mrs. Morgan, that you've chosen Happiness House as the place for Julie to complete her term."

Mama seemed encouraged and relieved as she reached to shake hands with Miss Oldenburg. By the time we'd finished having coffee and cookies, Mama was pouring out her upset over my pregnancy to this skinny woman who wore a black dress with long sleeves that looked like funeral attire and from whose French twist not a hair went astray.

It wasn't until Mama kissed me goodbye and the heavy oak door was closed and locked behind her that Miss Oldenburg revealed to me the realities of Happiness House.

"All right, Julie, get your bag and follow me. I'll take you to the sleeping area," she said, her drawling friendliness changing to a tone of brisk, no-nonsense when we were alone.

Even though I hadn't brought many items of clothing with me, the bag was heavy with school books so I could keep up with my class, my address book, two extra pairs of shoes because my feet were already swelling, and a few cosmetics to keep my spirits up. Mama had said, "If you let yourself go, you'll become depressed."

I struggled up the first flight of stairs with Miss Oldenburg throwing impatient glances over her shoulder at me.

"Couldn't we use the elevator?" I asked.

"That's for delivery men and the help. Exercise will be beneficial for you and the baby."

So I'd struggled on with my bag. As it turned out, there was no help and no delivery men either. The elevator was for parents or visitors who insisted on seeing the accommodations.

Miss Oldenburg got aggravated enough with my slow pace that for the last half of the third flight of stairs she gave me a hand.

"This bag is so heavy, one would think you were planning on making this your permanent home," she chided as we lugged it over the top step.

The door of one room was open off the hallway, and I automatically headed toward it. Inside, curtains of flowered chintz hung over the two windows, and a matching bedcover decorated the single bed. A private bath adjoined the room.

Miss Oldenburg jerked my arm as I took a step inside.

"That is only the model room."

She had led me into a long dormitory space two doors farther down the hall. At least twenty beds, ten on each side, lined the walls, with about six feet of space between the two rows and about three feet between each bed. Stopping midway into the room, she pointed to a small, iron bedstead with a thin, unmade mattress on a set of springs.

"I'm supposed to share a room with only one other girl. That's what my mother is paying for."

She jerked her chin up at my astonishment and gave a snort.

"Dream on. If you'd read your documents carefully, you'd have seen that was never stated. Sometimes there are only two girls in here, but this time of the year we usually have a houseful. Lots of lovey-dovey goes on during the cold months, and that, unfortunately for you, is the case. Yours is the last available bed. If you don't want it, you can call your mother and have her come back and get you. I have a waiting list a mile long."

I was too stunned to speak.

She tapped the toe of one high-heeled shoe.

"Staying or going?"

"Staying," came out, sounding half strangled when I answered, dumbfounded at the extent to which we'd been misled.

"Then make up your bed. You'll find clean sheets in the laundry room next door. It looks like someone has absconded with the pillow. Look around, and when you find a bed with two, help yourself to one."

"Where are the other girls?"

"In the rec room. They'll be here before you know it. The bell for lights out rings at nine thirty."

She walked, business-like, to the door, and the fading echo of her heels clacked out of the room.

The springs had squeaked when, left alone, I sank down on the bare mattress. I don't know how long I sat there, staring ahead without "seeing" anything.

How could this ever have happened to me?

I was in with the popular girls. I made good grades. I was from a good family. Even though Mama and my father were divorced, and my father was a drunk who had sired an illegitimate child, like Mama said, we had good bloodlines.

The answer came swiftly in the form of the memory of that night when I told Farrel, "I'm ready." With it came, at long last, the recognition of my ignorance and the naiveté that had allowed me to trust him. I put my hand on the bulge in my belly, the consequence of my terrible need for acceptance and love. I had brought this on myself. It was done and could not be undone.

In reality, Farrel bore half the blame, but that wasn't the way the world looked at it. The girl bore full responsibility to use the only sure-fire birth control in existence—the word "no." And following that dictum was the undisputed rule that failing to use that little word would bring all the blame down on her head. Farrel would never bear any culpability, and he would never suffer the consequences I had to suffer.

That thought had brought the remembrance of Frances lying in the coffin, so pale in her red dress. Maybe I would have been better off had I gone the route she went and was now lying in my own coffin.

Beneath my hand, there came a movement. For a moment, I didn't understand, and then a thrill the likes of which I had never known went through me. My baby had moved. The doctor had said it would move sometime between sixteen and twenty-five weeks, and then the child would become an inescapable reality for me. Now that had happened. The baby was a real person, and it was alive because I was alive. At least I was half alive.

That was what had saved me on that awful day and helped me to get the sheets and make up the bed so I wouldn't collapse on the stained mattress.

CHAPTER 21
Happiness House

When the girls came into the dorm from downstairs, someone commented that the empty bed was filled. Another said, "She's dead to the world."

I was faking. If I pretended to be asleep, I wouldn't have to deal with them when I was so tired. Besides, I wanted to be a fly on the wall and listen to what they had to say. It proved disappointing. The rest of their talk was broken pieces of conversations, and not much of that except from the girl who'd taken my pillow.

"Pilferer," she said.

"What?" asked another.

"She a pillow thief," the girl said.

"Didn't you steal hers?"

"Watch yourself," the accuser said. "There was nobody in that bed then."

The approaching clack of Miss Oldenburg's heels, followed by her police-woman's voice announcing "lights out" prevented my sneaking a peek at the true pilferer.

Gradually, the sounds of shifting to find comfortable positions and pillow fluffing changed into the regular breathing of sleepers.

I lay awake in blinding darkness until dawn streaked into the window next to my bed, comforting me enough to doze off. But after what seemed like only a minute I jerked upright, unable to remember where I was. Panic flushed through me until I saw the girl sleeping soundly in the next bed. She lay on her side, facing me, strings of her brown hair in clumps across her cheek. Along the rows of beds on both sides of the room, the other girls lay sprawled in slumber.

I eased up to make an urgent visit to the bathroom. At the door I looked back, fearful that with my futile efforts to keep the bedsprings from squeaking I had awakened someone. No one was stirring. The thought went through my head that they must have gone to bed completely exhausted to continue sleeping so soundly after the sun came streaming in.

The spotless latrine ran alongside the dorm room. I went in, as I had the night before, and used one of the twelve toilets in the long row. At least there were doors on the stalls. A row of sinks lay opposite them, and off to the side stood the shower stalls. Only two for twenty girls.

As I slipped back into the dorm room, a deafening siren went off. My frayed nerves made me flinch. The other nineteen continued drowsing until the siren jarred through the house a second time.

"What was that?" I asked the girl next to me as she swung her legs over the side of her bed.

"Miss Oldenburg's version of reveille. I noticed someone new had moved in when I came up last night. Welcome to the Hell Hole. Breakfast is at quarter to seven. If you miss it, you don't eat again until lunch, and believe me, by then you'll be starving. Hurry. It's six fifteen now."

"Surely, that gives us plenty of time," I began, but she cut me off.

"Not with twenty of us to shower and use the latrine. My name's Marty, by the way."

I stuck out my hand. "Julie."

"I bet you believed everything in the brochure, didn't you? The cooling system is the only good thing about this place. We better put our showers off till later." Marty began pulling on the clothes lying on the foot of her bed. "Yep. You ended up here because it was the cheapest, didn't you?"

I nodded.

"Don't feel bad. We all did. Get dressed, quick. I'll show you the dining hall, better known as the hog trough. You see, we don't dine there. We gobble down what we can in the fifteen-minute breakfast period."

There were no eggs and no meat on the menu this morning. Two cross-looking women servers, also pregnant, practically slung platters of pancakes on the tables. There were pitchers of milk and syrup and plates of butter.

"Do they bring us coffee?" I asked Marty.

"Coffee's not allowed. Not good for the babies. Wait'll you taste the milk. Powdered. Made up fresh every meal, though. At night you can get iced tea, but no refills, and no lemon." She seized the platter near us the instant the server put it on the table. "Grab what you want before someone else gets it."

The pancakes were runny in the middle. The little bit of syrup remaining by the time the pitcher came to me was all that made them palatable.

"Surely they serve eggs and bacon some mornings," I murmured to Marty.

The girl across the table heard me.

"On Sundays. The rest of the time it's like today, or cereal."

"You forgot grits day," said another girl, whose voice sounded like that of the pillow pilferer. "So called because that's all we get for breakfast on Saturdays. Fried grits, plain grits with a pat of butter, or cheese grits. Pick the cheese ones. The others suck."

She sat alone at the far end of our table. The top of her blonde head revealed dark roots. I thought she must spend a lot of time in the sun. Her skin resembled a tan leather pocketbook at home in Mama's closet.

"My name's Kay," she said. "I got knocked up in the backseat of the snazzy convertible my rich boyfriend drives."

I gave a sardonic laugh. "Backseats seem to be in vogue this year."

Her tough look softened. "Sorry I had your pillow. My back was hurting so bad I used it under my knees. Didn't help."

A bell sounded the end of breakfast. Miss Oldenburg materialized seemingly from nowhere and stood at the head of our table.

"Julie, come with me to my office. We have some things to go over. The rest of you, get busy."

I looked with questioning eyes at Marty.

"Don't let her push you around, and *don't* sign anything until you've read it over at least five times. Don't give in. She'll try to make you."

"What would she want me to sign?"

Marty's face registered surprise, but she had no time to reply. Miss Oldenburg moved behind me and gave me a slight push.

"I'll get you some maternity clothes and meet you at my office," she said. "Shake a leg. I haven't got all day."

I saw through the open door that Miss Oldenburg's office was in meticulous order. A few moments later she came down the hall carrying a stack of clothes—three skirts with tops and two pairs of slacks. She took a seat behind her desk and shoved a single page document toward me.

"Sign for the clothes. You'll be expected to return them after the birth."

Obeying Marty's instructions, I read every word before signing my name at the bottom of the page. The document was harmless enough, confirming that I had been given clothing, as promised in the brochure, and would return it when I left Happiness House.

She stuck the paper in a file jacket and retrieved another document with lots more pages.

"Your first work assignment is latrine maintenance."

"Work assignment?"

She looked at me with wide eyes. "Yes, work assignment. You didn't imagine you'd be sitting around contemplating your navel all day, did you?"

"I . . . I didn't know . . . we had to work. Nothing was said about that in the information papers."

"This is one of the least expensive maternity homes in the state. We require you work off the difference between what it costs to get in here and what it costs to get in a Cadillac version of a refuge for wayward girls."

I stood up. "I'm not a wayward girl. I only did it once, and with only one—"

She rapped her pencil on the desk. "Sit back down, and spare me your protestations of innocence. It's obvious from your condition you disregarded the rules of God and society by engaging in premarital sex, and now you must suffer the consequences."

"What about the boy? Shouldn't God and society put some of the blame on him?"

"A man can't help himself. A woman can. It was up to you to say no."

Her face reflected the same suppressed rage that echoed in her voice, making me wonder what her story was.

"In short, you've made your bed, Julie, and now you must lie in it, unless you want to leave here." She reached for the phone. "I'll call your mother right now to come get you, if you want me to."

I longed to say, "Yes, call her. I won't stay here another day." But thoughts of Mama wringing her hands in despair—and of the shame she and I would endure, and of my poor baby and the disgrace it would bear being labeled a bastard—made me shake my head and swallow the pain in my throat.

"Then you'll conform to the rules and regulations of Happiness House?"

I nodded.

"I can't hear your head rattle," she said and pressed her lips together.

"Yes, I will."

"Good. I suspect you have more strength of character than you've thus far revealed. You'll join the latrine team for this first week. You'll make it sparkle, as I am sure you found it to be upon your arrival."

At least I had an indoor job where it was cool.

"What other work assignments are there?" I ventured.

"Inside jobs include waiting tables, doing laundry, washing and drying dishes after meals, vacuuming and dusting, that sort of thing. Outside the girls water the grass and flowers, weed the beds, plant seeds, and sweep the walkways. I have a man come once a week to mow. I don't believe pregnant girls should be doing anything as strenuous as pushing a mower."

If I hadn't been so distraught, I'd have laughed in her face.

"Do we have any choice?" I asked, thinking that the blonde girl with skin the shade of tanned leather must have had all the outside jobs.

"No. I assign them. That's the way I run things. The latrine team gathers in the supply room in," she looked at her watch, "ten minutes. Before you go, I need you to sign these papers."

"What are they?" I asked as she passed them to me.

"Consent forms to give your baby up for adoption. There's no need for you to read them now. Just sign them. I'll give you a copy when you leave here that you can read back home at your leisure."

"I won't sign anything without reading it first."

"You do plan to give your baby up, do you not?"

"I . . . I'm not sure."

"What do you mean, you're not sure?"

"Just that. I'm not sure yet. I'll let you know later."

"You must sign them before you are allowed to leave here. The sooner you sign, the better . . . for your own peace of mind."

Wild to get out of her office, I snatched the papers and moved toward the door.

Her voice stopped me.

"If you have any idea of keeping the child, what are you doing here? If you go home with a baby, you'll suffer the same shame you would have if the town had witnessed your entire pregnancy."

"I'm still not signing the papers until I read them. And that's the way *I* run things."

CHAPTER 22
Any Place is Paradise

Four hours on the tile floor cleaning the latrine nearly destroyed my knees.

"Why didn't you wear knee pads?" Marty asked when I limped into the dorm and collapsed on my bed.

"Not knowing this place was a work house, it simply slipped my mind to pack a set."

She slumped at the sound of anger in my voice.

"I'm sorry. I rushed off so fast to lawn duty I forgot to tell you to grab a pair from the work room. I couldn't risk getting another demerit."

"A demerit for what?" I asked.

"If we're late for our jobs, we get demerits, and ten demerits means no watching TV for a week. Didn't Oldenburg tell you?"

I shook my head.

"The bitch. She doesn't tell the new people anything. Hey, listen, want to go for a walk after dinner tonight?"

Now flat on my back, I couldn't picture myself walking anywhere.

"It's nice to get away for a few hours," she said.

"Where will we get away to?"

"The shopping area. The diner to get a pop. The movie theatre to see what's coming."

"If I'm physically able, I won't care where we go," I said. "Any place away from here will be paradise."

Mama had left me some cash. "A girl should never be without her mad money," she'd said before leaving me here. She'd handed me a small drawstring bag, barely big enough to hold a few folded bills, one of which bore Benjamin Franklin's picture.

"Mama! A hundred-dollar bill! That's too much. Keep it yourself. What will I have need of, anyway?"

She'd given me her most serious look. "You never know what's going to happen. Pin it in your bra, and keep it there in case of an emergency, and don't tell anyone you have it. Use the small bills for pocket money."

I needed to spend some pocket money now, for my sanity. Taking care no one was looking, I sneaked a few ones into my pocket and pinned the bag back inside my bra.

Marty and I each took a fake wedding ring from the bowl on the small table in the foyer and set off on our walk shortly after dinner. Outside, the intense heat of a Texas afternoon had mellowed into the glow of evening. A sense of freedom strengthened me with every step we took away from Happiness House and filled me with exhilaration, as though we were escaping from prison. Had it not been for the baby in my belly, I might have felt carefree again. Despite my love for my unborn child, I'd have given anything to turn back time, if only to be just a Dilbert again in Nowheresville, but a virgin and not pregnant anymore.

We had barely set off when a voice called out, "Sluts! Whores! You must be the devil's wives. No one else would have you! Keep off my property. Don't look my way. Pray for forgiveness, if you know the meaning of prayer."

I stared, shocked, at the nicely dressed woman of about forty standing on the porch of her Southern bungalow next door shaking her fist at us.

"The neighbors hate us because they are convinced that Happiness House lowers their property values," Marty said, "and they believe our shame rubs off on them. Just walk on and pay no attention."

The neighbor's words set me trembling. I swiped at a tear and opened my mouth to yell at her, but Marty grabbed my arm.

"If you answer back, she has grounds to call the sheriff on us."

I wiped my face on my sleeve.

"Hey, girl, buck up," Marty said with a friendly poke in my ribs. "She's not worth it. Don't let her ruin your time away from the Hell Hole."

"Okay," I managed to say through a broken breath.

We walked on in silence for a while. The street was empty of traffic at this hour, except for the occasional carload of kids out for a summer evening. What I wouldn't give to be going to the Dairyette with the in-crowd tonight, even if Maylene were along. And surely she would be. The thought of her took me directly to thoughts of Carmen. How was she getting along? Had anyone seen through our ruse? Would she go out with Farrel? What about Justin? I was so homesick, I'd even agree to go out with Eugene Hoffmeyer if I could wake up and find this had all been a terrible nightmare.

I glanced at Marty's profile as we strolled along the cracked sidewalk. She looked to be about my age, but much more self-assured.

"When are you due?" I asked.

"Mid-September."

"So am I."

"Good. We can keep each other's spirits up. I can't wait to get this over with. Then I'm never going to look at a man again. Ever!"

"Where are you from?"

She turned sad brown eyes on me. "California. Hollywood. I was going to be a movie star."

She had a short, sturdy build, and with her brown hair straggling beside her round cheeks, she looked nothing at all like a slender, beautiful girl you'd expect to see in the movies.

"A producer got me in the family way," she said. "Promised me the moon. Said he'd put me in a movie with Elvis Presley. The one he's shooting now, *Jailhouse Rock*. Make me a star. Stupid me. I believed him. I never even got to meet Elvis Presley, never mind be in a movie with him. And the asshole producer could have introduced me. We were at a party where Elvis was before I left to come here."

"I met him," I said.

"You lie!"

I held up my hand. "I swear. Elvis is my friend. I met him at a concert he did at the football stadium in our town, back before he ever hit the top. He calls me his good luck charm because I was the first girl to scream at one of his concerts." My voice broke on those last words and must have lent credibility to my story, for Marty's entire aspect changed from scornful disbelief to awestruck conviction.

"You're not kiddin' me, are you? You really do know him?"

"I really do. We write each other, and he sends me his records—forty-fives—as soon as they come out."

"Well, I'll be horn-swaggled. What's he like?"

"He's just a good ole boy, and a real nice one."

Marty let loose a muffled scream. "Oh Lord. If you don't stop, I'm gonna drop this baby right here on the sidewalk."

We had approached the local movie theatre.

"Look, there's the poster for his movie, *Loving You*," I said, pointing to it. "Let's check when it's coming. We have to see it."

We stepped into the outside foyer of the theatre where posters of upcoming movies were displayed in glass cases on all three sides. The one for *Loving You* said only "coming soon."

"We can't miss it," Marty said.

"If we do, we can see it back home," I said.

"But I want to see it with you. Someone who actually knows him."

I thought back on that one night I was with Elvis.

"It's hard to believe it's been almost two years."

"How did you meet him?"

"The girls I went to the concert with left me stranded. Elvis saw me alone in the parking lot and gave me a ride home."

Her eyes searched mine. "That's it? He didn't take you anywhere first?"

"To the Old Hickory, to get himself a pig sandwich."

"Oh Lord!" She fanned herself with her hand. "What did you talk about to him?"

"I couldn't think of a word, at first. He broke the ice by asking me to dance."

I thought Marty really would miscarry on the spot. She grabbed her stomach and practically shrieked, "You *danced* with him?"

"In the parking lot of the restaurant. It's not nearly as glamorous as you might think. Everybody dances outside their cars while they're waiting for curb service. They have speakers that broadcast the music all around the place."

"But you danced with Elvis Presley!"

"Yep."

"He held your hand?"

"Only while we were dancing. He wasn't famous then."

"Were you slow dancing?"

"Yes, to 'Autumn Leaves.'"

"Then he must have put his other hand on your waist."

I laughed.

"Did he try to kiss you?"

"No. I wanted him to, but he didn't. He said his mama had raised him right. I think he might have kissed me at the door when he brought me home, but my mama chose that moment to materialize."

Marty took a step back and looked at me for a long minute, skepticism written all over her face.

"What if I said I don't believe a word you're saying? I bet all this trauma of being pregnant has scrambled your brains and you're hallucinating."

"Marty, at this point I am so miserable it doesn't make a hell's bit of difference to me. I did meet Elvis, he does write to me, and you can believe it or not. I really don't care."

She reached out to stop me, but I evaded her and continued on down the street.

"Wait, girl!" she cried, catching up and seizing my arm. "Okay, I believe you."

"Like I said, I really don't care."

We walked again in silence, my throat aching at the remembrance of that night that now seemed a lifetime ago. I was a different girl then, innocent, unaware of how one decision could ruin a person's life. On the heels of that memory came one of Farrel smiling at me in the oilfields. No matter how bitter it was, some parts of that night would always remain beautiful to me—the moon throwing its light on the clouds, the music, and Farrel's kiss that said the words "I love you" that he had never uttered to me.

A radio blaring from somewhere brought me back to reality.

"It's hard to believe that guy back there on the poster is the same guy I met when he was struggling to make it. Maybe somehow I am his good luck charm. He flew to the top after we met. Miracles do happen—to some people."

"The only miracle we're going to see is the miracle of birth," Marty said as we strolled along. "I wish to God I'd had an abortion while I could. Giving up my baby hurts a thousand times worse than that must."

"Why didn't you?"

She shrugged. "Lots of reasons, not the least being I was brought up to believe that sort of thing was not only wrong but dangerous."

"It is dangerous," I said. "You can't get a legitimate doctor to give you one. It's against the law. You have to get it done in some back alley. A friend of mine died from one that was botched in a place like that."

She shook her head. "I guess I made the right decision. And I guess giving the kid away will be the right thing, but God, I don't want to. Have you signed the adoption papers yet?"

"Miss Oldenburg tried to make me, but I insisted on reading them over first."

Marty's eyes lit. "I haven't signed mine either. Every time I see her, she tries to get me to. Hey, look, here's the newsstand I told you about. Want to go in?"

We stepped inside the little store. A skinny man needing a shave sat on a stool behind the counter.

"Help ya?"

"We're just browsing," Marty said.

"Browse, but don't read," he snapped. "You read, you pay."

I wandered to the newspaper rack. It seemed like eons since I'd read a paper. A newspaper banner leaped out at me. The *El Dorado Daily News*.

"My hometown paper is here!"

Marty turned a pleased smile on me. "I told you you'd like this place."

I pulled a copy from the rack.

"That'll be ten cents," said the man behind the counter.

I strode toward him, pulling out change from my pocket.

"Here, take twenty cents." I slung two dimes at him. "I'll buy one for my friend too. Marty, get yourself a copy, and let's go to that diner. You can read all my hometown society news. Then you'll have an idea of why I ended up here."

She grinned, and with light hearts we headed down the street toward the pink neon sign flashing "Diner" into the spring evening that was now fading into darkness.

CHAPTER 23
Always On My Mind

On June twenty-third, Miss Oldenburg shook me awake before her reveille siren went off.

"Shake a leg. There's a call for you in my office, and I can't have my phone tied up with you girls whining and blubbering all day."

Throwing back the covers, I jerked on my clothes, and ignoring other needs, I rushed down the steps to Miss Oldenburg's office on the first floor. She held out the receiver of an old-timey black phone and handed me a note printed in large letters. *Five minutes.*

"Give my best to your mother, Julie, dear," she said on her way out, loud enough to be heard on the other end of the line. Her voice reeked with phony cordiality.

"Hello?" I said when the door closed behind her.

"Happy Birthday!"

"Oh, Mama, it's so good to hear your voice."

I used all my strength to hold back the tears pooling in my eyes.

"Seventeen years old today," she said. "How are you, my darling?"

I forced brightness into my tone. "Fine. How are you?"

"I'm fine. Aunt Hattie's still here. She's just told us this morning, she may stay all summer. It's so hot in New Orleans."

"Isn't it just as hot in El Dorado?" I asked.

"Hotter than the hinges of hell. The attic and ceiling fans run day and night."

"How's Carmen?"

"She's fine. We sneaked off to the pay phone across the street from the high school to call you—the one by the Wildcat Café—so Aunt Hattie wouldn't hear. And we have to be careful. Carmen says that Bubba John Younger's mother says anyone who uses a pay phone must be having an affair." Mama's laugh sounded lame. "We don't have a lot of change either, so we can't talk long. And besides, we're having a party for Carmen later on this afternoon to celebrate your birthday."

"Oh." My spirits deflated like a punctured inner tube.

"Well, what else could we do, darling? All the carpool girls were asking what she was going to do on her birthday. We decided, if we didn't do something, it would arouse suspicion. Besides, you remember it's Aunt Hattie's birthday too. I'm making two cakes—a yellow with eight egg yolks and a white with the eight leftover whites. I'll use coconut icing on the white one and chocolate on the yellow."

I was missing out on everything.

"Mama, I wanted to talk to you alone, without Carmen standing there listening."

"Is something wrong?"

I could hear her breathing turn rapid.

"No, I just . . . I mean . . . I feel like I've lost you, not being able to have a private word."

"I'm sorry it was a bad time when you called. It has been like pulling teeth to escape from Aunt Hattie long enough to get to the pay phone and call you back."

The operator's voice broke in. "Please deposit another twenty-five cents."

"Oh, all right. Just a minute. Shoot! I dropped it. Julie, catch that quarter. It's rolling into the street. Hold on, operator."

I automatically glanced around the floor for the quarter before the shocking realization swept over me of what Mama had said.

The sound of money dropping into the slot rang in my ear.

"There now, I'm back," she said.

"Mama, you called her 'Julie'!"

"Oh dear, did I? I've gotten so in the habit of it with Hattie here. I live in terror I'll forget and call her Carmen."

"Mama, I've tried to call again, several times, but the lines for the two phones are so long, and people talk forever. I almost never get my turn before we are required to do something."

"They only have two phones?" she said, alarm in her voice.

I hadn't meant to tell her that. I swallowed hard.

"In addition to this one, but it's Miss Oldenburg's private phone. Next time call me on the house number she gave you."

We didn't say anything for a minute while I fought back tears.

"Listen, honey, Carmen wants to speak with you, but first, are you sure you're doing all right?"

"I guess."

"Have you been seen by the doctor?"

I had, but only once. "Yes. He said I needed to gain more weight."

"Then eat," she said. "Those words would be music to my ears."

She would die if she knew about the canned meat we'd been served last night.

"I don't dare send you a birthday package because I'd have to get it weighed, and with Happiness House's address on it, old Miss Daniels, the postal worker I always get, would be sure to put two and two together."

"It's okay, Mama. It's not much of a birthday anyway."

"Don't slip into self-pity, honey. You know I wouldn't neglect your birthday. I sent a card with a little something inside for your secret bag. Be on the lookout for it."

I glanced at the clock on the wall of Miss Oldenburg's office. Five minutes had gone by.

"The operator is going to come on wanting more money if we don't hurry," Mama said. "Here, I'm putting Carmen on. I love you, darling. Take care of yourself, and call. I'll practice my double-talk so, if Aunt Hattie overhears us, she won't catch on."

"Bye, Mama. I love you too."

"Hi, sis," came Carmen's voice over the wire.

"Hi. Have a happy birthday for me, will you?"

"That bad, huh?" she replied.

"Yep, but don't let on to Mama. How are things going? Do people believe you are me?"

"Seems like they do. I had to transfer out of French class, but Aunt Hattie speaks fluent French, and seeing as how she lives down there in New Orleans among all those Frenchies, she's teaching me some. And I found your clarinet in the closet, and I've been using the fingering chart to teach myself how to play."

"What on earth for?" I demanded. "I'll be back before football season starts. You'll never need it."

"Have you forgotten summer band practice? August nineteenth we start rehearsing the half-time show for the first game. I have to know how to play by then. The broken finger routine has long been put to rest."

"Oh." I looked at my own finger that had been broken. I could use it, but it was hard to bend. "Don't forget, your joints will be stiff," I cautioned.

"Righto. Listen, I'd better go."

"Carmen."

"What?"

I took a breath. "Have you seen him?"

"Who?"

"You know who."

"Honey girl, I've seen 'em all. You're the most popular gal in these parts. I'm seeing to that. Boys are beating down the door. Eugene, Justin, Bubba John Younger. Makes me wonder if old Farrel put out the word that you put out." She laughed at her own version of a joke. "Don't clam up on me now. I'm just joshing. Jesus, Mama E heard me say that. I thought she was reading the menu of the Wildcat Café. Julie knows I'm kidding, Mama E," she said, away from the receiver. "Don't get cranked."

"What did you call my mother?" My voice sounded wildly out of control.

A slight pause followed. "I called her Mama E. Get real, Julie. I can't call her Elizabeth."

I nodded to myself. I was being irrational. "Of course you can't. Mama E is fine, if it helps keep up the front."

"Good. Now listen, I gotta tell you something about Eugene. He shaping up. He might move into the cool category in another twenty years."

"That'll be the day. Is he still going with Rhonda?"

"Not when he can get a date with me. I mean you." Her voice dropped again into a whisper. "He's is so crazy about you, Julie. I couldn't turn him down. We went to the drive-in one night, and I let him, you know."

"No, I don't know. You let him what?"

"He'd never touched a girl's titties. He told me old Rhonda knocks him sky-west and crooked when he tries to touch hers. So I let him have a small feel. On the top of my shirt only. He asked if he could put his hand inside my bra, but I wouldn't let him, of course. If I did that, next thing you know he'd be trying to get in my pants, and I'm staying a virgin after seeing what's happened to you. But a little bit goes a long way toward keeping a girl popular, and besides, I thought he deserved a little thrill. Remember that when you get home and go out with him. He's played with your titties."

"I can't believe you would let him do that thinking it was me."

"Honey, he loved it."

"Carmen, have you seen Farrel?"

A beat.

"Sure, I've seen him. He's working in the oil fields with Dad, you know."

"With Dad?"

"They're on the same crew. He mentioned that one day Dad had a flask in his pocket. But it was only that one time because the owner of the rig caught him and gave him a warning."

"Where were y'all when Farrel told you this?"

"Hmmm. Let me think. The Dairyette, I believe."

I could tell she was trying to evade the question. "Carmen, have you been out with him?"

"I cannot tell a lie."

"You have. I knew it! How could you do this to me? You promised you wouldn't go out with him."

"I had my fingers crossed."

Her answer left me numb.

Miss Oldenburg opened the door to her office. "Hurry up," she mouthed.

I held up a finger. "One minute more."

"No."

I put my hand over the mouthpiece. "Please, Miss Oldenburg, just one more minute. Or I'll tell Mother you're using us instead of paying staff to run the place."

"Make it snappy," she said, and giving a snort, she left the room again, slamming the door behind her.

"Okay, back again," I said to Carmen. "Why did you go out with Farrel?"

"Look, it would have been suspicious if I hadn't. I had to prove to him that I'm . . . I mean that *you're* not pregnant."

"Did he try anything?"

"Well, you know how guys are. Listen, Justin has the hots for you, big time. You ought to focus on him when you get home."

"Did Farrel try to kiss you?"

"Deposit twenty-five cents, please," the operator said.

"Did he?"

"What do you care? You don't love him anymore, do you?"

"No . . . I don't, but he's always on my mind."

"That doesn't sound like 'no' to me. Well, if you do love him, you shouldn't. And don't worry. He thought he was kissing you, and I kept it to one kiss, I promise."

How could I trust her promises now?

"Listen, sis, I gotta go. We're running out of quarters. Call in the afternoon between two and four. That's when Aunt Hat takes her nap. Don't write. She checks the mail every day looking for a letter from Elvis. She'd be sure to see anything you sent."

"Have there been any letters from Elvis?"

"Yep, one. It's in Mama E's envelope to you."

"Twenty-five cents," demanded the operator.

"Bye, Jules. Chin up. Gotta get ready for your birthday party."

A click on the line and they were gone. A click of the door and Miss Oldenburg was back in the room, glaring at me.

"Except for the fact that it's your birthday, you'd have extra KP duty, miss. I'll let you off this one time. But don't try it again."

"I won't, Miss Oldenburg. I'm sorry. I hadn't talked with my mother since I got here."

Tears I couldn't stave off ran down my cheeks.

For once, Miss Oldenburg's face took on a look of sympathetic understanding.

"I hope you've learned your lesson, Julie. You can't engage in irresponsible sex and not pay the penalty. All you girls have to learn that."

"I know," I said through a sob.

A thought occurred to me as I looked at her looking at me. Maybe she'd had a child out of wedlock herself. Maybe she was punishing herself for it by being so mean to us. Someday I might get up the courage to ask her.

"And Julie," she said as I moved toward the door, "I'll expect you back here after breakfast tomorrow to sign the adoption papers. It's time to resolve things about this baby."

CHAPTER 24
In My Own Skin

A manila envelope came in the mail that morning shortly after my phone call. I ate a hurried lunch and made the climb upstairs to the dorm to open it before the other girls came up. Inside were Mama's birthday card with a twenty tucked inside and a letter from Elvis.

I sat staring at Elvis's letter. The shock of having been violated hit me. A small rip on the edge of the flap, as well as excess glue on the seal, betrayed that the letter had been opened. Neither Carmen nor Mama had said a word about having read it. Translated, that meant they didn't want me to know.

Even though Mama usually asked what Elvis said in his letters, she had never, and I knew she would never open mail addressed to me. She'd read mail I'd already opened and hidden under my mattress, but to her, actually opening another person's mail was tantamount to stealing.

Carmen was another story. I didn't know her convictions about such things. Still, it might not have been Carmen. With me gone, maybe Mama had felt it her duty to censor what was sent to me at the home. No matter who it was, I felt violated. Someone had read *my* letter from Elvis.

I removed the little bag from my bra and stuffed the twenty in with the hundred-dollar bill. When it was pinned safely back in its place, I stared out the window by my bed, wishing I had enough to escape from this place, get on a plane, and fly to Memphis or California, wherever Elvis was, and pretend for a time I was the girl I used to be. The thought swelled my throat. Most likely I would never see Elvis again, except on the big screen. And no way under heaven would I ever again be the girl I used to be, for no amount of money would permit me to escape from myself.

My baby moved inside me. A surge of love so great it was indescribable went through me—overpowering the desolation I'd felt after reading Elvis's letter and distracting me from thoughts of escape. No, I would stay here and have my baby, Farrel's and my baby. There was no escape anyway, even if you did have a big movie star for a friend. I still had to live in my own skin.

"Julie, come quick!" Marty burst into the dorm. "Miss Oldenburg is doing a presentation in the dining hall, and everyone is required to attend."

I set Mama's card on my bedside table and stuffed Elvis's letter in the drawer beneath it.

"Hurry up! She'll pitch a fit if we aren't there when she starts," Marty said between heavy breaths as we hurried from the dorm. "I saw you put that letter in your drawer. Is it from Elvis?"

"Yes. I'll show it to you later."

Silence pervaded the dining hall. The girls had adjusted their chairs to see the screen Miss Oldenburg had set up at the head of the room.

"*Tempus fugits*, Julie and Marty. Make haste and take a seat," Oldenburg said. "You're holding up the works."

The projectionist flipped the light switch, and the room was left with only sunlight leaking through the shades. The clicking of film threading through the projector sounded, and the screen lit up with a picture of a little boy running toward a jungle gym on a school playground. A male narrator pointed out that the child was dressed in the latest style of kids' clothing. We watched other children playing in the background who were similarly dressed—all but one. Off to the side stood a little girl, watching with a wistful face. A close-up showed a rip in her dress and dirt on her cheek. She was alarmingly frail.

A man and woman, obviously husband and wife, waved to the well-dressed boy. Leaping off the jungle gym, he ran into their wide-open arms.

The scene shifted to a woman in a factory, working with shoes as they passed on a conveyor belt. Her hands moved so quickly they became a blur. Her hair was stringy, and her dress hung askew on her bony frame.

The scene faded to a shot of the husband and wife walking up to their front door, each holding a hand of the well-dressed boy between them. All three laughed with joy. The man tossed the child and caught him. The child crowed with delight. From that scene, a picture flashed on of the factory mother trudging home to a tenement building at the end of the day. As she opened her door, the skinny little girl could be seen placing knives and forks on a table cluttered with junk. She brought two bowls and a box of cereal to the table and filled the milk pitcher with water.

The film took twenty-five minutes to contrast the luxurious life of the well-dressed boy and his parents with the tattered child and her mom. When the dining hall lights came up again, several girls were wiping tears.

Miss Oldenburg stood before us.

"The man and woman you saw with the little boy were two heart-broken people who had received the fatal verdict that they could never have children. Then, a miracle happened. A girl, just like one of you, chose to do the right thing and give up her illegitimate baby for adoption. The factory worker represents you, if you follow the selfish path and refuse to do what is best for you and your child."

Murmurings and whispers followed Miss Oldenburg's next words. "Would you deliberately choose to hurt the child you are carrying?

"Most of you aren't equipped financially to raise a child," she went on, "and none of you are equipped morally. If you were, you would be married now with your condition acceptable to God, your families, and the world. But you are seen as lacking in character and moral values. And it isn't necessarily your parents' fault. I've met at least one parent of each of you. They are as different as night and day from you."

Miss Oldenburg took a step toward us.

"Your parents are devastated by your careless actions. You have brought shame down upon their heads and upon your own. And when your baby is born, if you try to keep it, you will bring shame down on its head—shame and suffering. For ask yourself: what can you give a child? Your baby will be branded a bastard to all the world, and you will be branded a slut for the rest of your lives."

Miss Oldenburg moved among us, touching various girls on the shoulder as she passed.

"If you think some nice man will come along and marry a fallen woman, you are sadly mistaken. You don't even see the natural fathers of your babies asking to marry you and take care of the child, do you? What makes you think an adoptive father would do so? If you keep your child, you must prepare to rid yourselves of the idea that a decent man will marry you later. Your lives will be ruined."

I gave an involuntary jump as she planted her hand on my shoulder. Looking up at her, I searched for something that would reveal what kind of person this woman was. A pair of brown, marble-like eyes looked back at me, eyes that held no compassion, no understanding. What they did hold was something I could not identify. I vowed to my-self to make every effort to learn exactly what she was about—pressuring us like this to give our babies away—so that, God help me, I could make the right decision about the small human inside of me, whom I was growing to love more deeply every day.

Miss Oldenburg's aspect changed abruptly. She fairly danced to the front of the room again. Her face took on a brightness I had never be-fore seen in her. When she spoke again, her words were so filled with enthusiasm and joy she sounded as though she had seen the Rapture.

"If, however, you sign the papers to give your baby up," she smiled upon us, "you can move on from this tragic occurrence, forget about it, and continue with your life as if it never happened. Think about it, those of you who are reluctant to sign. You are the ones this presenta-tion is aimed toward."

She wiped her nose with her handkerchief.

"Would those of you who have already signed please come forward and stand before the recalcitrants so they may see examples of true bravery and goodness and join me in applauding your willingness to do the right thing."

More than half the girls straggled up and stood near her at the front of the room. Their puckered brows and anxious faces belied her promise of happiness and relief that was supposed to follow the signing of the papers. One raised her hand.

"Yes, Lucy?" Miss Oldenburg said.

"I don't think I'm all that brave and good. I don't want to give my baby up. I just don't have any other choice."

Miss Oldenburg beamed. "That's entirely correct, Lucy. You don't have another choice." She turned to face us. "And the rest of you don't either. I will be calling you one by one into my office during the following week and giving each of you the opportunity to prove your love for your baby. Prove it by signing the agreement to give it a good life, one that you can never provide."

Many girls silently wept as we filed out of the dining hall. Marty and I shed no tears. Nor did Kay, the pillow pilferer, who wore a resolute face as she stepped along with us back to the dorm to get ready for our work details.

"All Miss Oldenburg and the owners of this home want is money," Kay said. "Those adoptive parents are willing to pay big bucks to get a child. No one at this place gives a hoot about us or our babies. They don't care how we feel. To them, we don't deserve to have feelings."

"Who else is there, besides Miss Oldenburg?" I asked.

"The doctors, the nurses, and the social worker who stops by every once in a while to help Oldenburg put the screws to us about signing."

"Come on, Kay," Marty said. "Let's hurry it up so Julie can show us her letter from Elvis Presley before we have to go to the salt mines."

Kay's eyes grew large. "Elvis Presley? Is he your baby's fa—?"

I cut her off. "No! He's only my friend."

They plopped down on my bed while I got out Elvis's letter. I read it to them, then they each wanted to hold it.

"Just think," Marty said when it was her turn. "Elvis the Pelvis wrote this letter. His fingers touched it."

"It really bothers him to be called that," I said.

"Nooo!" they chorused.

"But he said the worst thing was when they accused him of destroying us kids' morals." I gave a sad laugh. "It would take more than a beautiful voice like his to destroy anyone's morals. I've been trying to sort this out in my head, and I'm almost there. I think moral standards are so slanted in favor of the boys that girls don't have a chance to be normal human beings like God created us to be."

"I like that," Marty said.

Kay handed the letter back to me. "So do I. God created me to have sex and get pregnant."

The two of them laughed.

"Well, He did, didn't He?" I said. "And the boys. That's all they think about. Why doesn't anyone call them sluts?"

They stopped laughing.

"I mean, isn't that one reason we're here on this earth, to 'be fruitful and multiply'?" I said.

Kay moaned. "Oh God, now she's dragging the Bible into it."

"Will you sign, Marty?" I asked.

She chewed on a hangnail and shook her head.

"I don't want to."

"Kay?" I said.

"I don't want to either, but what choice do we have?"

I struggled to find the right words. "I mean, I live in this body, this skin. I know what I am, and I'm not a slut. I feel the same way I felt back when people saw me as a good girl—except for the shame. I don't know if I can ever get past the shame."

"We won't, if we don't sign the papers," Kay said.

Marty nodded.

"But will we even then?" I asked. "What about the *secret* shame, never mind the pain we'll bear for what I am afraid will be the rest of our lives because we abandoned our babies?"

CHAPTER 25
THAT SAME MOON

Driven by the thought of that secret shame, I grabbed a wedding band after dinner and went to the little park down the street in the other direction from the newsstand and movie house. A vacant bench beneath a pine tree reminded me of El Dorado's neighborhoods, whose stately homes stood beneath tall pines with needles fanning against skies that, in my mind, were always blue, even when it rained.

Tonight, looking through the needles of this pine, I watched the moon travel the summer night up to its eight o'clock perch in the sky. That same moon was shining on my friends back home—on Farrel and on Mama—and somewhere it was shining on Elvis.

Homesickness wrenched my insides. Closing my eyes, I pretended I was there, wandering the streets of home. From the high school, beneath its soaring white columns, to War Memorial Stadium, where I saw Elvis, and where, for fame and glory, our Wildcats waged football wars. From where the band stepped off, playing a Sousa march and leading floats in parades to the square, to where its anchor, the white courthouse with its flags flying, surrounded by Woolworths and other hometown stores, watched over the throngs gathered to pay homage to the Homecoming Football Queen. Maybe I would be back in time for it.

My thoughts shifted to our house with its green shutters and wraparound porch, and inside, Mama sitting in her favorite chair. The crepe myrtle trees bloomed this time of the year back home. I longed to wake up innocent and in my own bed again on a summer morning with the sight of the watermelon-red blossoms filling my eyes. I longed to be soothed by the whirring sounds of fans suspended from our twelve-foot ceilings, making bearable the suffocating summer heat.

Before that night at the concert—the night when I met Elvis and first saw Carmen, the night that robbed me of my unrecognized state of bliss—I thought I was miserable with no boyfriend and only three Dilberts to run around with. In those days before Farrel, I lived in to-tal oblivion of my happy existence. I had Mama, and my father was nothing more than an occasional annoyance. But the old adage, "Be careful what you want, you might get it," proved true. I got what I had so deeply craved—acceptance in the in-crowd, the boy I loved, and the tenuous beginnings of a relationship with my father—and with it all came the true meaning of misery.

What had happened during the weekend Carmen stayed with our father and pretended to be me? She would have told me on the phone if he had seen through the ruse. It was clear: he couldn't tell us apart. Although that was what we'd hoped for, with it came the bitter real-ization that he cared so little that neither of us was identifiable in his mind. We did not look *exactly* alike. There were small differences, if he had taken the time to notice.

When I had finally gotten up the courage to risk his temper and drunkenness and had gone to see him, he'd left me on Christmas Eve to go to a saloon. Although he'd expressed concern about whether I had seen through Farrel before it was "too late," I felt I was only a trophy to him, instead of his child to whom he would devote his life. He had al-ways made me feel that my value to him was no more than the winner's cup of gold plastic he'd won in a fishing contest. He might care more about me if he could put me on the mantle next to it.

Sitting there in that Texas park, I searched every clue I'd ever been given in the effort to decipher what had destroyed our family. Of course I knew Mama's side of the story. He had cheated on her with Carmen's mother, while Mama was pregnant with me, no less. What I didn't know was why. On Christmas Eve, he had hinted there was more to it than that, but he wouldn't tell me what.

The sound of a kid yelling "wheee" as he zipped down the slide jarred me from my reverie. I eased up and headed back along the path leading out to the street. I hadn't gone far when a woman's voice spoke from a bench nearby.

"When are you due?"

I looked over at her. She was young, but older than I, and wore a sleeveless yellow blouse and matching skirt.

"September," I said.

Her eyes held eager friendliness.

"Seems like forever, doesn't it?" She patted the empty side of the bench. "Sit and talk awhile?"

It was still early. Why not?

"Mine begs to play on the slide every night before bed," she said. "Thank goodness the park is well lit and just across the street from our apartment. Do you want a boy or a girl?"

"Either will be fine," I said, forcing myself to sound casual. "But I believe it's a boy. I feel it! I already have a name picked out. Nicholas."

"That's a good name. I wanted a boy. And that's what I got." She nodded toward the kid on the slide. "Michael. He'll wear himself out, then he'll be willing to go to bed. I remembered to bring the bread wrapper this time."

"I used to slide on bread wrappers from the Colonial Bakery," I said without thinking. "They were the best for going fast. More wax, I guess."

"What part of town is that bakery in?" she asked with questioning eyebrows.

I fanned myself with my hand. "Oh, it's not around here. I don't live here."

She nodded, her inquisitive expression demanding an explanation. The need kicked in to enlarge the secret self I was creating.

"My husband is on business out here for a while. We're from Little Rock."

"We're here temporarily too," she said. "Are you in the apartment house across the street?"

This was getting beyond my control.

"Uh, no. We're with my husband's aunt, a few blocks away."

Her brow relaxed. "I almost took you for one of the girls from the home."

"Girls from your home?" I asked, deliberately changing *the* into *your* to feign ignorance.

"Oh, no! Girls from Happiness House."

I called up a clueless face.

"The home for unwed mothers," she said, her voice low, as if she feared someone might accomplish the impossible and hear her over the traffic and other city noises.

"Oh, is that around here?" I asked.

"Just down the street. I'm surprised you don't know about it. I wish it wasn't in this neighborhood. They say the girls are all sluts. I guess they'd have to be to get themselves in that situation." She waved at the boy with the bread wrapper. "He's having so much fun. Better hope you're right and it's a boy. If it's a girl, you'll have to play with her until you have your second. Boys are much more independent. He'd slide by himself all night if I let him."

I made a point of angling my wrist so she could see me check my watch.

"I've got to go. Farrel will wonder where I am. He had to work late tonight, but he'll be coming home about now. It was nice talking with you."

"I wish you didn't have to leave so soon," she said. "Maybe we'll meet again sometime. Do you walk here often?"

"I will from now on," I said, forcing brightness into my smile and making a mental note to never return. "Good night."

She gave me a small wave. "Good night."

I moved away from her as fast as I could and still maintain a casual air. If it hadn't been for the baby, I would have thrown myself on the ground and howled to the orange moon now floating above the park. But I didn't want to be arrested, so I pushed down my wretched sadness and kept walking back to Happiness House to further plan my future—no, my present—life of duplicity. My baby, Nicholas, kicked hard, reminding me I had no other choice.

CHAPTER 26
TELL ME WHY

The next morning, I received a summons to the examining room to see a different doctor from the young one who had examined me previously. Grey hairs around his temples suggested that this one was about forty-five, maybe even fifty.

"Let's see how you are doing," he said. "Don't be shy, Julie, is it? Your name is Julie?"

I lay back and tried to relax as he conducted his exam, but his manner was rough and careless. At one point, a cry escaped me.

"I'm not hurting you," he snapped. "You got yourself into this situation. If you'd kept your legs together, we wouldn't be doing this."

The lump in my throat broke. I could not hold back a sob.

"Tears won't do you any good now. What are you, fifteen? Sixteen?"

"Seventeen," I managed.

"Old enough to know better. There now, all finished. You can get dressed. Miss Oldenburg will see you in her office in ten minutes."

"How is he?" I ventured.

"Who?"

"Nicholas. My baby. Is he doing all right?"

"I can't believe you've named this little bastard. Better forget about that. It'll make it all the harder when the time comes for you to part company with it."

His words cut through me. Part company? Of course that was the whole idea of my coming here, but the further along I got in my pregnancy, the more wrenching became the thought of parting company with my baby.

I surmised that Miss Oldenburg planned to put the pressure on me to sign the surrender papers. I dressed as quickly as I could, all the while planning my strategy to delay the signing a little longer.

Seated in her office, I waited ten, fifteen, almost twenty minutes before she came in, her stockinged legs swishing beneath her skirt, her heels clacking. She settled into her chair and, opening the file she had brought in with her, she looked at me over the top of her glasses.

"I hear you've named the baby."

"It's not definite," I stammered. "He just seems like a Nicholas to me."

Miss Oldenburg looked back at the file. "It could be a girl, you know."

"Boy or girl, my baby is sweet," I answered without hesitation.

"Boy or girl, it's not yours to keep. You do understand that, don't you?"

"I know what you mean."

"I'm not sure you do. You haven't signed the adoption papers yet. That's the objective of our meeting this morning."

"I figured that."

"Good. Then I assume you brought them with you?"

"No. I didn't know I was meeting with you until the doctor told me, and he didn't state the reason for the meeting."

A dripping sound drew my eyes to the window air conditioner. A brimming bucket sat beneath it. Her tone aggravated, Miss Oldenburg said, "The man is coming to fix it today. Keep your attention on pertinent matters."

Passing a fresh set of the adoption documents across the desk to me, she said, "Here's a pen. You've had plenty of time to read these. Sign them now, and let's be done with it."

The heading across the top of the document read "Permanent Surrender of Child." The papers appeared to be the same documents she'd given me to read earlier, but I skimmed them nevertheless. Above the signature line were the words "By signing below I hereby forfeit all rights as parent to the child I have birthed."

Yes, the documents were the same. I laid them on the desk.

"I can't sign my baby away. It hurts too much."

"It's not about your feelings," Miss Oldenburg said. "It's about what the child needs that you can't give it."

"I am the only one who can give my baby a mother's love. There's nothing more important than that."

"The adoptive parents can give it a better kind of love."

"What kind of love could that possibly be?"

"Turn the papers over to the back side," she ordered. "Take the pen, and at the top of the page make two columns. Label one 'Things I Can Provide for the Baby.' Label the other 'Things the Adoptive Parents Can Provide for the Baby.'"

I did as she asked, and then sat staring at the page.

"I don't want to do this."

"Your mother is paying her hard-earned money to keep you here, is she not?"

I gave a dumb nod.

"Tell me why."

I looked up at her. "To escape the shame, of course, if anybody found out."

"Who brought this shame down on the heads of you and your mother?"

Tears welled in my eyes.

"You did, did you not?" She sounded like a bleating goat. "Your mother is suffering because you made a decision to have carnal relations when you weren't married."

I cried harder. Miss Oldenburg passed me her box of tissues.

"I didn't do it to hurt my mother," I said, blowing my nose. I looked squarely at her and tried to speak with a conviction I did not possess. "We . . . Farrel and I . . . loved each other."

"Is that so?" she cut in. "Then where is he now? Why aren't you in his home as his wife, the two of you awaiting your first child?"

"We're so young!"

"Precisely," she said.

I shifted in the chair. "I didn't tell him about the baby. He would have married me. I didn't want to ruin his life. He's working in the oil fields to pay his way to school next year."

"Oh yes, of course." Her smile was cynical. "Does he really love you, Julie? Are you entirely sure he would have married you, had you deigned to tell him?"

My arguments dried up and flaked into nothingness as I thought back on Farrel's excited face when he told me the driving force of his life was to lift himself out of the poverty he and his family were mired in.

"Ahhh," Miss Oldenburg said. "You're not sure. You say you didn't tell him because you didn't want to ruin his life. I suspect another part of the truth is you didn't tell him because in your heart of hearts you knew he didn't love you and you feared he wouldn't marry you. And who knows? Maybe in your heart of hearts you didn't want to marry *him*."

My courage flailed. She was right. I knew he didn't love me. I knew he didn't want to marry me, or anyone at this time in his life. And I didn't want to marry him either, not the way it would have been. If we were ever to marry, I wanted it to be because we wanted each other for better or for worse, not because we had to.

"Now that we've come to terms with that little issue, kindly list in the column labeled 'Things I Can Provide for the Baby' all you know you can give it with no education, no job, no home—"

"I have a home!"

"Your mother wouldn't have sent you here if she'd harbored any inclination at all to raise an illegitimate grandchild. Go ahead, write. And after the two seconds it will take, kindly write in the other column the things the adoptive parents can give the baby."

In my column I wrote "My love." After several minutes of being able to come up with nothing else, I focused on the column for the adoptive parents. That list flowed more easily: "A home, clothing, food."

When I paused, Miss Oldenburg prompted me. "Don't forget a college education."

"I'll be on my feet by that time. I'll be making enough to put him through school myself."

"On the salary from a menial job?" She laughed. "I highly doubt it."

I frowned in confusion, unable to grasp her meaning.

"How quickly we forget," she said. "You won't have a decent job because you won't have an education. You won't be able to return to high school if you keep the baby, and likely no college will accept you. And as we've said before, no decent man will marry you."

I shook my head in despair. The pen leaked a drop of ink on my finger. In my mind it became a symbol of my blemished self. I was a blot on the world.

Miss Oldenburg continued with her litany. "To that list in the adoptive parents' column, add toys the baby will eventually want, such as Madame Alexander dolls, and a prom dress, if it's a girl, or a basketball and goal to practice with, and a bicycle with gears, if it's a boy. And how about travel to widen the child's experiences? The couple I have in mind for your baby can take the child to Europe someday. Most important of all, add respectability to the list. With these fine people, the baby won't be a bastard."

The realities she was pounding into my brain stunned me. Everything she said was true.

"The adoptive parents will be college educated. They'll own their own home and have good incomes. They'll give the baby everything you cannot. You are unfit because you aren't married. You did wrong. You are not worthy of keeping the child."

She stepped from behind the desk and, coming closer to me, tried a different tact.

"It's God's will, Julie. God chose you," she gestured to the dorm room above her office, "and all you girls, to bear children for these women who can't have them. You girls are all miracle workers."

Still staring at the columned back page, I laid the pen on the desk.

"Don't put that pen down. Turn the paper over and sign. Don't add another mistake to your list. Do the right thing for once in your life."

I knew I was ill-equipped, not just to care for and raise a child, but to perform almost any job other than the cleaning and maintenance chores she had me doing at the home. I knew I had made a terrible mistake by having sex with Farrel. But somewhere in the dark well of my essence, a small flame of the self-confidence that had come to me after the Christmas Eve visit with my father flickered and held steady. That small light was enough. Enough to reveal to me I wasn't all bad. Like him, I had made a mistake, but also like him, there was good in me too. That feeble light was enough to give me the guts to stare straight into her eyes and say, "I'm not ready to sign away my child. I don't know if I'll ever be ready."

CHAPTER 27
Loving You

Elvis's new movie, *Loving You*, came to the neighborhood movie theatre toward the end of July, and all the girls in the dorm went to see it together. I sat between Kay and Marty, and we screamed every time Elvis sang, especially when he sang to Dolores Hart, the ingénue who played his girl. A part of me envied her, being in a movie with him. It must have been wonderful playing the role she played and being around him every day on the movie set.

The featured song, "Loving You," made me wonder if anyone would ever love me for always. Carmen's latest letter said Eugene Hoffmeyer would, if I only gave him a chance.

When I answered the letter from Elvis that Mama had sent in my birthday envelope and used his new Graceland address, the girls begged so hard to hear my reply that I broke down and read it to them before sealing it. I'll always remember that afternoon with everyone huddled around me, intent on hearing every word.

July 26, 1957
Dear Elvis,

Sorry I've taken so long to write. I will try to do better next time. My boyfriend and I have broken up, so I'm no longer two-timing you. Ha!

I went to see your movie Loving You. *Elvis, you really have made it all the way to the top. You did a great job, and I'm proud of you. Everyone in the theatre cheered when you sang. You've got all the girls screaming over you now! But I was the first, and I'll always treasure that title, along with being your good luck charm.*

You will never know how much it means to me that you still remember. Just so you know, I still remember too. Take care, my friend.

Juliet

The girls were no longer squealing and saying they were going to fall out dead on the floor when I finished. They were long-faced, and some had tears.

"You're lucky to have a friend like him," Kay said. "He has restored my belief that there are still some nice guys in the world."

"Yeah, but how long will he stay that way?" asked cynical Marty. "Hollywood does things to people, and they're not always nice things."

"I believe Elvis will always be good at heart, no matter how rich and famous he gets, and no matter what dissipated people he might fall in with out there," I said. "I only hope he meets a nice girl someday who'll be his true love."

"Don't you ever wish it had been you?" Kay asked.

I shook my head. "No. I like Elvis, but I love . . ." I broke off.

Marty peered into my face. "Who?"

"Someone else, whom I wish I hated."

Everyone got quiet after that and drifted off, either in groups of three or alone. I put the letter in a manila envelope with no return address and sent it back home for Mama to forward to Elvis. Then I joined the other girls to try to make it through the rest of this day, and the next, and the next, until we finally would give birth and get out of this miserable place.

Kay was the first to leave us. She went into labor in the middle of the night and woke everybody up with her screams.

Miss Oldenburg came clacking into the room and immediately snapped into business mode.

"Marty, help her get her suitcase packed. Julie, go down to my office and telephone them we're coming. The number is on the top of my desk in plain view."

I was out of the room and headed for her office before they could get Kay downstairs and into Miss Oldenburg's car. I fumbled around the doorframe, searching for the light switch. When I couldn't find it, I felt my way in the direction of her desk. Her headlights shot into the windows as they backed away, illuminating the room enough for me to find the small lamp that sat next to the phone.

It took forever, but finally a receptionist answered. She spoke with a disgruntled voice. Maybe I'd awakened her.

"You're calling from Happiness House?"

"Yes, one of the girls has gone into labor. Miss Oldenburg said to let you know she's bringing her right over." My breath was coming in fast jerks.

"Cool it, sweetheart. A baby pops out every day. We'll let the doctor know."

A click, and she was gone.

My fingers lingered on the receiver when I put it back down. Except for the few letters I'd gotten since I came here, telephones had become my lifeline, my only connection to home and the known quantities of my life, and I so seldom got the chance to make or receive a call. This was it. No one was here to stop me. The hands of the desk clock pointed to one in the morning. It wasn't too late, I hoped. Did I dare?

With cold hands, I lifted the receiver again and dialed the operator. Up until a moment before, I'd intended to call Mama. I have no idea what steered me in that other direction.

"I need information, please," I said into the phone.

"City and state?"

"Memphis, Tennessee. The number for Elvis Presley."

"Have you lost your mind, honey?"

I wondered that myself. "He's a friend of mine, operator. Get the number and put me through, please."

"Who shall I say is calling?"

"His good luck charm."

The operator laughed. "I can't tell Elvis Presley that!"

"Just do it. You'll see. He'll accept the call."

A long few minutes later, I heard the phone ringing. I tried to imagine Graceland and where the phone was located. With a silent laugh at myself, I suddenly realized he probably had many phones. What if the ringing woke his mom and dad, or his grandmother? A voice I didn't recognize answered, "Hello."

"Long distance for Elvis Presley," the operator said.

"Who's calling?"

The operator told him with an apologetic laugh.

"Hold on."

As the guy moved away from the phone, I could hear him calling to Elvis.

"Says she's your good luck charm."

Then the familiar voice came through the wire. "And that's exactly who she is. This is Elvis Presley."

"Elvis? Is that really you?"

"It's me, little Juliet. I've never been so glad to hear from anyone in all my life. How are you, honey?"

That did it. I burst into tears and could barely speak.

"I'm okay, just a little lonely tonight."

"What's the matter, honey? Missing your boyfriend?"

"That and a few other things I can't go into," I said.

"Operator, hang up on your end," Elvis said.

"Yes, sir," murmured the operator.

"Don't need anyone eavesdropping. Now we can have some privacy. Listen, honey, why don't you hop a bus and come on up here? You can stay at Graceland. We've got twenty some odd rooms. You can swim in my pool. I'd love to see you, and Mama and Daddy would be thrilled to death to meet a fine Southern girl. And so would Grandma. You'll love her. I call her 'Dodger.'"

That made me cry even harder.

"Tell me what's troubling you, Juliet. I can't help if you don't, and I may not be able to help even then, but I'm willing to listen. Sometimes all a person needs is a friend to listen."

My desperation drove me to trust him. "You have to promise you'll never, ever tell a soul."

"You got it."

"Elvis, I . . ."

Moments passed during which I could not speak.

"You can trust me, Juliet."

I covered my mouth to muffle my sobs.

"Is it your boyfriend?"

I nodded.

"Are you still on the line?" he asked.

Oh God, don't let him hang up. "Yes! Don't go away, Elvis. I'll get hold of myself in a minute."

"It's all right. Take your time. I'm right here."

In the background from his end, I could hear music. "What's going on there?"

"Nothing. A few of the boys are jamming in the other room. No one can hear me. Now you tell me what going on. Did that jerk of a boyfriend do something to hurt you?"

"It's not his fault, Elvis. I was the one who pushed it. Only once, and only with him, but that was enough."

A heavy pause followed. At last he said, "I see."

"Do you really?" I didn't want to spell it out, if I didn't have to.

"Yeah, honey. I think I do. You've got a little bundle of trouble. Am I right?"

"You're right."

"What about Mama? How's she taking it?"

"You know the disgrace that goes with this. Mama sent me away."

"Sent you away? At a time like this? Now is when you need her the most."

"She's trying to help both of us escape the shame."

"Where are you? Want me to come get you?"

My heart pounded. "No, Elvis! Don't even think of doing something like that. People would believe it was yours. It would ruin you."

"Tell me where you are."

"I'm in a home, but don't try to find me."

"What kind of home?"

"You know, for the unwed. It might as well be for the undead because we're all existing in a sort of living death."

"Oh my lord. I'm so sorry, Julie. You must be suffering something awful."

Elvis and Mama were the only ones to deduce that fact.

"I know you'll never like or respect me again," I said, "but I had to talk to someone, and as it turns out, you're my only real friend."

"Wouldn't he marry you?"

"I didn't tell him."

"Why on earth not?"

"I knew he didn't love me, and I didn't want to be married on those terms."

There was a long minute of silence from him. In the background, the boys were playing "Loving You." Finally, he spoke again.

"That was mighty generous of you to do for him, and smart on behalf of both of you. I could tell from the first minute I met you that you're a fine girl, and I'll always think that. You don't have to worry. This won't change a thing about me respecting you and us being friends. In fact, I respect you even more after what you just told me. And I'll never tell, even if someone puts a gun to my head."

I swiped a tissue from the box on Miss Oldenburg's desk and blew my nose.

"That's the spirit," Elvis said. "Blow those tears away, and look to the future. When will you be out of there?"

"I'm not due until mid-September. Elvis, this is the worst part. They want me to give the baby up for adoption."

"Is that so?"

"Do you think I should?"

"Isn't that why Mama and you decided you should go to the home? To keep it all hush-hush?"

"Yes, but . . ." I couldn't find words to explain.

"It's not that simple when there's someone else involved, is it?" he asked.

"That's just it. They keep telling me I'm not fit to keep it. Not good enough."

"Don't believe a word of that. You're a fine person, and any baby would be twice blessed to have you love it and raise it."

I reached for another tissue.

"Honey, don't go tuning up again. That won't help in the least. If you want to keep it a secret and go on with your life, you better give it up."

"I don't know if I can. Thinking about it hurts so much. How much more will it hurt to actually do it?"

"If you want to keep it, you'll have to give up that secret. Bottom line, Julie, you'll have to do what you believe is right. I can't advise you, but I can be your friend, no matter what."

"Do what I think is *right?* Or what I think is best for *me?* Or what is best for the *baby?*"

"What you think is *right*, honey. Follow your gut. It will tell you the way to go."

Car lights flashed through the windows in the office.

"Elvis, I've got to go. The matron's back. I can't be caught using her phone."

"Where should I write you?" he asked, drawing a quick breath.

"Send it to my home in El Dorado. Mama's forwarding everything to me. I have to hang up. Thanks for talking to me, Elvis. Thanks for being my friend."

I hung up and scooted upstairs. On the way, I realized that Elvis had called me Julie, instead of Juliet, after I told him about the baby. Our friendship had grown stronger. I also remembered that I had not reversed the charges. Miss Oldenburg's bill would reflect my call to Memphis.

CHAPTER 28
The Last Goodbye

Days passed, but Kay did not return to the home to collect her things. Word filtered back from the hospital through the social worker who visited us periodically that she'd been in labor for two days before they'd finally done a C-section to deliver the baby. When we asked how she was doing, Miss Oldenburg told us it was none of our business.

When Kay had been in the hospital for three days and we still hadn't heard a word, everyone agreed to let Marty be first in line for the phone so she could call and inquire. The hospital staff refused to give out any information, even though Marty pretended to be a relative. The consensus was that we had to go to the hospital and find out for ourselves.

Everyone wanted to go, but a crowd would never be able to sneak in. It was decided that, since Marty and I knew Kay best, we should be the ones to go.

It was too far to walk, so we were left with no alternative but to do what was strictly forbidden—take a cab. All the girls chipped in on cab fare, and we made another secret call. Marty told the cab company to have the driver park a block down the street from the home. When we got there, he was waiting. For an extra-large tip, he promised to hang around while we went inside the hospital.

Although our hearts were beating hard and fast, we faked an air of confidence that got us past the information desk without being questioned. We bustled through the marble foyer, concocting meaningless chatter and phony laughter and pretending we knew exactly where we were going.

A wall sign listed maternity on the third floor. We found the elevator and rode up, sharing our speculations that being pregnant might be helping us get past hospital staff. We must have been right, for no one seemed to notice us, although visiting hours were not until two o'clock, and it was only noon. We'd come during lunch so we could get back in time for afternoon chores.

We proceeded off the elevator with our heads high and our walks purposeful, as if we had every right to be there.

In the middle of the maternity floor, we encountered our first stumbling block. Kay was not on the south end of the corridor. To search for her on the north end, we had to pass the nurses' station.

Ducking into the ladies' room to reconnoiter, we smoothed our hair, blown awry by the open windows in the taxi, tugged on our maternity tops to straighten them, then stepped boldly back out into the corridor to make our move. Just as we were breathing sighs of relief that we'd passed the nurses' station without notice, the one on duty at the desk called out, "Can I help you?"

"We're fine," I called back, and we doubled our speed.

It didn't work. She was after us faster than a hot knife through butter, as Mama would say. Her piano legs carried her toward us, her pudgy cheeks jiggling with every step.

"What do you girls want?"

"We're here to see someone," Marty said in an authoritative voice.

The nurse came back using the same tone. "And who might that be?"

"Kay," I said.

I hadn't meant to say anything, and certainly nothing lame, but Marty had turned a greenish shade of pale, and I'd used up all my meager store of fake confidence.

The nurse raised her eyebrows. "Kay who?"

I didn't have a clue who. We didn't share last names at the home. I finally came out with, "We've been here before, and no one gave us the third degree. We just want to see our friend Kay for a few minutes."

The nurse's gaze dropped to our bellies. When her eyes sought our faces again, they conveyed that she knew we were from the home.

"Be quick," she said in a low voice. "Down the hall, room three twenty-two. You have five minutes before I call security."

We murmured our thanks and rushed to the third door on the right.

Propped up on pillows, Kay lit up when she saw us come in, and she reached out with both hands.

"How you doing, girl?" Marty asked.

Kay shook her head. "This having a baby smarts."

"Don't they give you pain medication?" I said.

Kay started to say something but, with a forced laugh, backed off.

"You gals'll find out soon enough. You're big as elephants. You won't have as much pain as I've had with a C-section."

"Is it a boy or a girl?" I asked.

I could see that she was fighting tears. "A little girl. They let me hold her once. She was perfect."

"Was?" Marty said hesitantly.

"They won't let me see her anymore," Kay said, brushing away a tear. "They said it's easier that way."

"You signed her over for adoption, then?" I said.

"I did, yes. You'd better be prepared to sign too." Her voice dropped to a whisper. "They won't let you—"

A nurse entering with a new IV bag interrupted her.

"Time for you girls to skedaddle," she said. "I understand the nurse at the desk took pity on you, but don't abuse the privilege. Say your goodbyes."

"We just need a minute more," I said.

"Some other time," the nurse replied. "Now, shoo!"

"When are you getting out of here, Kay?" Marty asked, turning back when we were halfway to the door.

"In a few days," the nurse answered for her.

Kay gave us a longing look and a feeble wave.

"It means so much to me that you came. I'll never forget it."

We were almost out into the hall when she yelled, "Remember, it's all about money!"

We turned back into the room, but the nurse pushed us out and shut the door in our faces.

"So she was right," I said. "The adoptive parents pay the home big money for our babies."

Marty grabbed my arm. "Look, no one is around. Let's see what else is on this floor."

We cased the remaining length of the north hall. It paid off. At the very end was a large room where they kept the newborns. We stood at the observation window and watched them sleeping in their bassinets. My heart twisted.

"They're so tiny, so vulnerable."

"Look, over there in the corner," Marty said. "That one's in an incubator. It must be a preemie."

"Wonder which one is Kay's." I said, straining to read the names on the identity cards.

"The name cards here up front say they're all boys. And see, they're using only last names, so it's hopeless that we'll ever find her little girl."

I turned to Marty. "Kay was about to tell us something when the nurse came in and interrupted her."

"I know. She said, 'They won't let you.'" Marty wrinkled her forehead.

"They won't let you what?" I mused.

"They won't let you stay here another minute longer," came a voice behind us. It was the younger of the two doctors who visited us at the home. "If you girls don't want me to report you to Miss Oldenburg, you'd better leave, right now."

Marty and I took him at his word and left the hospital as fast as we could. The taxi driver, true to his word, was waiting for us, his radio blaring Elvis's latest hit, "Teddy Bear."

"Would you tell me what all you gals see in that dude?" he asked, putting the car in gear.

"I couldn't make you understand it in a thousand years," I said.

He jerked his head around and threw a grin to us in the backseat.

"Oooh," he said. "So that's it, huh? Well hey, I've got a little of that sex appeal myself. The girls used to go nuts over me when I was younger and didn't have this paunch . . . and a few other things. Do you reckon, if I let my hair grow, I'd kick up as much dust as he does?"

"Sure," I said and gave him a good-hearted pat on the back.

When he dropped us off, we gave him all the extra money we'd brought with us, thanked him, and walked the block back to the home to report to the others.

Miss Oldenburg met us at the door and waved her latest telephone bill in my face.

"Julie, I know it was you who placed this call to Memphis. You owe me a dollar seventy-five. Pay up, or you'll be looking for a hotel room before dark."

I still had three ones pinned in my secret bra bag, plus the hundred-dollar bill I'd never broken.

"I'll go up and get it for you," I said, partly ashamed of having it when we'd taken money from everyone to cover the taxi fare, but on the other hand, I'd contributed my fair share.

"You're not allowed to make any calls for the rest of the time you are here," she told me when I came back down with the money. "In case of emergency, I'll deliver messages between you and the involved parties."

"That's not fair!" I cried.

"What's not fair is that you haven't signed the adoption papers," she said back to me. "Your mother would be very distressed to learn of this."

I knew she was right. During our most recent phone conversation, Mama had implored me to sign the papers and get it over with.

It was during that conversation that I'd asked her, "Did you have any feelings for me, like love or anything, before I was born, when you were carrying me?"

"Why do you think I divorced your father and saw to it that he would play hell seeing you and ruining your life like he ruined mine? You must sign those papers, or all our efforts, everything we've done to protect you—to hide this embarrassment and the shame and to ensure that you can start over and look forward to a bright future—will have been in vain."

"Mama, I know you were angry and wanted to get even with my father for what he did, but what I'm asking is something different. Did you have a strong and deep love for me while I was still in your womb?"

"Of course I did. I loved you beyond measure and still do."

"Then you know how I feel now and why I'm not ready to sign my baby away."

"I do understand, darling, but once you have the baby, you'll see how much it needs parents who can provide for it. Promise me you will do what is right and sign it over for adoption."

"I can't promise that, Mama. Maybe at some point I'll be able to, but not now."

She had said nothing more, except goodbye. We hung up, and we hadn't spoken on the phone since.

CHAPTER 29
BETWEEN THE LINES

We never saw Kay again. Miss Oldenburg finally told us that her family had come and taken her home. We were never told where.

I wanted to go home too. I lived for the day. But at the same time, I didn't want to go into labor because I still couldn't bring myself to sign the adoption papers, and I knew I couldn't take my baby home.

At over a hundred degrees in the shade on Labor Day, the heat was murderous. Miss Oldenburg excused us from chores when our due dates were two to three weeks away, so thankfully I got to abandon my latest job, weeding the flower beds.

With all the other girl slaving away at chores, I was bored with nothing to do all day and anxious because I hadn't heard from Mama in almost a month. Still forbidden to make a call, I waited until Miss Oldenburg was out to use one of the two house phones.

Carmen answered. When she heard my voice, the first thing she said was, "This isn't a good time to talk."

"Why?"

"It's just not. I'm getting ready to go out."

"Let me speak with Mama."

A long silence, then, "She's not here. She and Aunt Hattie are . . . not here."

"Aunt Hattie is still visiting us?"

"Yeah. She was having so much fun socializing with all her old friends, she decided she'd stay on."

"For how long?"

"Indefinitely."

"How can I come home with her still there?"

"We haven't figured that out yet."

I was astounded at what she was telling me. On top of that, she sounded remote and not the least bit glad to hear from me.

"Is something wrong?" I asked.

Her voice came back with a ring of false gaiety. "What makes you think that?"

"I don't know. You just sound odd."

"When are you having the baby?"

"Not till September thirteenth."

"That's a Friday!" she said. "I'm staring straight at the calendar. You can't have the baby on Friday the thirteenth. It's bad luck."

"That's all I needed to hear," I said under my breath. "Have you seen Farrel lately?"

"Not really."

"What does that mean? You've either seen him or not."

"I've seen him around, but we haven't been out. You asked me not to go with him, didn't you? Well, I'm doing what you asked."

"Has he asked you out?"

"Look, Julie, this discussion is ridiculous. When you get home, you can work things out with him yourself. Leave me alone about it, okay?"

If she had slapped my face, I couldn't have been more stunned.

"Have Mama call me the minute she gets home, will you?" I said.

"I'll deliver the message. I can't guarantee she'll call."

"Why not, in heaven's name?"

"I've got to go, Julie. Be good. I hope everything goes well for you when the baby comes."

I hung up, more despondent than ever. Anxiety gnawed at me. Something was wrong. I knew it. I wanted to scream and throw things. I was trapped out here in this house of hell, about to have a baby at only seventeen years old, and I couldn't even talk to my mother.

Marty found me sitting alone in the rec room, tapping out a song of Elvis's with my fingers and staring glassy-eyed at nothing while I waited for Mama to call. Marty urged me to help her in the kitchen, which I did, and she suggested we go out for a walk after dinner.

"We haven't been to the newsstand in a week or so," she said. "Let's go buy your hometown newspaper. Maybe that'll make you feel better."

"Mama should have called by now. I'm afraid she'll call while we're gone."

"Oldenburg's back. She wouldn't let you talk to her anyway."

"She wouldn't dare tell my mother she can't talk to me," I said.

But by the time dinner was over, I couldn't bear waiting around any longer. With my nerves still edgy, I nonetheless grabbed a wedding ring and left with Marty on our walk.

"I don't believe Carmen gave her my message," I said as we waddled along.

Marty frowned. "Why wouldn't she?"

I shook my head. "I can't imagine, unless Aunt Hattie was always around and she didn't get an opportunity. When we were talking, I got the distinct feeling something was wrong."

"What did she say to make you think that?"

"Not anything, really. I just read between the lines."

"I'm sure it's not," Marty said, squeezing my hand. "Your mother would have contacted Miss Oldenburg if something was wrong."

"One thing I know for a fact. Mama would have called me back, if Carmen had told her."

"Maybe she hasn't had a chance yet," Marty said.

"With the baby so close to arriving, she'd make a chance. I just know she would have called if she'd gotten the message. I can't explain it, but I have one of those nauseating premonitions I always get when something is wrong."

At the little newsstand, I headed straight for the *El Dorado Daily News*.

The skinny man behind the counter began his litany, "You read, you—"

"I know, I know," I shouted. "You read, you pay. We've got it down pat now. You can save your breath."

He glowered at me from beneath lowered lids. He still needed a shave, only worse than usual, and his hair had grown below his earlobes.

I tried biting my lip to keep from letting loose with my rude remark, but it didn't work.

"What have you heard about the barbers' strike?" I said, giving him a snide smile as I slapped a dime down on the counter.

His jaw went slack before fury ignited his eyes.

"Get outta here, both of you! Those dime store rings don't fool me, you pregnant whores."

Marty and I waddled as fast as we could back out onto the sidewalk, howling with laughter.

"Good for you," she cried, clapping her hands.

"I'm surprised he got it," I said.

At the diner, we found a booth and squeezed in. I pushed the table toward her to make room for my belly.

"Don't do that. You'll squash my baby. I'm as big as you are."

"Sorry. I'm so squeezed in here I can barely breathe."

"Take small breaths," she said with a grin.

We each ordered a coke, all we could afford, and I unfolded the paper to read while we waited. Marty reached across the table.

"Reading your hometown newspaper all summer has gotten me hooked. I can hardly wait to see what's in the Society Section today. I bet I know everything there is to know about the Junior League ladies, the DAR members, the PTA, which lady gave the most elaborate tea this summer, and who took the kids to Europe on the grand tour."

"You forgot the United Daughters of the Confederacy," I said, "and don't forget who attended what piano recitals, which church is having a supper this Sunday, and what's being served at the county fair food booths."

The thought of the Union County Fair made my throat ache with homesickness.

"Every year, each elementary school has a food booth," I told Marty. "There's a big competition between them to see who can make the most money at their booth. Hugh Goodwin always wins. They make fabulous chili."

The front page of the news section announced that the Rialto Theatre would be getting Elvis's movie *Jailhouse Rock* as soon as it was released. The story went on about how the Southern boy had made good after playing concerts right there in town before he hit the top.

I turned to page two, but as my eyes flicked over the paper searching for the continuation of the story about Elvis, they came to rest on the Obituary column. At first I thought I must be seeing things. The top of the column in bold type read "Elizabeth Lawrence Morgan."

The letters danced before my eyes. It couldn't be true! Not Mama! There must be some mistake.

"Marty!" I said. "My mama's dead!"

Marty looked up, her eyes wide with shock. "What?"

"She's dead! The paper has my mother's obituary in it! My mama's dead!"

"She can't be!"

"You girls need to keep it down," the waitress said, setting icy cokes in front of us.

"My mama," I said, barely able to sound out the words. "She's dead."

"Give me that!" Marty said, snatching the paper. "Which one is it?'

Marty did not know my last name.

"The first one."

"Elizabeth Lawrence Morgan?"

I nodded, numb with shock and still not able to believe it.

"Oh my God." Marty read, "'Departed this earthly life on Sunday, September first, after a brief illness.' That was yesterday."

I clawed my thighs through my cotton skirt.

"No one even called me to tell me she was sick! And on the phone today, Carmen didn't say a word. Not that Mama'd been sick or that she had *died*. Oh God, it can't be true!"

"Who else knew you were here?"

"Only Carmen and her mother, and she's in London. Why in God's name didn't Carmen tell me?"

"Calm down, Julie. Let me read the rest. I still can't believe it's really your mom." Drawing a quick breath, she continued, "Born December 11, 1914."

"That's Mama's birthday! It is her! She's dead, Marty. My mother is dead."

A rigor ran through me.

"You're shaking. Take it easy," Marty said, reaching across the table and grabbing my hand. "You'll traumatize the baby."

"It can't be true," I cried. "What did she die of? Does it say?"

Marty scanned the column. "No, just that business about a brief illness."

"She's dead, Marty. My mama's dead." I broke down, unable to control the tears.

Marty picked up the glass and held it out to me. "Here, take a sip of your coke."

As I raised it to my lips, it slipped through my fingers and spilled all over the table. Coke and ice cubes splashed on my maternity top and my skirt. I pushed myself out of the booth.

"I've got to get out of here!"

The waitress came running with rags and a mop, but we shoved past her and headed for the door. The man at the cash register yelled at us. Marty threw a dollar bill on the counter.

"Wait! Don't you want your change?" he called.

Neither of us broke our stampede out the door to answer.

Once outside and walking as fast as I could back toward Happiness House, I said, "I've got to get home, but I can't! Everyone in town would find out about the baby. When is the service? Did the paper say?"

"I didn't get that far."

Stopping right there in the middle of the sidewalk, she flipped back to the Obituary Section and read aloud.

"'Services will be held at ten A.M. on Thursday, September fifth, at the First Methodist Church, 201 South Hill Avenue. Interment will follow in Arlington Memorial Cemetery.'"

Tears streamed down my face. Over and over my brain repeated, "My mama's dead! She's dead!" But my mind refused to accept it.

My body did not refuse, however. We barely made it inside the door of the home when I felt liquid running down my legs. The next instant, I doubled over in pain.

CHAPTER 30
THE DARKEST HOUR

When the pain subsided, I looked down at the puddle on the floor.

"I've wet myself," I said to Marty and hid my face in embarrassment.

In the doorway of her office, Miss Oldenburg stood, frowning at the mess I'd made in the foyer.

"Your water broke."

I turned a clueless face toward her.

"You're in labor," she said in an exasperated tone. "Go up and pack your bag. I have to get you to the hospital."

"Miss Oldenburg, Julie's mother has died," Marty said, her face pale as she put an arm around my waist.

Oldenburg blinked. "Her mother . . . Julie, your mother is dead? I can't believe it! No one has contacted me. When were you notified?"

Seeing that I was unable to answer her, Marty held out the newspaper.

"She had to read it in the obituaries. Her mom died Sunday."

Oldenburg's face reflected disbelief. "But she was a young woman." She clucked her tongue and studied me. "The shock of it has thrown you into labor. When is your due date?"

"Not till the thirteenth," I managed to say.

"Just get her packed," Oldenburg said to Marty.

That was it. Not a word that she was sorry to hear about Mama. I struggled to get adequate breath as Marty and I made our cumbersome way up the stairs. I clung to the railing and pulled myself from step to step.

"I could pack for you," Marty offered.

"No. I want to do it, if I can get up there."

The one thing I knew about having a baby was that I'd have to take off all my clothes and put on a hospital gown. My money bag containing the hundred-dollar bill had to be kept safe while not in my bra.

I searched inside the suitcase for a place to hide it. What I needed—a secret compartment—didn't exist in my hand-me-down bag. Then I thought of the pocket in the blue and white suit-dress I'd worn when I first came to the home.

The other girls, having heard the news, were gathering around my bed in the dorm room. Without privacy, there was no alternative but to unpin the bag from my bra in front of them. With a knowing smile, Marty moved to block their view.

She carried the suitcase as we made our way back downstairs where she begged to ride with us to the hospital. Miss Oldenburg flatly refused.

As we backed out of the driveway and into the street, another pain struck me.

"Don't carry on so," Oldenburg said through her teeth. "You'll make me wreck the car."

"Sorry." I wiped my sweaty forehead with the back of my hand. "I didn't know it would hurt so."

She chuckled. "You don't know the half of it."

"So reassuring," I said under my breath.

Oldenburg slammed on the brakes, pitching me forward. I threw my hands out to keep my chest from hitting the dashboard.

"One more sarcastic word and you can get out and walk the rest of the way."

I knew she wouldn't put me out, and I knew why. Kay had confirmed for us that adoptive parents paid a high price to get a baby. Some of that money must be part of Oldenburg's salary. She might even own an interest in the business. Pregnant girls, like me, were valuable to Oldenburg. She wouldn't dare put me out on the street.

When we pulled up to the emergency entrance of the hospital, she tapped her fingers on the steering wheel.

"Well? What are you waiting for?"

I turned shocked eyes on her. "Aren't you going in with me?"

"I never go in with a girl. My jurisdiction ends right here. You're on your own."

My throat swelled. "Miss Oldenburg, my mother just died and my half-sister didn't bother to let me know. I had to read it in the newspaper."

"I sympathize with you. I lost my mother at a young age too. It's tough to take. I know you want someone to hold your hand through this ordeal, but there isn't anybody. You should have thought of that when you decided to have premarital sex."

"Oh, please. Haven't you lectured me enough about that?"

A pain hit me. I doubled over, moaning.

"You'd better go on in. Give them your name and tell them someone called ahead to let them know you were in labor. I need to get going."

I shook with anger. "If you can spare one more minute, I'll get my suitcase out of the backseat."

I slammed the car door and hauled the bag up the walkway. When I reached the emergency room, I looked back toward the car. She was still sitting there, watching me. At least she had the decency to wait until I got inside.

A nurse wasted no time getting me into a wheelchair and up to the maternity floor. She wheeled me into a labor room and, handing me a hospital gown, told me to undress.

"It ties in the back," she said, picking up my suitcase.

"Where are you going with that?" I asked, my voice too shrill.

"It'll be here in this closet until you deliver and we put you in a room. No one will bother it."

I was under such duress about Mama's death and the labor pains that I didn't fully grasp what was happening. No one at the home had told us what to expect during the birth process. I was shocked when the nurse proceeded to shave me "down there" and give me an enema. The humiliating procedures completed, she flicked the light switch and started out of the labor room.

"Wait!"

"Yes?" She stuck her head back inside the room.

"Please, don't leave me here in the dark. I'm scared."

She looked surprised. "You want the lights on? I thought you'd try to sleep."

"Who could sleep? Leave them on and the door open. Somebody needs to tell me what is going on."

"You're having a baby."

"No kidding!"

I wanted to be stoic in front of her, but hard as I fought, the tears kept coming. When she saw them, her expression softened.

"You're in the first stages of labor. It'll be a while."

"How . . . how long, do you think?" I asked through a hiccupping sob.

"Hard to tell." She glanced at the chart. "It's your first, I see. It could take anywhere from eight to twelve hours. I'll be back to check on you in a bit. You're not the only gal in labor here, you know."

And she was gone.

I had mistakenly supposed that someone would be in the room with me, constantly monitoring my progress. Frightened, I lay there, tense and waiting for the next pain to strike. When it didn't come right away, I relaxed enough to check out my surroundings.

Two sinks were directly behind me. The bed I was on was equipped with leather straps and wheels to raise it up and down. A round mirror hung above me. I supposed it was there to allow me to see what the doctor did, if he ever came to do anything.

The next pain caught me unprepared. I managed to moan instead of crying out, even though it was sharper than the first ones. For the next hour, the pains came every fifteen minutes or so, according to my wrist watch, which I'd kept on.

The door was barely open, but I could hear footsteps and voices as they passed by in the corridor, and occasionally a scream.

At one point, I eased myself off the bed and crept to the door to look out. A doctor came striding along the hall, followed by a man wearing khaki slacks and a navy shirt and wringing his hands. As they strode into the room across the hall from mine, I caught a glimpse of a nurse standing beside the bed and holding the hand of another woman in labor.

"Your husband is here, Mrs. Robins," the doctor said. "How are we doing?"

A moment later, another nurse came toward me from down the hall, her white, rubber-soled shoes squeaking on the tiled floor.

"Get back inside and shut the door," she ordered.

"Are women with husbands the only ones who get the attention around here?" I asked, holding my stomach with both hands.

She gave me a condescending smile. "You're one of the girls from the home for unwed mothers, aren't you?"

Shame flushed through me. My face grew hot.

"I thought so," she continued, apparently judging from my scarlet cheeks that she was correct. "We'll get to you soon enough."

Clutching her clipboard to her chest, she steered me none too gently back inside my room to the bed.

"Now stay there. If they catch you out of your room, they'll strap your legs down, and you won't be able to get up. They'll do that anyway for delivery."

"Who are they?" I asked.

"The interns and doctors."

"I need some medicine for the pain. Can't you give me something?"

"We give twilight sleep, but I don't know if you qualify for it." She lifted the top sheet of paper on her clipboard and studied it. "Julie Morgan, aren't you? I see you haven't signed off on the adoption papers yet. May I ask why not?"

"I'm not sure about giving my baby up," I said, skimming my fingers over my bulging tummy.

"Then what, pray tell, are you doing in a home? Didn't you go there to hide the fact that you are pregnant out of wedlock?"

"Yes, but I—" Another pain struck me, this one much harder than previous ones. "Oh God," I cried out. "Please make it stop. I can't bear it!"

"Don't yell like that. You'll scare the other mothers to death. You'll get twilight sleep, if and when you sign the papers."

"I don't have them with me. I left them back at the home," I said.

"The social worker from the adoption agency should be here any minute. She'll have a set of documents with her. Sign them, and you'll get something for pain."

Two hours later, the social worker peeked into my room, catching me in the clutches of a terrible pain.

"Help me, please," I cried out. "Please make them give me something for this pain."

"You haven't signed the papers turning the baby over for adoption," she said with a toss of her head.

I dug my fingernails into my thighs.

"You surely can't expect me to do that now."

"You won't get out of this hospital until you do," she said, "and certainly you won't get anything for the pain. Now, don't you think signing would be the reasonable course of action? I can hold the papers so you can do it without even sitting up."

"If I do, I surrender my baby permanently, don't I?"

"That's correct."

"What if I change my mind?"

She shook her head and sighed. "Miss Morgan, there is no changing of your mind in a situation like this. Think what it would do to the adoptive parents, who've spent their hard-earned money to get a baby. Think how devastated they must be that they can't have a child of their own. If you took your baby away from them, it would . . . I don't know, but I imagine it could very well break their hearts. I realize that for some of you girls it is difficult to give up your babies, however, if you sign now, we will allow you to hold it before we take it away."

"The baby is not an 'it,'" I said. "My son has a name. It's Nicholas, and I'll thank you to call him that."

"Oh, for heaven's sake! It could very well be a girl."

"It's a boy and . . . I . . ." Pain seared through me. "I want my mama!" I cried out. "Oh God, help me."

The woman looked at me with cold eyes.

"I'll leave the pen and papers here on the night table. I'll stop by again to collect them before I leave. If you're smart, you'll sign and salvage what you can of your life."

After she left, no one came in to check on me for over an hour. Finally, a young intern appeared.

"Doing fine," he said, lowering the sheet. "It shouldn't be too much longer now."

"Please, give me that twilight sleep the nurse was talking about. Knock me out, in the name of God. I can't bear this pain."

"No can do, honey. Not till you sign off on the kid."

Hours later, when the sun was backlighting the leaf pattern on the closed chintz curtains, I was still alone and no one had checked on me since he left. My body shifted into another mode that set off a need to push. The pains were now only about three minutes apart and had increased in intensity to the point that I thought I would surely die. An excruciatingly hard one hit. Gritting my teeth, I pushed so hard the veins strained in my neck.

The next moment, the baby was in the bed.

CHAPTER 31
THE GREAT ESCAPE

The baby was a boy, and even with no one there to give him the customary spank on his bottom, he wailed lustily, battling the air with his tiny fists. I managed to pick him up and cradle him close. My Nicholas, my baby, Farrel's baby—surely there never was a more beautiful child.

Some part of my exhausted body reminded me that it was important to note the time. My watch said nine o'clock.

I could not stop the baby's wails. They must have heard his cries out into the corridor, for the nurse who had prepped me rushed in and was followed a moment later by a retinue of nurses and interns.

"Oh my God!" said the first nurse. "Didn't anyone monitor this girl? She had the baby right here! Why wasn't she taken to delivery?"

No one answered.

She seemed to register for the first time that Nicholas was in my arms.

"You're not supposed to hold that baby!" She reached for him.

"Don't touch my baby! Don't any of you try to take him away from me!"

The group around my bed took subtle steps backward. No one said anything more until the younger doctor who examined us at the home came into the room. The crowd parted to let him through. By this time, I had lifted the baby to my breast, and his little lips were pulling on my nipple.

"Don't nurse him!" the doctor said. "The cord isn't cut."

The next few minutes were total chaos with nurses rushing in and out and the doctor taking care of the cord.

When the excitement had died down, I again lifted the baby to my breast.

"You are not allowed to nurse him, Miss Morgan," the doctor said.

"Why not, in God's name?"

"Because you won't be able to continue with breast feeding. He'll be bottle-fed. We'll give you some pills that will dry up your milk."

Much as I despised hearing those words, I knew they were true. I had to leave here to go to Mama's funeral, and there was no way I could take him with me without exposing the shameful secret. At the same time, the idea that there was any way on earth my precious baby could be considered shameful made me feel unglued.

When I tried to ease Nicholas's lips away from my nipple, he broke into a deafening squall.

"Here, let me take him," another nurse said, stepping forward.

"No!" I said, moving the baby back to my breast. He stopped crying instantly.

The doctor waved the nurse back and moved closer to my bed.

"He's a fine little fellow, Julie, but he needs to be cleaned up, and you need more attention, yourself."

"It's about time somebody decided that," I said, ripe with anger and hurt.

"I apologize that you had to give birth to him all alone and without medication. That was an oversight." He reached for the papers of surrender, still on the bedside table. "But you haven't signed these yet, and that is part of the reason why. Now give the baby to me. You can hold him again when they are signed."

"No!'"

The doctor cleared his throat. "I have to take him now, Julie."

"You will not!" I said, twisting so that Nicholas was out of his reach.

The doctor threw a helpless look toward the nurses and interns, but no one offered a suggestion.

"Am I going to have to call psychiatric services?" he said, turning back to me.

That stopped me cold. At the home, there'd been rumblings about girls who'd refused to sign the adoption papers being put in mental institutions until their parents arrived to get them out. I had no one to come for me.

Gathering my courage, I played my only trump card.

"It's about the money, isn't it?"

He gave a start. "Wh-what?"

"The money people have to pay to adopt a baby. You and the home and the adoption agency all get a cut from it, don't you?"

His eyes shifted away from mine. I knew I had him.

"What about my rights?" I rushed on. "Don't I have any? What about my baby's right to have his own true mother?"

"Do you intend never to sign, Miss Morgan?" he asked.

"I don't know right now this very second! I've just given birth with no one to attend me. My mother died suddenly, and I had to read about it in the newspaper. If I signed now, it would be under duress, and one thing I know for sure because my mother worked for a law firm, a signature under duress wouldn't hold up in any court of law."

Inside, I quaked with fear, but the bold face I put on worked. The doctor nodded, solemn-faced. The room went silent except for the small sounds of my child feeding.

"Again, I apologize, Miss Morgan," the doctor said, "and I offer my sincere sympathies for the loss of your mother. We were under the assumption that you came here in order to conceal your pregnancy and give up the baby. We'll give you a day or so to rethink the matter. Just let us attend to both of you. No one can take him away from you permanently until you sign him over for adoption."

When Nicholas and I were clean and comfortable, they put him back in my arms. Apparently, my fit had made an impression on them.

With the nurse tagging along, two male staff workers moved me with the baby in my arms to a room down the hall from the labor and delivery area.

"We don't put you girls from the home in with our real mothers," the nurse said, "and since no one else from there is delivering right now, you get a private room. Lucky you."

I flared. "You're trying to say I'm not a real mother?"

"You know what I mean," she said with a toss of her head.

After she'd left us alone, I fed Nicholas again and, following her instructions, put him on my shoulder to burp. He was so precious. The longer I held him, the more in love with him I grew.

A meal was brought to me long before the regular kitchen personnel came around with lunch. After I ate, I slipped under the sheet and cuddled my baby close. I hadn't meant to fall asleep, and when I awoke, he was gone.

The hospital was quiet. My watch said ten o'clock. I thought back. Marty and I had gotten the newspaper on Monday, the second of September, Labor Day. Mama had died the day before. Those words remained horrifyingly unreal. Miss Oldenburg had brought me to the hospital around eight o'clock the night of the second. I remembered my watch reading nine A.M. on Tuesday when Nicholas was born. Mama's funeral was scheduled for Thursday, the fifth, but what day was it now? It must still be Tuesday, the third.

I pressed the call button. The squeaky shoes nurse arrived so quickly I wondered if she'd been hovering outside my room.

"Is my watch right?" I asked. "Ten o'clock?"

"That's right," she said. "Ten P.M."

"On Tuesday the third," I said.

She shook her head. "Ten P.M. Wednesday night, September fourth."

"Wednesday night!" Alarm flushed through me. "That's impossible!"

She drew back the curtains. It was dark outside.

"No, honey. You slept round the clock, and we let you. Your bed needs straightening. Do you feel like getting up and sitting in the armchair for a few minutes?"

I threw back the covers. Mama's funeral was only twelve hours away. I had to get home. As I swung my legs over the side of the bed, I saw the surrender papers still lying on the table. I remembered someone saying during all the chaos that the hospital wouldn't release me until I signed. I couldn't take the baby with me, or everyone at home would know, but I couldn't sign those papers either.

"Would you please bring my baby to me?" I asked Squeaky Shoes as I took a few tentative steps. I didn't know how painful it would be to move. Fortunately, it was only mild discomfort and soreness.

"I'm sorry, honey. I can't do that."

She looked up while smoothing the bed covers. "You'll need to get right back in bed. It's not good for your body to get up too soon from childbirth."

I decided not to argue.

While she finished tucking the sheets, I eased over to the mirror. Grasping a handful of hospital gown in back, I pulled the front tight across my body. My stomach had gone down somewhat but maybe not enough for me to squeeze into the blue and white travel dress. I opened the door to the closet. It was empty.

"Where is my suitcase?" I asked Squeaky Shoes, who by this time was fluffing the pillows.

"We'll get it for you later. Right now you need your rest. The bed is ready."

My heart skipped a beat. Without my little money bag, I was dead in the water. That hundred-dollar bill was my ticket to freedom and home.

Squeaky Shoes kept her eyes riveted on me, like she thought I might vanish. To allay her suspicious, I crawled between the sheets and lay down, as if to go back to sleep. I let her put out the light and close the door. When I heard her footsteps fading down the corridor, I threw back the covers and got out of bed again.

I opened the door of my room a crack and peeped out. The hospital lights were dimmed for night. With my rear end probably showing through the gap in the back of the hospital gown, I tiptoed barefooted down the hall in search of the room I had been in. The door stood open wide to the empty darkness inside. Without flipping the light switch, I went straight for the closet. Reaching around in the dark, my fingers located my suitcase where the nurse had left it.

I took the bag with me into the adjoining bathroom and locked the door. I hadn't bathed since the day I went into labor, but I didn't want the nurses to hear the shower running, so I made do with a sponge bath in the sink. After cleaning up as well as I could, I focused on fitting into the blue and white suit. It lay on top, where I'd packed it. A quick feel in the pocket relieved my anxiety. The money bag with the folded bill was still there.

The more I tried to hurry, the more everything went wrong. First, my lipstick slipped through my fingers and into the toilet. No alternative but to fish it out and wash it and my hands under water as hot as I could bear.

Next, the waistband of my skirt proved too small to fasten. I rolled up my handkerchief and threaded it through the button hole. I sucked in my stomach and used the money bag pin to secure the two hanky ends to the button side, providing an extra four inches to the waistband. I had to have that money in my purse from here on anyway. The zipper would only come up halfway, but the peplum-style top hid the gap, as well as the outline of the sanitary belt.

I stuck a few pads into my purse, along with Elvis's letter, and was ready to go when I remembered my bare feet. In a frenzy, I rummaged through the suitcase. My black pumps with the little heel weren't there. I took a deep breath and thought back. I had worn them to the hospital. Maybe they were in the plastic drawstring bag they made me store the maternity outfit in when I undressed to give birth.

I fumbled all around the closet until I felt the bag in a back corner. Not bothering with hose, I pulled out the shoes and, slipping my feet into them, I shoved the suitcase back into the closet. I couldn't be burdened with it on an attempt to escape. Maybe someday I could come back for it.

I opened the door an inch or so to check the corridor. No one. I eased out and had taken only a few steps when I heard the squeaking rubber soles. I ducked back inside the room, leaving the door slightly ajar to see out. Squeaky Shoes hurried by on her way toward the observation room.

I still couldn't decide what to do about Nicholas. No way could I take him home with me. Keeping him a secret was the least I could do for Mama's memory, and for myself. But neither could I bring myself to surrender him for adoption. The one thing I must do was get home and see Mama one last time before they put her in the ground. The thought hurt so much my throat felt like it was ripping all the way down into my guts. But there was no time for crying.

Soft hospital sounds accentuated the still darkened corridor. I could not risk going past the nurses' station to the elevator. At the far end of the hall was a red-lighted exit sign. Hoping it was the stairs, I headed for it, not realizing until I was almost there that I'd have to pass the observation room.

As I approached the wide window, I paused. Round-the-clock nurses tended to the newborns. I knew that much. Someone was bound to be on duty and would surely see me if I stopped to get a glimpse of Nicholas. But I had to risk it. I had to see my baby. Maybe no one would pay attention to me. After all, I was dressed like a visitor.

As usual, the boy babies were up front, close to the window. I was quickly able to locate the name "Morgan" on the card attached to the end of a bassinet. Even without it, I would have recognized his adorable face.

The one nurse in attendance was occupied in the rear with her back to the window. I waved to my baby. I knew he could not focus his newborn eyes enough to recognize me, but seeing him and touching the window comforted me.

"Been released?" a voice asked.

Squeaky Shoes stood behind me. I slumped.

"Oh, I see, you're making a getaway?" she said. "What are you thinking? That you'll run away without signing the papers and leave him in limbo? Or were you planning to shatter the glass and take him with you?"

"My mother's funeral is tomorrow. I have to be there. And I know I can't take him with me."

"Honey, why don't you do what is right for him and sign those papers so he'll be provided for? Then you can get on with your life."

"I simply can't right now with Mama dead and all. He's a part of me. Don't you understand?"

As she gazed at me, her face underwent a change from authoritative nurse to sympathetic friend.

"What will happen to him if I leave without signing? Please tell me, please."

She took a long breath. I could see her debating with herself.

"They'll put him in a foster home until they can put enough pressure on you, wherever you are, to make you sign."

I thought hard. Maybe I wouldn't ever have to sign. Maybe I could go home and figure something else out. At least I knew he'd be all right if I left him there.

"Are you going to blow the whistle on me?" I asked.

"I'll have to sound the alarm, but with your mom dead, you've got a lot on your plate," she said. "I'll give you a head start. There's a pay phone booth right outside the hospital. The number for Yellow Cab is stuck on the inside wall. I was on my way to dispense the medication to dry up your milk. Here it is. You'll need it. Take the staircase and hurry."

I took the vial of pills and gave her a quick hug.

"Have you got enough money for your ticket?"

"I have a hundred-dollar bill, but no change for the pay phone."

She fumbled in her pocket and handed me a dime. With murmured thanks, I fled down the stairs, across the lobby, and out into the night.

I was on my way home.

CHAPTER 32

TRAILWAYS HOME

"The bus station," I told the cabby.

"Greyhound or Trailways?"

Road block before I'd even begun my trip.

"Oh, Lord. I don't know."

"Where ya headed?"

"El Dorado, Arkansas."

"Trailways," said the driver.

"Please hurry. I have to be home tomorrow morning, and I don't know the bus schedules."

"Then we'll agitate the gravel," he said.

Elvis had used that same expression the night he gave me a ride home. The remembrance filled me with nostalgia for the lost girl of that magical time.

The cabby was nice enough to turn the meter off while I went inside to break my large bill.

I'd never been inside a bus station late at night, and hardly ever during the day. No women were there, and no one young. Spittle dotted the floor, and cigar smoke coming from a man sitting clear across the waiting room made it hard to breathe. A few other men, all in bedraggled clothes, sat reading or dozing.

"When is the next bus to El Dorado?" I asked the ticket agent.

"Departing one A.M., scheduled to arrive at eight in the morning."

He took the hundred-dollar bill and studied it.

"Is something wrong?" I asked, my voice shaky.

"This the smallest you've got?"

I nodded.

His eyes narrowed. "Where'd you get this bill?"

"My mother gave it to me."

"Sure it's not counterfeit?" the agent said, his face suspicious.

"Yes, I'm sure. Just give me a ticket and my change. The cab driver is waiting to be paid."

"Don't know if I can break it," he said, fumbling in the cash register.

"Sir."

He met my gaze.

"Please. My mother died unexpectedly." My throat swelled. "I've got to get home."

With that, he counted out my money and gave me a ticket. I rushed back outside.

"There is a bus," I told the cabby, handing him the fare. "Keep the change."

"Thanks. I was going to drive you myself, if there wasn't a bus," he said. "I've got a daughter about your age. Be careful, and good luck."

My watch said ten after midnight. Taking a seat in the waiting room as far away from anyone as I could get, I ticked off the minutes until the bus would leave.

It crossed my mind that I had enough time to call Carmen. I looked around. A pay phone hung on the wall next to the rest rooms. I was halfway to it, change in my hand, when I had second thoughts.

She had done the unthinkable by keeping Mama's death from me. I couldn't imagine why she would do such a cruel thing. Maybe she was trying to protect me. She knew that I was quite literally trapped out here. There was no way I could come home hugely pregnant. Or maybe she'd feared such news would bring the baby on early, which it had. No matter what, news like that had to be given immediately to the next of kin. Because simply nothing made sense, I decided to catch her off guard by showing up without warning.

At twelve forty-five, my bus pulled in. I visited the restroom and then bought a soda pop and a sandwich to take with me. I was starving. The call over the public address system to board the bus for El Dorado,

Arkansas, with stops in Texarkana and Magnolia, didn't come until one o'clock, the time we should be leaving.

I took the first seat up front across the aisle from the driver. The man smoking the cigar was the only other passenger. He took a seat midway back. I thanked my lucky stars to see a compartment at the rear of the bus labeled "Restroom."

The driver had collected our tickets and gone back inside when I noticed a black car pulling into the parking lot. My window on the bus was nearer the passenger side of the car, so I wasn't able to immediately see the face of the woman who emerged from the driver's side. As she circled around the rear of the car and headed toward the entrance to the bus station, her face came into full view. It was Oldenburg. In one hand she clutched a manila envelope. The papers.

With brisk steps, she went through the swinging doors, nearly colliding with our driver on his way back out to the bus. Reason told me she'd case the waiting room first, then check the ladies' room. I had enough time to get away, if the driver moved fast.

He sprang up into his seat and turned the ignition key. The bus rumbled to life. Through the plastic window of the swinging door, I saw a distorted version of Oldenburg rushing toward the restrooms. I looked back at the driver. He was thumbing through paperwork.

"When do we leave?" I asked. "It's already ten past one."

"We're going. Keep your pants on," he said.

Shoving the gear stick into reverse, we crept backward out of the parking space and away from the loading dock. Just as he put the bus in drive, Oldenburg came flying out through the swinging doors, waving the envelope.

I could see her lips moving, but I couldn't hear her over the roar of the bus's engine. The driver, intent on negotiating the long vehicle out of the lot, appeared not to be aware of her at all.

I watched her shaking her fist as the bus pulled out. I watched her until we began our turn onto the next street. I watched for as long as it was possible to keep her in sight. Just before she slipped out of my line of vision, I saw her open the car door and crawl back inside. Pressing the lever on the side of my seat, I leaned back and tried to relax.

I had escaped.

The Dallas lights had passed by for only about a half hour when the driver turned hard and we pulled into another bus station. I sat straight up.

"Why are we stopping?" I asked him.

Not answering me, he called out, "Fort Worth."

"Why are we stopping here?" I repeated as he got up and started down the steps to exit the bus.

He looked up at me like he thought I didn't have good sense.

"Pick up passengers, of course. And let some off. This'll be a quick one."

The two passengers joining us boarded quickly, and within minutes the driver was back in his seat, starting the engine. Just as we were heading out, I saw the black car barreling into the lot, the horn blaring in the garish lights of the station. Oldenburg leaped out and ran toward the bus, waving the envelope above her head.

This time the driver saw her and braked. He reached for the hand lever to open the door of the bus.

I rushed down the aisle and into the cubicle restroom. Inside, I slid the latch on the door and held my breath.

"Where is she?" Oldenburg's brassy voice demanded.

"Who's that?" the driver asked.

"The young woman. Is she on this bus? She's trying to skip town without signing these papers. She has to be stopped."

"Ma'am, you can see there ain't but three folks sitting in here. What kinda papers you got? A warrant for somebody's arrest?"

"No, no! Adoption papers, if it's any of your affair. She's refused to surrender her baby for adoption."

"Well, if that don't beat a hen a peckin'!"

She challenged him. "Are you sure there's no one else on this bus?"

His voice dropped. "There is another passenger in the restroom, but it ain't—Stop, ma'am. You can't go no farther down this aisle without a ticket. And you sure can't go charging into that restroom."

"Is it a woman?" Oldenburg asked. "In the restroom?"

I was done in. I had my hand on the latch when I heard the driver say with a chuckle, "Not to my way of thinking."

I could imagine Oldenburg's perplexed face in response to that. After a beat, she said, "Oh, well, why didn't you say it was a man? Sorry to hold you up, sir."

Sounds resonated back to me of her going down the steps of the bus and the door closing. I waited until we had been moving for quite a while before coming out of the restroom. Thrown one step backward for every two steps forward by the rhythm of the bus, I made my way up the aisle and fell into my seat.

In a while, the driver looked over at me.

"How old are you, girlie?"

"Seventeen."

"Right. You're a girl still, by my way of thinking. I knew you weren't no woman."

He lowered his voice. "Are you the one that dame was ahuntin'?"

"What dame was that?" I replied.

He smiled.

We bumped along in the night through stretches of oilfields and scattered clumps of pine forests. We traveled down Main Street in every little town on the road and picked up passengers in most of them. We sailed over asphalt and bounced over gravel and potholes. Sleep was impossible.

My reflection rode beside me in the window. I watched her smooth her hair and tuck it behind her ears. I struggled along with her to get comfortable on the hard seat. It was as if Carmen were sitting with me. I longed for her to be real so I could ask her why she hadn't called to tell me about Mama. But she remained only an illusion, reflected in the window by lights turned low for sleep that would not come.

Mama's ghost flitted in and out of my mind—her every gesture, her arched eyebrow of disapproval, her infectious laugh that I'd heard too seldom, her soothing words of comfort when I was distressed. She had never been sick a day in her life. Had a stroke taken her, as it had taken her own mother before her? Or had there been an accident? The paper surely would have made a front-page story of a car wreck. But no matter the details, the biggest question remained—why Carmen hadn't called to let me know?

I had just managed to doze off when a loud pop sounded from under the bus, followed by sounds of flapping. We swerved. The driver wrestled with the wheel as we wobbled to a stop in a clearing by the side of the road.

"Must have lost a tire," he said, rushing down the steps and jumping off the bus.

A male passenger sitting in back got off with him, and from the window I watched them squat to check the tires, then stroke their chins. In a few minutes, they got back on the bus.

"Ladies and gentlemen," the driver said, "we've had a blowout. Fortunately, we're only two miles out of Texarkana, so we ought to be able to limp on in if we take it real slow."

And slow it was. It took us almost thirty minutes to get to the station in Texarkana. Once there, the driver told us to get off the bus and wait inside.

"How long will take to get us back on the road?" I asked the ticket agent.

He looked up at the clock on the wall behind him.

"Maybe upwards of an hour," he said, looking past me at a customer in line to get a ticket.

It was already going on four thirty. The funeral was at ten. I wanted someone to erase from my brain the indelible reality of Mama's death. I wanted someone to hold me and tell me everything was going to be all right. But there was no one to do either. So I took a seat and waited, and waited, and waited.

At seven that morning, they called us to board the bus. One more stop in Magnolia made it ten forty when we pulled into the Trailways station in El Dorado.

I was late for Mama's funeral.

CHAPTER 33

THE SEARCH FOR MYSELF

I was too exhausted to walk the five blocks to the Methodist church. I had never ridden in a taxi in El Dorado, but when I saw one letting a passenger out in front of the bus station, I hailed him.

"Where to?"

"The First Methodist Church, and hurry."

Traffic was congested around the square. It was ten of eleven by the time we arrived.

"Wait for me," I told the driver.

I dragged myself up the long flight of steps. Inside, vapors of smoke lingered above extinguished candles. The sanctuary echoed my footsteps. A janitor sweeping between the aisles looked up at me.

"The funeral, is it over?" I said, struggling to catch my breath.

"Gone to the graveyard," he said. "'Bout ten minutes ago. You just missed 'em."

I moved as fast as I could back outside to the cab.

"Can you take me to the cemetery?" I asked the driver.

"It'll cost you."

"Just drive."

For a moment, my mind registered as odd the bustling streets, as if it were an ordinary weekday. But of course, the town wouldn't shut down for my mother's funeral.

We crossed over the railroad tracks on Main Street by the ice house and headed east. Along the way, front yard gardens wore the fading blooms of summer zinnias and cosmos. Every house, even the run-down ones, looked beautiful to my homesick eyes.

The driver turned onto Mosby. From the cab window, I could see the stream of cars moving along inside the cemetery gates toward the tent erected beside the grave. Today the bright sun mocked the sad occasion, unlike the time I was here for Frances's burial. On that sorry day the "rain of fools," as Mama called it, would have soaked us through were it not for a stray umbrella half hidden under the car seat.

"You want me to get in that line of cars inside the cemetery?" the cabby asked.

I hadn't thought this through. Was I going to barge into the graveside service and announce that I was the real Julie and Carmen was an imposter? I could picture the shocked looks that would take over people's faces. Where would I say I'd been? Maybe I should hang back and watch from behind a tree. But how dreadful to have to snoop on my own mother's burial.

"The tent is not far," I told him. "I'll walk. Would you wait here for me outside the gates?"

"How long?" he asked.

Still weak from childbirth and barely able to think from the exhaustion of the bus trip, I didn't have the mental or physical wherewithal to sort out this dilemma. It would depend entirely on what happened when I got closer to the grave.

"For as long as it takes."

"You pay, I wait."

"Here." I yanked some bills from my purse and stuffed them into his hand. "Now, wait."

"Hey," the cabby called as I started my difficult walk up to our family plot. "You some kind of a black sheep in the family or something?"

How accurate the uninformed can be. "I guess you could call me that."

He shook his head and reached for his cigarettes.

Like someone learning to walk all over again, I negotiated my way up the slight incline, my lower back aching with every step. I was behind the procession and could watch the people pouring out of their cars parked half on the grass and half on the edge of the narrow cemetery road. A large mausoleum sat between me and the ivory tent. I stood partially behind it and peeked around to watch the happenings.

There was no place for me at my own mother's funeral. The only thing I could be thankful for was at least I had on a decent dress, although the blue and white fabric in no way approached the appropriateness of Carmen's black dress, pillbox hat, and gloves.

I could see her standing front and center beneath the tent beside Aunt Hattie, also dressed in black. The carpool girls hovered on the sidelines—Maylene, Darcy, Laura, Lynn, and even Eugene Hoffmeyer, without Rhonda. Mama's bridge club crowd, with Mavis in front, stood clumped together near my schoolmates.

I wished I could just back my ears and go out there in front of them all, squeeze between Carmen and Aunt Hattie, and grieve openly for my mother, but that would ruin everything she had wanted so badly for me.

The minister took his place in front of the mourners, which also included the lawyers Mama typed for. My cousins and our many distant relatives from all over the county stood, wiping their eyes, some of whom had barely known her.

Although I scoured the crowd from face to face, I did not see my father. That was no surprise. None of the Morgans would have dared show up. Had Carmen wired or called Claudia in England to let her know?

My life, before the day we left on the drive to Dallas, had been fairly constant, unchanging, sometimes even boring. The days had strolled by from one year to the next with only the predictable changes that happened while one was growing up. Changes that people had progressed through for millennia. But in the short span of five months that I'd been away, my world had collapsed, almost as if our house had fallen down, leaving me mortally wounded in its rubble. A tornado of events had blown to pieces the walls of my security. My world had vanished, almost as completely as if it had never existed.

The pastor intoned the ritual words of the burial service. With cracking voices, the crowd sang "In the Sweet By and By." Carmen laid a white rose on the coffin. Mama should have had red roses. The Lawrence family always buried our dead with red roses covering the casket. But Carmen wouldn't have known that. She was not of our blood. But why hadn't Aunt Hattie insisted? There were no answers for me.

At the end of the song, the pastor announced that lunch would be served back at the church, and the crowd dispersed.

A man offered his arm to Aunt Hattie. I strained to make out his face. To my stunned senses came the realization that it was Farrel. I should have known by his lean, tall body. I couldn't piece together why he would have taken off from work to be at Mama's funeral—busy Farrel, so in a hurry to pull himself away from his roots on the wrong side of town and acquire acceptance by people who thought they were made of finer fabric. My own mother had cherished the idiotic idea that we were descended from Ireland's blood royal. For all I knew, maybe we were, but it hadn't made the slightest difference in the circumstances of our lives.

Carmen appeared to be thanking Farrel. I flinched as he leaned over and kissed her lightly on the lips. He put out his arm and led Aunt Hattie away. After that, the in-crowd girls and Eugene spoke briefly to Carmen and went to their cars, leaving her standing there alone.

I could not bear this exile a moment longer. Taking quick steps, I moved toward her as she turned to follow Farrel and Aunt Hattie. She paused and glanced around, as if sensing that something was about to happen. She turned to look in back of the tent. Seeing only stragglers going to their cars, she looked again toward the coffin.

"I'm over here," I said from a few feet away, in the direction she hadn't looked.

Her mouth fell open. "What are you doing here?"

"I've come to my mother's funeral. Why didn't you let me know she was dead?"

"Oh my God," she gasped, sinking into a chair.

"Answer my question, Carmen. Why didn't you contact me?"

She stammered, looking first one way, then the other.

"I didn't know what to do. I thought you weren't due for another week."

"Two weeks."

"Well! I knew you couldn't come here *pregnant*," she said under her breath. "And I knew you'd be so upset you might do just that."

"I read in the newspaper about Mama. It brought on the baby early."

"I can't believe it's you," she said through a half sob.

I walked over to her. "But it is. Take my hand. See, I'm real."

She did not respond. Instead, she got to her feet, her eyes darting around at the cars as they pulled away and joined the caravan creeping out to the street.

"You have to go."

I frowned. "Go where?"

"Anywhere, but you can't stay here. I have to go to the church and take my place beside Aunt Hattie at the luncheon. If anyone sees you, we're in deep shit."

"You never quite learned to talk like I do, did you?" I asked, anger rising in me.

"Seriously, Julie, you have got to disappear. Go away somewhere."

"Give me the key to the house. I'll have the cab driver take me there."

"You can't go to the house!"

Her words bounced off my brain. "Why in heaven's name not?"

"You can't let Aunt Hattie see you."

"But where else can I go? Maybe it's time to confess to her what has happened."

"If you do, you'll never get that 'little something' from her will. Isn't that what you and Elizabeth wanted?" Carmen's voice was shrill, her face fraught with anxiety.

"I'd forgotten about all that. It doesn't seem so important anymore."

"You might change your mind down the road," Carmen said. "At any rate, you can't make an appearance until we change places. You'd still have to account for your whereabouts all this time."

"But where will I go? And when are we going to change places? I want to be myself again. Aren't you tired of being me all the time? It must have been awfully stressful."

"It was hard at first," she said. "But now I've become pretty good at it. We'll have to meet secretly somewhere and figure this all out at another time, but right this minute, you've got to go. Git! Vamoose."

"But where? I have no place to go and not a whole lot of money left."

"That's not my problem."

I stared, not believing she had uttered those words. Guilt flashed across her face.

"I'm sorry," she said. "I shouldn't have said that. Listen, go to Dad's. Pretend you're me. Say you wanted to go to school here this year, so Mother let you come back."

"Without any luggage?" I said, tears of exasperation springing into my eyes.

"Tell them your bag got lost on the flight. I have the key to grandma's old house on East Third Street. We'll plan to meet there in a day or so and get some of my clothes and an old suitcase for you. Tell them . . . Oh hell, I don't know what you can tell them. Make up something, if my story doesn't suit you."

"Why can't we meet at your grandma's old house in a day or so to get some of your clothes for *you* and make the change?" I was becoming hysterical.

"We can, we can. But for now, you've got to cool it. How did you get here anyway?"

"I literally escaped from the hospital and rode all night on the bus. I caught a cab here." I pressed on my abdomen to get a deep breath. "The driver's waiting by the gate."

"Then go back and make him take you to Dad's. We'll figure out how to do the switch as soon as everything quiets down from the shock of Elizabeth dying."

Much as my mind rebelled against it, I knew that was the only answer.

"What is Farrel doing here, Carmen?"

"I . . . he asked if he could drive us to the church and out here and all."

"Then you've been seeing a lot of him?"

"No, not really. He would like me to, but no. I stayed away from him, for you. You've gotta go, Julie."

"Wait, first you have to tell me, Carmen."

"Tell you what?"

"How did Mama die?"

"She had an aneurism that burst. The doctor said she'd known about it for years, but it was inoperable and there was nothing that could be done."

"She never said a word about it to me," I said, unable to hold back my tears any longer. "I don't even know what an aneurism is."

"Neither did I."

"But why didn't she tell me?"

"She didn't want to worry you. The doctor said she knew it could burst at any time, but she also knew it might never happen. He said she didn't want me, uh, you, to know, 'cause if you did, you'd never have another peaceful day. I really have to go."

She stuck out her hand and patted mine. Mama's diamond ring she'd inherited from my grandmother flashed a prism of light. I seized Carmen by the wrist.

"Take that ring off and give it to me, right now!"

"Have you lost your mind? Keep your voice down. People will hear you."

"Why are you wearing my mother's ring?" I said in a harsh whisper.

"To keep up the deception. Why else? Aunt Hattie gave it to me. I couldn't very well say, 'I can't wear it. I'm not really Julie.'"

"I want that ring. It belongs to me."

"You can't wear it before we make the switch. I'll give it to you then." I let go of her. "You didn't ask about the baby."

"Oh, yeah. What was it? A boy or a girl?"

"A little boy. It killed me to have to leave him out there."

"Well, it's over now. You can forget about it and move on."

"I suppose it wouldn't be hard for you to forget about him. He's only your nephew. But he's my son."

She looked down.

"I guess I don't quite get the full impact of what you've been through."

"No, I guess you don't."

I looked beyond her. I could never forget Nicholas. Nor could I ever move on.

My eyes focused. Farrel had put Aunt Hattie in the car and was approaching us with hurried steps.

"Julie," he called. "Your aunt says we need to get to the church."

He drew closer. His eyes connected with mine. His expression changed into confusion as Carmen faced him and we stood side by side. He shook his head, as if to clear it.

"Carmen," he said, coming over to me and giving me a quick hug. "I'm blown out of my tree to see you here. I thought you were in England. When did you get back?"

"This morning," I replied, hoping he would somehow see through the charade we were enacting. "I, uh, wanted to go to school here this year."

He took a moment, seemingly to digest that.

"Are you going to the lunch?"

"No." I nearly choked on my next words. "I barely knew Elizabeth."

"Oh, right. Well, we gotta get going, Julie," he said, taking Carmen's arm and tossing a look at me. "See you around, Carmen."

I watched as, without a backward glance, Carmen let him escort her to his car. He put her in the passenger side and started around the front of the car.

A noise drew my attention away from him. The gravediggers were about to lower my mother into the ground.

"Stop! I want to see her," I said to the men. "I got here too late for the funeral."

They shrugged. "It can't be done."

"But she's my mother."

"Sorry, miss. We've done sealed the vault. It can't be done."

Maybe it doesn't matter, I thought. Mama had always said she wanted to be remembered the way she looked in life, not in death. Stooping, I took a handful of earth from the mound they'd dug out. It was cold, making me wonder what they had dressed her in for the long sleep. Holding the dirt above the gaping hole, I allowed it to sift over the white rose lying on the vault. "Ashes to ashes, dust to dust," the pastor had said. And so it was. I felt like I had lost everything—my mother, my sister, my aunt, the father of my child, even myself.

A motion from the direction of Farrel's car caught my peripheral vision. He had paused on his way to get in, and he stood, staring at me. His face still wore an expression of confusion. He took long strides toward me.

"Do you need a ride somewhere?" he called across the grassy spaces between headstones.

I shook my head.

He started back to the car but hesitated after only a couple of steps and, turning, came toward me again. As he stepped close, his eyes took in my hair, tangled from traveling all night on the bus, and my wrinkled dress with a coke stain on the front of the skirt.

Thank God my breasts weren't leaking.

"How have you been?" he asked.

"Okay."

It took all my strength to commit to the deception. I had to turn my face away. The sweating gravediggers labored at shoveling the dirt onto the vault, burying my mother facing the east, as was the custom, so that her first sight upon rising from the dead would be of Christ with his angels, coming in glory.

Farrel shifted his weight, drawing my attention back to him. He squinted in the harsh sunlight.

"She's taking it better than I expected."

"Who?"

"Julie, of course," he said, a quizzical note in his voice.

"Oh, right."

Awkward space hung between us.

"Where will you be staying?" he asked.

"At my father's house."

"Could I come over and see you sometime?" His voice had a hollow ring.

My throat ached. I did not want to deceive him.

"I guess you and he could talk about your work in the oilfields," I finally said.

"It's you I want to talk to."

When I said nothing, he pressed. "So can I . . . see you sometime?"

"Maybe—sometime."

I looked at this man, the father of my child—our child. My eyes embraced him, for my arms could not. I watched him go back to the car and drive away with Carmen as the false Julie sitting beside him.

I took a step to go myself but turned back for one last look at Mama's grave. For the first time that day, I noticed the crepe myrtle tree she had planted near our burial plot. Its blooms were shriveling, now that it was September, but a few stragglers still held their summer splendor.

The gravediggers had mounded the earth until it resembled a nest for giant ants. A breeze sent a flurry of the watermelon-red blossoms fluttering down onto the grave. Mama would like that.

I started back along the cemetery road toward the waiting taxi that would take me to the home of my father, the next destination on the journey in search of myself.

The End

BUT WAIT—THERE'S MORE!

DON'T MISS
In Those First Bright Days of Elvis,
Book I in the Days of Elvis series
And Book III: In Those Glory Days of Elvis,
coming in 2018

In Those First Bright Days of Elvis

by Josephine Rascoe Keenan

One trivial decision can change your whole life.

On an October night in 1955, fifteen-year-old Julie Morgan decides to attend a free talent show and concert at the football stadium of her Arkansas hometown. At the concert, Julie encounters three strangers: a lookalike, who could pass for her twin; a college boy, who will be the love of her life; and Elvis Presley, who befriends her and whose casual comment about a light bulb becomes a driving force in her pursuit of love and self-worth.

But in that pursuit, Julie goes down the wrong path, seeking popularity and an older boy's affection as substitutes for her missing father's guidance and support, unaware that her longing to feel loved and valued stems from her need to have her father in her life.

Growing up is never easy. The birth of rock 'n' roll, a growing standard of living, and the culture of automobiles brought a feeling of freedom and ease. But the phrase "Duck and Cover!" meant the possibility of nuclear war and death was now a fact of everyday life.

Josephine Rascoe Keenan masterfully weaves a story of human anguish and betrayal, love and loss, recrimination and regret, and shows how choices, once made, can change one's life forever. She meticulously recreates the "golden days" of drive-in movies, screen-wire petticoats, and flashy American cars, when the world seemed brighter and more innocent than today.

But was it?

Available in ebooks and paperback at:
www.Pen-L.com/InThoseFirstBrightDays.html

If you'd like to hear more about Josephine's upcoming books,
free deals, and other great Pen-L authors,
sign up for our Pals of Pen-L Newsletter here!

www.Pen-L.com/OptIn/Thanks.html

THANKS TO:

Tracey Buswell Simmons, for providing information on Continental Trailways Bus Company.

Lorraine Kay Lorne and Randy Thompson of the Young Law Library, University of Arkansas, for their help with legal research.

My colleagues at the writers group, whose sharp perceptions and unfailing support helped to guide the journey in creating this book.

My husband, Frank, whose insight and probing questions helped guide me to the finished product and who listened with rapt attention to each chapter as it sprang to life.

And to those fans of *In Those First Bright Days of Elvis* who accosted me with the singular demand: "Hurry up and write Book II."

For a complete bibliography see www.KeenanNovels.com/blog

SOME OF THE SOURCES CONSULTED IN THIS BOOK:

Butler, Brenda Arlene, *Are You Hungry Tonight?* Avenel, N.J.: Gramercy Books, 1992.

Clayton, Marie. *Elvis Presley Unseen Archives.* Bath, UK: Paragon Publishing, 2002.

Fessler, Ann. *The Girls Who Went Away: The Hidden History of Women Who Surrendered Children for Adoption in the Decades before Roe v. Wade.* New York, NY: The Penguin Group, 2006.

Lowell, James Russell, (author), H. Garrett (illustrator). *The Vision of Sir Launfal.* Boston and New York: Houghton and Mifflin, 1890.

Presley, Priscilla Beaulieu, and Sandra Harmon. *Elvis and Me.* New York, NY: G. P. Putnam's Sons, 1985.

Yancey, Becky and Cliff Linedecker. *My Life With Elvis.* New York, NY: St. Martin's Press, 1977.

DISCUSSION QUESTIONS FOR
IN THOSE DAZZLING DAYS OF ELVIS

1. What are the social attitudes today regarding unwanted pregnancy? How have these attitudes changed since the 1950s?

2. What do you think this change in attitude says about our society?

3. Do you think Julie should have told Farrel about her pregnancy?

4. For many years adoption records were sealed and birth mothers could not find out who had adopted their children; neither could adopted children get information about their birth mothers. Today, in some states, adoption records are available for adopted persons when they reach age 18. In your opinion, should adoption records be available to both birth parents and the adopted children?

5. What do you think Julie should do about her child?

6. *Confirmation bias* is the tendency to accept evidence that confirms our beliefs and expectations and to reject evidence that contradicts them. How does this phenomenon work with regard to Carmen and Julie changing places? What does their scheme of switching places reveal about the observations and perceptions of people around them?

7. Research shows that many people resemble each other, whether or not they are related. What do you think of the girls' changing places? In Carmen and Julie's world, it works; would it work in the world today?

8. When Julie agrees to change places with Carmen, does she open herself up to any dangers? What are the risks?

9. If there had been such a thing as social media back in the 50s, do you think it would have made it easier or more difficult for Julie and Carmen to change places?

About the Author

Josephine Rascoe Keenan grew up in the little town in Arkansas where all three books in "The Days of Elvis" series are set: El Dorado, city of "black gold." After reading *Gone with the Wind* when she was eleven, she decided to become a writer someday. That day came after she had worked many years in the entertainment industry as a director and an actress with many talented people, such as Johnny Cash in the made-for-TV-movie *The Pride of Jesse Hallam*.

Josephine wanted to tell a story of what life was like in the '50s when Elvis was first coming on the scene. Elvis had done a few concerts in El Dorado before he hit the top, and she thought it would be great to create a story about a girl who met him before he became the King of Rock 'n' Roll. The result was a three-book series entitled "The Days of Elvis."

Josephine is a versatile writer. *Cricket* magazine has published two of her short stories: *The Petticoat Skipper* (March 2016), about Mary Greene, one of the first female riverboat captains, and *Ohoyo Osh Chisba: the Unknown Woman* (November 2007), about the coming of corn to the Choctaw people. Her poem, "A Ride on Grandpa's Foot," appeared in *Modern Maturity Magazine* in August 2005, and *Reader's Digest* published her submission for Humor in Uniform. Three of her plays have been produced in regional theatres: *Friends* and *Life's a Butter Dream*, both of which toured with Artreach Touring Theatre, and

The Center of the Universe, a three-act play chosen as a winner of Ensemble Theatre of Cincinnati's New Play Contest.

Josephine enjoys oil painting, and her work will be featured as the cover art for all three books in "The Days of Elvis" series. She and her husband love traveling, square dancing, and gardening.

VISIT JOSEPHINE AT:

WWW.KEENANNOVELS.COM

FACEBOOK JOSEPHINE.KEENAN1

TWITTER @FJKEENAN1

Dear Readers,
If you enjoyed this book enough to review it for Goodreads, B&N, or Amazon.com, I'd appreciate it!
Thanks, Josephine

Find more great reads at
Pen-L.com

CPSIA information can be obtained
at www.ICGtesting.com
Printed in the USA
LVOW12s1505030817

543710LV00001B/114/P